Alice-Miranda
in Egypt

Books by Jacqueline Harvey

Kensy and Max: Breaking News
Kensy and Max: Disappearing Act
Kensy and Max: Undercover
Kensy and Max: Out of Sight
Kensy and Max: Freefall
Kensy and Max: Full Speed
Kensy and Max: Take Down

Alice-Miranda at School
Alice-Miranda on Holiday
Alice-Miranda Takes the Lead
Alice-Miranda at Sea
Alice-Miranda in New York
Alice-Miranda Shows the Way
Alice-Miranda in Paris
Alice-Miranda Shines Bright
Alice-Miranda in Japan
Alice-Miranda at Camp
Alice-Miranda at the Palace
Alice-Miranda in the Alps
Alice-Miranda to the Rescue
Alice-Miranda in China
Alice-Miranda Holds the Key
Alice-Miranda in Hollywood
Alice-Miranda in Scotland
Alice-Miranda Keeps the Beat
Alice-Miranda in the Outback
Alice-Miranda in Egypt

Clementine Rose and the Surprise Visitor
Clementine Rose and the Pet Day Disaster
Clementine Rose and the Perfect Present
Clementine Rose and the Farm Fiasco
Clementine Rose and the Seaside Escape
Clementine Rose and the Treasure Box
Clementine Rose and the Famous Friend
Clementine Rose and the Ballet Break-In
Clementine Rose and the Movie Magic
Clementine Rose and the Birthday Emergency
Clementine Rose and the Special Promise
Clementine Rose and the Paris Puzzle
Clementine Rose and the Wedding Wobbles
Clementine Rose and the Bake-Off Dilemma
Clementine Rose and the Best News Yet

Alice-Miranda in Egypt

Jacqueline Harvey

PUFFIN BOOKS

PUFFIN BOOKS

UK | USA | Canada | Ireland | Australia
India | New Zealand | South Africa | China

Penguin
Random House
Australia

Penguin Random House Australia is part of the Penguin Random
House group of companies whose addresses can be found at
global.penguinrandomhouse.com.

First published by Puffin Books, an imprint of
Penguin Random House Australia Pty Ltd, in 2021

Cover and internal illustrations by J.Yi
Cover design by Mathematics xy-1.com © Penguin Random House
Australia Pty Ltd
Typeset in 13/18 pt Adobe Garamond by Midland Typesetters, Australia

Printed and bound in Australia by Griffin Press, part of Ovato,
an accredited ISO AS/NZS 14001 Environmental Management
Systems printer

A catalogue record for this
book is available from the
NATIONAL LIBRARY OF AUSTRALIA
National Library of Australia

ISBN 978 1 76 089104 6 (Paperback)

Penguin Random House Australia uses papers that are natural and
recyclable products, made from wood grown in sustainable forests.
The logging and manufacture processes are expected to conform to the
environmental regulations of the country of origin.

penguin.com.au

For Ian – whose travels have continued to inspire me – and for Sandy, as always – much loved and missed.

Who could have imagined the places Alice-Miranda would take us all!

Prologue

The boy pressed his ear to the door and willed his heart to stop beating so loudly. His mother had banished him to his room an hour ago for asking too many questions, but now his father was home with answers.

'Akil, please tell me, what did they say?' he heard his mother's voice.

There was a long pause.

'Masud's blood is not a match,' his father replied.

For a moment the world was silent – the house was still – and then his mother let out an agonising cry.

How was this possible after everything the doctors had said? Surely they were wrong. Masud angrily wiped his eyes and flung open the door, charging into the sitting room where his parents stood opposite one another. His mother was shaking, tears streaming down her face.

'Baba!' The boy clenched his fists in front of him and ran towards the man. 'It is a mistake. I know it!'

Akil slowly shook his head. 'Your brother is in God's hands – there is nothing more we can do.'

'No!' Masud shouted. 'If it cannot be me then there must be someone else – we just need to find them and then Jabari will be well again.'

Esha Salah's tears fell to the floor.

Jabari was the baby she never dared hope for after doctors had told her she was unable to bear more children. Somehow he came anyway – a ray of sunshine in all their lives. Seven-year-old Masud had been besotted, and as soon as Jabari could walk the little boy became his big brother's shadow. For eight years, the pair had been the best of friends but then Masud began to notice things. Jabari was often covered in bruises, though he was not in the least bit clumsy. He was always cold, even in the height of summer, and he was constantly tired. The diagnosis of leukaemia had been as unexpected as it was shocking.

Esha wiped her eyes and straightened her back. 'I must go to the hospital,' she said to her eldest son. 'Your grandmother has been there all day.'

'I'm coming with you, Mama,' Masud said.

'No,' Esha whispered. 'You must stay here and help your father. There is a group arriving tomorrow.'

Masud stared at the man, his brown eyes aching.

'Please, Baba, can't you take someone else on the tour?' the boy asked. 'I want to be here for Jabari.'

Akil looked tenderly at the boy and clutched the knotted prayer rope that was rarely out of his hand.

'There is no one else, Masud. I need you,' Akil said. 'We must work so that we can pay for your brother's treatment.'

'But Jabari needs better medicine. There is a hospital in Philadelphia in America – they have the best success rates in the world and there is a special register of donors. There must be a match. I have been doing research,' the boy said.

'Stop it, Masud!' his father shouted. 'We cannot afford such things!'

'Then what is the point of working at all,' Masud yelled, 'if there will never be enough money to cure him?'

Esha spun around and glared at her son. 'How dare you speak like that? While there is breath in your brother's lungs we must pray for a miracle.'

'There *are* no miracles, Mama!' Masud yelled. 'What we need is a fortune.' The boy's face crumpled and he ran back to his room.

Chapter 1

Alice-Miranda zipped the suitcase and hauled it from her bed to the floor.

On the other side of the room, her best friend Millie was grunting and puffing, trying to close the lid of her own luggage – but with a lump like a camel's hump in the centre she wasn't having much success. Beads of perspiration peppered the girl's brow.

'Would you like some help with that?' Alice-Miranda asked.

Millie sighed and wiped her forehead with the back of her hand. 'Yes please! You'd think after all the travelling I've done in the past few years I'd have learned a thing or two about packing.' The girl gave up and slumped onto the bed. 'But I'm hopeless!'

'I'll say,' another voice replied.

'Hi Sloane,' Alice-Miranda said with a smile.

The older girl wandered into the room and sat down on Millie's desk chair, spinning herself around like a top.

'Are you already packed?' Alice-Miranda asked.

'An hour ago,' Sloane replied. 'Caprice is driving me crazy with her non-stop singing. I know she has her exams soon, but I'm really hoping that we don't have to share a room on this trip – all those trills and runs are getting on my nerves.'

'At least she has a beautiful voice,' Alice-Miranda said. 'It could be worse.' She opened the lid of Millie's suitcase and moved the contents onto the bed before rolling all of the clothes tightly and placing them carefully back into the bag like a three-dimensional garment version of Tetris. 'I'm so excited to visit Egypt. I've been reading as much as I can about the Pharaohs and all of the monuments, and watching videos too, but I'm sure I've only just scratched the surface. The Queen's Colours program has given us some wonderful opportunities – I'm so glad that we all worked hard to get to Gold – it would be horrible if anyone was left behind.'

Millie picked up the guidebook her grandfather had sent her and waved it in the air. 'Don't worry – I have everything we'll need to know and more right here.'

'I love that your grandfather has made the guidebook a tradition between you,' Alice-Miranda said. Millie's bookshelf held a growing number of the tomes for many different countries.

'It's going to be an amazing trip, although the weather might be a bit hot for my liking,' Sloane said.

Jacinta appeared in the doorway, still in her tennis clothes. 'Can you come and pack for me too, Alice-Miranda?'

'Of course.' Alice-Miranda nodded before noticing the anxious look on her friend's face. 'Are you okay?'

'Don't tell me – you've just heard that Lucas isn't coming?' Sloane teased.

'What?' Jacinta gasped, her jaw gaping. 'When did you find that out? What's happened? He told me this morning he was all set. His mother sent a parcel of new clothes over from New York especially.'

'I'm just teasing you,' Sloane said with a grin.

The colour began to return to Jacinta's cheeks.

'Well, please don't. The conversation I just overheard Miss Grimm and Mr Grump having is bad enough,' Jacinta said.

The other girls looked at their friend expectantly.

Jacinta sat down on Alice-Miranda's bed, a row of frown lines on her forehead.

Millie stood in front of her, hands on hips. 'Well, out with it.'

Jacinta shook her head. 'I shouldn't say anything. They didn't know I was there and they were clearly having a *very* serious talk about *very* serious things. I only stayed hidden because I didn't want them to see me and think I was eavesdropping on purpose.'

'That's extremely noble, Jacinta, but you can't tell half a story then leave us hanging,' Sloane said. 'Besides, if you keep it to yourself it sounds like you're going to be a misery guts. Where were you, anyway?'

'The toilet in the tennis pavilion. They were right outside,' Jacinta said. 'I'm sure they didn't think anyone was there. Miss Grimm said she'd seen the team leaving with our coach but I had an urgent call of nature and ran back.'

Alice-Miranda bit her lip. 'If it's a secret then you shouldn't tell unless someone is going to get hurt.'

'It's worse than that,' Jacinta said.

'How?' Millie asked.

'If I tell, you have to promise that it stays between us,' Jacinta said.

The girls nodded.

'I mean it, you can't say a word to anyone. Because it's big, really big – and terrible. Probably the most terrible thing I've ever heard.'

'Come on – enough with the suspense,' Sloane said, jumping up to shut the door.

Alice-Miranda looked at her friend. 'You don't have to say a word if you think it's the wrong thing to do.'

'It really doesn't matter what I think,' Jacinta said, and sighed deeply. 'Because unless there's a miracle, our lovely school is going to be closed by Christmas.'

Chapter 2

'Are you sure that's what you heard?' Millie asked. She, Alice-Miranda and Sloane were standing side by side staring at Jacinta, who was sitting on the bed, nodding.

'Why would I make it up? It's too awful for words,' Jacinta replied.

'Did they say *why* the school has to close?' Sloane asked. 'There's not some silly charter like at Fayle is there? Oh no – please don't tell me my mother's been up to no good again. Surely she learned her lesson the first time!'

'I don't know.' Jacinta shook her head. 'They didn't mention specifics. Miss Grimm said things were even worse than she had first thought and Mr Grump asked her how long until closure and Miss Grimm said Christmas. Mr Grump asked if any of the staff knew and Miss Grimm said that Miss Reedy was aware that there was a problem but she hadn't told her the extent of it yet. Miss Grimm said she was still too cross. They both agreed it would be best to keep it between themselves for as long as possible – just in case there's any chance of making things right. Miss Grimm said something about the news hitting the headlines and what a disaster that would be, but then they walked away and I couldn't very well follow them.'

'It sounds like money problems,' Millie said.

'Or perhaps the government has decided to take the land for an airport or something,' Sloane said. 'Dad says things like that happen quite a bit. He had a parcel of land he was planning to develop into a housing estate, and then suddenly the roads authority told him they needed it for a freeway corridor.'

Alice-Miranda tapped her finger against her lip. 'Is it possible they were talking about another school?'

'Anything's possible,' Jacinta said, 'but honestly I don't think so. They sounded very upset. I can't imagine they'd be too worried about somewhere like Sainsbury Palace closing down – that could only be good for business here.'

'True,' Alice-Miranda agreed. She grabbed a jacket that was lying on the end of her bed. 'Come on then.'

'Where are we going?' Sloane asked.

'To investigate,' the girl said.

'Definitely not!' Jacinta objected. 'We can't just troop into the headmistress's office and ask her if she's lost all of the school's money – she'd know I was listening.'

'Really? You *have* met Alice-Miranda, haven't you?' Millie said. 'Don't you remember that she'd been here less than a week when she marched into Miss Grimm's office and asked what was wrong with all of the staff and why everyone here was so miserable?'

'That's not what I had in mind this time,' Alice-Miranda said. 'We have to help if we can. There must be a way to make some subtle enquiries while keeping Miss Grimm's secret.'

'What are you up to?' Millie looked at her friend. Something was brewing behind those innocent brown eyes.

'Let's go for a walk,' Alice-Miranda said. 'Mrs Clarkson mentioned she had to take some documents over to the office. We can save her the trip.'

'But it's Saturday afternoon and Miss Grimm probably won't be in her office,' Sloane said, before realising that was just the point. 'We're not breaking into the headmistress's office, Alice-Miranda!' She was aghast at the thought.

'Of course not,' the child replied. 'I'm just dropping off some papers.'

A wry grin appeared on Millie's face. 'But if there should be anything lying about that gives us a clue, we can start figuring out what's wrong,' she said, nodding. 'I see what you're doing.'

'We could get into terrible trouble,' Jacinta said.

'No one will be getting into trouble ever again if Miss Grimm doesn't ask for help until it's too late,' Alice-Miranda said.

'Miss Grimm sounded scared,' Jacinta admitted. 'What if someone has been extorting money from her and now there's none left?' The girl gasped as another thought entered her mind. 'What if she accidentally killed someone and somebody else found out and they've been making her pay to keep the secret and –'

'You need to stop watching all those crime shows, Jacinta,' Millie said, cutting her off. 'Or maybe you should start writing a novel – it sounds like you have the perfect plot for a thriller.'

'This is going to put a dampener on the Queen's Colours trip,' Sloane said. They were leaving the next day.

'We can't let that happen,' Alice-Miranda said. 'I'm so looking forward to seeing Neville and Britt *and* Alethea and Gretchen. I am sad that Lucinda and Ava and Quincy aren't coming, but it sounds like they've had a ball being part of the Model United Nations.'

'Who'd have ever thought we'd be looking forward to seeing Alethea Goldsworthy?' Millie said. 'But I agree.'

'Is that horrible cousin of yours coming?' Sloane asked.

Millie frowned. 'I haven't heard, but I can't imagine Maddie would have managed one hundred hours of community service and learnt a new skill to an accomplished degree in order to achieve her Gold level. From what Chessie has told us about her time at Bodlington, Madagascar is bone lazy.'

'I guess we'll find out,' Sloane said. 'Come on, we'd better get moving.'

Ten minutes later, having picked up Mrs Clarkson's envelope, the girls had trekked most of the way down the path that linked Caledonia Manor with the original campus at Winchesterfield-Downsfordvale. There was a slight chill in the air, though it was hard to say exactly if it was due to the weather, or the pall of gloom that had descended over the group since Jacinta's revelation.

'Has anyone heard how Mrs Derby is?' Sloane asked. The headmistress's personal assistant was nearing the full term of her pregnancy and the poor woman had suffered with morning sickness the whole time. She'd done her best to keep working, but six weeks ago the doctor had ordered her to stay home. The girls had seen Constable Derby in the village the weekend before last and the man had reported that his wife had been back in hospital being treated for dehydration.

Since then, the school had already been through at least half a dozen replacements, most of whom hadn't lasted more than a day or two. While Miss Grimm was a much happier person in recent years, apparently she still wasn't the easiest boss.

The girls walked across the driveway to the main school building. A group of junior boarders was playing a rowdy game of tag on the oval while Mrs Howard, the housemistress, sat on one of the benches on the edge of the field, a trail of knitting beside her.

'There's Charlie,' Jacinta said, pointing at the gardener, who was wheeling a barrow towards the greenhouse. 'I think I'll go and have a chat – see if he needs some help with the weeding. I'm sure he'd appreciate it.'

'Oh no you don't,' Millie grabbed her friend's arm before she could sidle off. 'You're coming with us. You're the one who started all this.'

Jacinta reluctantly followed her friends through the rear doors of Winchesterfield Manor, past the entrance to the library and into a hallway filled with portraits of stern-looking former headmis-tresses and trophy cabinets glittering with treasure.

Millie tugged on Alice-Miranda's sleeve. 'Look,' she whispered. Miss Grimm had just walked out of the boardroom, which was at the far end of the passageway, near the front of the manor. She was followed by two men in dark suits with equally dark expressions on their faces.

'I wonder who they are,' Sloane asked.

'They don't look like prospective parents,' Jacinta muttered.

The headmistress led her guests out through the grand double doors. Millie and Sloane bobbed down behind a large potted palm while Alice-Miranda and Jacinta ducked in beside a cabinet.

As soon as they were gone, Alice-Miranda scurried from her hiding place and into the sitting room down the hall, the others right behind her. A relic from the days when the boarding school was a private home, it had been retained in its original state and was only used every now and then for parent functions, or special morning or afternoon teas. Alice-Miranda and the girls slipped inside and hid behind the brocade drapes, giving them a clear view of the driveway. Miss Grimm shook hands with the men before they hopped into a navy blue Mercedes and drove away.

'I can't believe the school is closing,' Sloane said. 'I know it's taken a while, but this is where I feel happiest in the whole world.'

The other girls nodded. They knew exactly what she meant.

Moments later, Miss Reedy appeared from around the corner of the building. She approached the headmistress with a taut smile, but the expression on Miss Grimm's face was anything but agreeable. From the girls' vantage point, it looked as if there was a terse exchange.

Alice-Miranda took a deep breath. 'Stay here. I'll be back in a minute.' She exited the room, leaving the other girls concealed in the drapes.

'Oh no,' Jacinta moaned when she caught sight of their friend heading towards the teachers, who were still mid-discussion on the driveway. 'She promised not to say anything.'

'Don't worry – she won't just blurt it out,' Millie said.

Miss Grimm and Miss Reedy both seemed surprised by the sight of Alice-Miranda. They smiled at her tightly as the girl held out Mrs Clarkson's envelope to Miss Grimm, who shook her head and pointed towards the manor. Then the woman looked at her watch and raced away in the direction of her flat just as Mr Plumpton drove around the circular driveway and Miss Reedy hopped into the passenger seat without a backwards glance.

'Well, that was weird,' Sloane said. She untangled herself from the curtain and walked across the room, flopping onto the ruby velvet chaise lounge in the corner.

'What happened?' Millie said when Alice-Miranda re-entered the room.

'Did you ask who those men were?' Sloane said.

'I started to, but Miss Grimm cut me off and said it was none of my business. Then she said I should just put the envelope from Mrs Clarkson on Mrs Derby's desk. They were both completely distracted. Miss Grimm said she was late getting Aggie to a birthday party and Miss Reedy mentioned she was going to the shops. It felt as if something was really off between them – they seemed to be avoiding eye contact.'

'At least you've got permission to go into Mrs Derby's office,' Millie said, raising her left eyebrow above her green glasses.

'Which is very important,' the girl agreed. 'Come on then.'

Chapter 3

The foursome left the sitting room and headed down the hall to Mrs Derby's office. While the likelihood of anyone being inside was slim at best, Alice-Miranda still knocked, just to be sure.

The girls waited a few moments and Alice-Miranda was about to try the handle when there was a grunting noise on the other side, followed by loud huffing and panting.

'What's that?' Sloane whispered.

'Don't you mean, who's that? Mrs Derby's on

leave and Miss Grimm's taken Aggie to a birthday party and we just saw Miss Reedy head off in the car,' Millie said, her green eyes wide.

Suddenly there was a loud exclamation. 'Oh no you don't! You're not getting away from me, you little monster,' a voice threatened, followed by a whacking noise and a thud and another grunt.

Millie grabbed an umbrella from a stand in the hallway. It was the only weapon she could find within arm's reach.

'It sounds like someone needs our help,' Alice-Miranda said, and pushed open the door. She charged inside, the other girls right behind her.

'What on earth?' Millie exclaimed in horror as she surveyed the mess in front of them.

The office looked as if it had been ransacked. There were papers everywhere – on the floor, the desk and just about every other surface – but there was no one in sight.

'You won't get away from me!' the voice boomed again. It was coming from under the desk. Alice-Miranda raced around to see a broad bottom sticking up in the air.

'Mrs Parker! Is that you?' the girl cried.

There was a loud bang on the underside of the furniture followed by a pained, 'OW!' Myrtle Parker backed out, rubbing her crown, before flopping against the chest of drawers behind her.

'What were you doing under there?' Millie demanded, then realised that she was still brandishing the umbrella. She lowered it down beside her.

'And hello to you too, Millicent,' Myrtle tutted. 'He's well and truly got away now thanks to you girls and your highly inconsiderate interruption.'

'Who?' Sloane asked, peering under the desk. She was glad not to spy some poor child holed up in the corner.

'That wretched mouse I found in the back of the filing cabinet,' Myrtle replied. 'The one I've been pursuing around this office for the past hour.'

'I didn't know you were a pest exterminator,' Sloane said with a giggle.

Myrtle cast the child a glare.

'You know very well that I am no such thing, but I can't stand the thought of sharing an office with a rodent,' the woman replied. She hauled herself to her feet.

'Sharing an office?' Millie said, then studied Mrs Parker's very professional-looking outfit.

The woman was dressed in a purple twinset with a navy skirt and matching shoes. A long strand of pearls was draped around her neck and pearl earrings bobbed on her earlobes. While Mrs Parker was always immaculate, her outfits usually looked as if they were made from floral curtains, so this was something of a departure.

A horrible thought entered Millie's head. 'Are you working here?'

Jacinta laughed loudly then made a pffing sound with her lips. 'Of course not. She's far too old.'

'Excuse me, young lady – since when have I been too old for anything?' Myrtle demanded.

Jacinta frowned. 'Since we met you.'

Myrtle gasped. 'Well, what else would I expect from you, Jacinta Headlington Bear – with a father like yours?'

Jacinta gave her own outraged gasp. 'That's not very kind, Mrs Parker.'

'Well, ditto from you,' the woman replied. 'And if you really want to know, I wasn't trying to be kind.'

Alice-Miranda jumped between the pair, extending her arms and holding up her hands. 'That's quite enough. I think you need to apologise.'

'Yes, she does,' Myrtle said with a firm nod.

'I meant both of you,' Alice-Miranda said, lowering her hands to her hips and glaring first at Mrs Parker, then Jacinta.

Myrtle's eyebrows furrowed and Jacinta's top lip trembled.

The pair eyed one another warily.

'Sorry!' Jacinta exclaimed and Myrtle mumbled – but at least it was in unison.

'And?' Alice-Miranda looked at her friend first.

'I didn't mean to offend you, Mrs Parker. It's just that you and Mr Parker have been retired for a long time, haven't you?' Jacinta said. 'I thought you were pensioners like my granny.'

As far as the girls knew, Myrtle Parker had long filled her days with volunteering on committees and at village events. Between those and looking after Mr Parker when he was ill, surely she hadn't had time for a job.

'Yes, well, I shouldn't have brought up your father. It's not your fault he's a dastardly rogue,' Myrtle said.

'I think you should hug,' Millie said.

'And *I* think *you* should mind your own business, Millicent,' Myrtle snapped. 'For your information, I never officially retired from anything and if it's good enough for Reginald and Stanley to resurrect that old rock band of theirs, then it's good enough for me to fill in for Mrs Derby until the woman is well enough to return to work. The poor girl mentioned that Miss Grimm was having the devil's own time finding anyone reliable when I visited her last week, so I offered the head-mistress my services. Honestly she will have no one better until Louella returns from her maternity leave. I would advise that you do your very best to stay in my good books. We all know it's the headmistress's personal assistant who actually runs the school.' Myrtle raised her eyebrows so high it looked as if they might leap from her forehead.

'Good for you,' Millie said with a decisive nod. 'My father always says that retirement is a death knell and you've got plenty of life in you yet.'

'Except she won't be here for long if what we heard is true,' Jacinta whispered to Sloane, who nodded.

'What was that, girls?' Myrtle asked primly. 'You do know that whispering is the height of rudeness.'

'Sorry, Mrs Parker,' the pair chimed.

'I'm sure that Miss Grimm will be very grateful to have you, Mrs Parker,' Alice-Miranda said, though she was wondering why the headmistress hadn't mentioned anything about the situation. Then again, the woman had been distracted.

'Yes, I'd just started reorganising the filing when the mouse appeared. Honestly, what a mess. I don't know how Louella found anything,' Myrtle said.

Millie looked at Alice-Miranda and pulled a face. Mrs Derby had always been meticulously organised and now the place was a complete disaster.

'What are you lot doing here anyway?' Myrtle asked.

'We brought some papers from Mrs Clarkson to Miss Grimm,' Alice-Miranda explained.

'I'll take them,' Myrtle said, snatching the envelope from the girl's hand.

'I think it would be better if we left them on Miss Grimm's desk,' Millie said. 'Mrs Clarkson said they were important.'

'You'll do no such thing,' Mrs Parker retorted. 'If it's *important*, then it's a job for the head-mistress's PA. I hardly think that students should be giving themselves access to the headmistress's office on the weekend. That wouldn't be appropriate at all.'

'You're very keen to be here on a Saturday afternoon,' Sloane said. 'I know Miss Grimm's a hard task master, but still.'

'Actually, Ophelia has no idea. I thought I'd make a start on things today and then I could be ready for action on Monday morning,' the woman said. 'Surprise her.'

'That's brave of you,' Millie said.

'Why do you say that?' Myrtle asked.

'Miss Grimm hates surprises, but she hates mess even more. If she were to arrive and see this then I think you might lose your job before you even start,' Millie said.

Myrtle Parker ran her tongue around the inside of her dry mouth. 'Well, I've been interrupted by you lot and that wretched mouse and now I'm hours behind. Is Miss Grimm likely to come into the office?'

'Probably,' Millie said, eyeballing the other girls, who immediately cottoned on to her reasoning.

'We can help you, Mrs Parker – we help Mrs Derby with her filing all the time, and Mrs Clarkson too,' Alice-Miranda said. 'Many hands make light work.'

Myrtle turned and looked around, suddenly feeling completely overwhelmed.

'Otherwise you'll be here for ages,' Millie said. 'What will Mr Parker think if you don't arrive home in time for dinner?'

Myrtle huffed. She picked up some pages, then walked to the filing cabinet before shuffling back to the desk. She was beginning to feel dizzy just looking at the place. 'You're right. Reginald and Stanley were having a rehearsal this afternoon and I promised to make something tasty for their tea. So yes, you can assist, but you have to obey my instructions to the letter. I want everything in alphabetical order. The lot! And Jacinta – you can bring me a cup of tea and some of Mrs Smith's lovely scones with jam and cream. I could smell them when I walked past the kitchen earlier. Chop, chop!'

The girls exchanged glances. Hopefully, something among the mess might tell them why their beautiful school was on the brink of extinction.

Chapter 4

Maryam Moussa placed the telephone back in its cradle and picked up her coffee cup. She had just checked the department's diary for the week and was relieved to see that Dr Hassam would be off again soon. That the Minister for Antiquities spent most of his time hosting novice archaeologists on dig sites thousands of miles from Cairo was highly irregular, given the scope of his position. However, money talked. Dr Hassam's introduction of a program that allowed enthusiastic amateurs on excavations – when previously only fully qualified archaeologists had been able to participate – had been ill-received until the expeditions began to unearth some real treasures. A young Italian student had stumbled upon an entire new burial chamber in the Valley of the Kings – to the horror of the professional team who had been chipping away on the same site for years – while an elderly gentleman from Connecticut had uncovered a cartouche said to belong to Thutmose III.

Maryam preferred it when her boss was away, given his demands often ran to unreasonable. Not that anyone would have believed it outside the office. The man was revered by all and sundry – except perhaps the archaeologists who quietly hated that he was selling out their profession for the sake of a fast buck.

Maryam yawned and stretched her neck. Her job as Director of Archives, which primarily involved cataloguing antiquities, was hardly inspiring – but then she'd always seen it as a means to an end. And she was increasingly certain that the end was in sight. She'd recently made some innovations that would enable her to speed things up.

Dr Hassam's deputy, Fadil Salib, was easier to

get along with, though he would be away on his honeymoon for the next six weeks. His gorgeous wife, Jamila, came from a very wealthy family and her parents had insisted the couple take time to enjoy the beginning of their new life together. Dr Hassam had not been happy about it, but Fadil was due holidays and the minister couldn't very well stop him. Maryam had gone to the wedding – along with half of Cairo, it seemed. The event was impossibly glamorous with no expense spared and for a moment Maryam had found herself wondering what life might have been like, if only . . .

She absently rubbed the bridge of her nose. It still surprised her sometimes that the bump was gone – how long had it been?

A sharp knock on the door refocused her attention.

'Come in,' Maryam called, her stomach tightening when she realised who it was. Usually she would have been summoned to Dr Hassam's grand office on the top floor. She wasn't a fan of the intimidating space, lined as it was with priceless antiquities and various examples of the man's archaeological conquests. She honestly couldn't remember the last time he'd come down here.

Maryam went to stand up but the man motioned for her to stay where she was.

'Good afternoon, sir,' she said.

'Hello Maryam,' Mustafa Hassam replied. His face was red and there were beads of perspiration dotted along his brow. 'There is something important we need to discuss. I have noticed several discrepancies in the . . .'

Maryam's stomach tightened further as her boss's eyes rolled back.

'Dr Hassam, are you feeling all right?' she asked. But before the man could utter another word, his legs buckled beneath him and he crashed to the floor.

Barclay Ferguson twitched with excitement. He hadn't visited Egypt in a long time and now he would be there tomorrow. Albeit accompanied by a group of students undertaking the Queen's Colours' newest and highest Diamond award. Only participants who had attained their Gold certification had been invited to take part in the ten-day tour, which would involve amateur archaeology, community service and a variety of cultural experiences.

When Barclay's assistant, Morag Cranna, had suggested Egypt as the destination for their trip, Barclay had initially been hesitant. Not because he didn't love the country – it was one of his favourite places in the world – but in recent times civil unrest had created concern, particularly for tourists. Morag had returned armed with the most up-to-date facts and figures, at which point it was decided that, on balance, the rewards of the trip still far outweighed any potential risks. She also had a distant cousin who ran an animal shelter caring for horses, donkeys, mules and camels that the children could volunteer at. The clincher was that Morag had secured the services of Barclay's old friend Akil Salah as their tour guide. When Barclay consulted Her Majesty about the idea, the monarch had been thrilled to bits.

While the man was the CEO of the Queen's Colours Leadership Program these days, he had made his fortune in the adventure travel business. At a time when most people believed that taking a caravan to the Scottish Highlands was the most exciting thing they would ever do in their lives,

Barclay had introduced the world to a new way of holidaying: by taking action-packed vacations to less travelled destinations around the globe.

Upon his graduation from university, and long before the idea of a gap year was fashionable, Barclay had surprised his conservative parents by taking off with no more than a backpack, some traveller's cheques and a spirit of adventure. The trip turned out to be one that would change the entire course of his life.

Barclay had successfully negotiated his way across continental Europe before hitchhiking through Turkey and into Egypt, where he'd run into some petty thieves. The bandits had stripped him of his worldly possessions before dumping him in the desert, where he wandered for hours in the searing heat. It was merely good luck that he chanced upon a camel herder called Sefu Salah and his son Akil, who had undoubtedly saved Barclay's life.

In snatches of Arabic and English, Sefu and Barclay had struck up a friendship. When Barclay established his travel business, Sefu had become one of his most trusted guides. Akil had taken over the business when Sefu retired and, to this day,

Barclay's Adventure Travel often engaged the man's services. The last time Barclay had seen Akil and his wife, Esha, was at Sefu's funeral more than a decade ago. As far as he knew, Sefu's wife, Rana, was still alive and well, and Akil and Esha had been blessed with a second son, Jabari, who had come some years after their older boy, Masud. Barclay felt like a child on Christmas Eve knowing that he would soon be reunited with his friend. They always had a wonderful time together and surely this occasion would be no different.

Chapter 5

'Well, that was a total waste of time,' Sloane said with a sigh as the girls exited Winchesterfield Manor. They'd spent the past two hours filing, dusting and organising under the dictatorial supervision of Myrtle Parker. The woman could have given Stalin a run for his money, barking orders while she sat at the desk, sipping tea and scoffing scones.

Millie's stomach growled. 'Mrs Parker might have shared her afternoon tea with us, at the very least, after all that free labour we provided.'

'I think that's what Mrs Smith had in mind,' Jacinta said. 'She told me there was enough for everyone.'

'I'm sorry,' Alice-Miranda said. 'I didn't imagine the afternoon would turn out quite like that.'

The girls had filed absentee records, copies of the weekly newsletter, daily running sheets, time-tables and parent details, as well as student reports, invoices and business paperwork from the school accountant and other suppliers, but nothing had pointed to any trouble.

'Hello girls,' Mrs Howard called from the front porch of Grimthorpe House. 'What have you been up to all this time?'

'Hello Howie,' Millie called back. The girls headed towards the woman. 'We had to make a delivery to the office and ended up helping Mrs Parker.'

'Mrs Parker? Myrtle? What's she doing here?' Howie asked.

'She's taking over from Mrs Derby,' Alice-Miranda said.

'Really?' the woman replied, her lips twisting in a way that suggested this wasn't an entirely welcome thought. 'I hadn't heard.'

'I know,' Jacinta said. 'It's shocking. Mrs Parker is positively ancient and super bossy – I don't think Miss Grimm has thought this through very carefully.'

Howie frowned. 'Actually, dear, I think Mrs Parker is a year younger than I am, so enough of the ancient, please. But yes, Ophelia will have met her match with that one.'

'Mrs Howard, you didn't see Miss Grimm earlier with some men in suits, did you?' Alice-Miranda asked.

'As a matter of fact I did. I've been wondering who they were,' the woman replied. 'They spent an hour or so inspecting *everything*. I was mildly mortified when they headed inside Grimthorpe House, given I know some of the girls hadn't exactly left their rooms spick and span. Poor Ophelia looked as if she'd just lost her life savings.'

'Has she?' Millie asked.

Mrs Howard frowned at the girl. 'Has she what?'

'Lost her life savings? Or Fudge? Or maybe the entire school?' Millie said.

'Fudge was inside with the junior boarders last time I looked, and I haven't heard anything about Miss Grimm losing the school or her life savings. This place is as safe as houses. It's been here for over one hundred years and I'm sure it will be here for hundreds more to come.' Mrs Howard smiled. 'Now hadn't you lot better get back to The Stables and finish packing for your trip? What I wouldn't give to be off to Egypt tomorrow. I know Mr Plumpton is very excited, but when I asked Miss Reedy if she was looking forward to it, she really didn't seem particularly thrilled at all. I'd happily go in her place.'

'We'd love if you could come,' Alice-Miranda replied.

Jacinta's stomach growled loudly.

Howie recoiled. 'Good heavens, what was that?'

'We didn't get any afternoon tea,' Millie said, aware that she was feeling a bit lightheaded herself.

'Well, that won't do. Wait there a moment,' the woman said. She disappeared inside the boarding house, returning with a large tin full of Toll House cookies. 'I baked this morning. Help yourselves.'

They tucked in and bade Howie farewell.

'Have a wonderful time away, girls. And don't worry about a thing here. I'm sure that Mrs Parker will have everything under control,' Mrs Howard said. She gave them a wink and a wave.

'If only that were true,' Millie whispered.

Alice-Miranda had a strange feeling. Surely there had to be a rational explanation for what was going on. Mrs Howard was right – schools like Winchesterfield-Downsfordvale didn't just close. Still, something was amiss and they needed to find out what it was before it was too late.

Chapter 6

Livinia Reedy was frazzled. If it wasn't for Caroline Clinch coming down with a sudden and rather inconvenient bout of gastro, she wouldn't even be here – not that she'd told Josiah she'd tried to arrange a replacement for the trip. He would have been upset, of course, but there was something terrible happening back at school and Livinia had a feeling that somehow she was at the heart of it.

A couple of days ago, Ophelia had asked her some odd questions about the school accountant and if she had signed any forms while the head-mistress was on maternity leave. The problem was, those days had been such a frenzy of activity, Livinia couldn't remember exactly what she'd signed, or when. There had been one day that the man had been quite insistent about something she had to get back to him urgently – so she did – but it was just for a rollover of a term deposit, nothing more.

When Livinia had asked Ophelia what the matter was, the woman had clammed up, refusing to share any further details. In fact, Ophelia had been extremely curt. Livinia had felt sick to her stomach wondering what she had possibly done wrong. Josiah had noticed her bad mood and was constantly asking if there was something awry, but Livinia didn't want to worry him. The last time she and Ophelia had gone through a tense time, the poor man hadn't coped well at all. She was sure she could sort it out – it was just that, being in Egypt, it was going to be much harder to do.

The flight had been long and bumpy – hardly relaxing – and now Livinia had become a target for every tout in the airport, setting her even more on edge. 'No, I do *not* need a taxi!' the woman exclaimed, waving a man away. He grinned, revealing a row of tombstone-like teeth under his bushy moustache. Clearly she was ripe for the picking, looking every inch a tourist, given he was the fifth fellow to approach her and the most insistent one yet.

Livinia had left Josiah at the baggage carousel with the girls from Winchesterfield-Downsfordvale and the two lads from Fayle School for Boys. Their flight had been running late and she didn't want to leave Barclay Ferguson or Morag Cranna waiting a moment longer. Though now she wasn't sure that she should have left the group at all. There were several exits and, while the itinerary said to meet in the arrivals hall beneath a large clock, she was completely confused as there were several identical timepieces hanging up and down the pavilion. Right at the moment she felt like a meerkat on watch – her head twisting this way and that, trying not to miss anyone. There was no sign of Barclay or Morag, and on top of *that* her phone had run out of charge. Livinia decided to take a look outside in case she'd misunderstood the instructions.

Meanwhile, back inside the baggage hall, Mr Plumpton was counting heads for the umpteenth time and checking that every case was now in the possession of its rightful owner.

Only students who had achieved their Queen's Colours Gold award were eligible for the trip. Susannah Dare and Sofia Ridout had been part of the leadership conference in Scotland but had decided to defer the program for a year, while Francesca Compton-Halls had worked doubly hard to get through all of the levels required, along with Alice-Miranda, Millie, Sloane, Jacinta and Caprice.

Lucas Nixon and Sep Sykes were flying the flag for Fayle.

'Right then, we're off,' Josiah announced.

'Excuse me, Mr Plumpton, we can't go yet. Caprice is still waiting for another bag,' Alice-Miranda said.

'But she has a suitcase big enough to hide a body.' He looked over at the girl, who was standing beside a giant case. 'I thought everyone was limited to one piece of checked baggage – in a manageable size.'

'It's Caprice, sir,' Millie chimed in. 'She has no limits.'

'I heard that!' Caprice snapped.

The man shook his head and glanced at his watch. 'Miss Reedy's not answering my calls. I hope she's all right.'

'I'm sure the bag won't be long – there's hardly anyone else waiting,' Alice-Miranda said. She paused for a moment then looked up at the man. 'Is there something else the matter, Mr Plumpton?'

The Science teacher frowned at her.

'You just seem tense, that's all,' the child explained.

'Honestly, I don't know,' he said, scratching the top of his head.

'Is it Miss Reedy?' she asked.

'Why would you think that?' He looked at her curiously.

Alice-Miranda shrugged. 'She didn't look very excited on the plane.'

'No, she didn't, did she? Miss Reedy has been terribly distracted the past few days,' the man said with a sigh. 'I think there's something going on between her and Miss Grimm, though she says everything is fine. I have a feeling she's not telling me the whole story and I don't know why.'

Alice-Miranda bit down on her thumbnail. 'Do you have *any* idea what the matter is?'

Mr Plumpton shook his head. 'No. Perhaps you do? You're a very perceptive girl, Alice-Miranda.'

She smiled at the man. 'I'm afraid I don't but

I'm sure they'll work things out – it's probably just a misunderstanding.'

'I hope so. Livinia seems to be under more stress at the moment than ever and it's not good for her health – or mine,' Mr Plumpton said, mopping his forehead with his handkerchief.

Alice-Miranda nodded and looked along the carousel. 'Caprice has her bag.'

'Good. Now come along, children,' the man said, motioning towards the exit, where he expected his wife would be waiting with their tour leaders.

'Here, let me take that.' Lucas grabbed the handle of Jacinta's suitcase. He had his own in the other hand.

'You really don't have to,' Jacinta said with a smile.

'No, you really don't have to,' Caprice snarled from behind. 'I'm the one who could do with the help here.'

Jacinta turned around and glared at the girl. 'We were all told to bring what we could manage ourselves.'

'Tell someone who cares,' Caprice replied, rolling her eyes. 'At least I have enough clothes so that I won't smell like a hairy armpit after the

46

first day. By the look of that teeny bag of yours you must be planning to wear the same outfit the whole time. And that's just gross.'

'Did you say you had a hairy armpit, Caprice?' Millie asked. 'I've got a razor if you need one.'

'Very funny, Millie,' Caprice huffed and tried to race ahead – except the wheels on her bags locked together and she went down like a sack of potatoes.

'There's Miss Reedy!' Alice-Miranda called, pointing towards the woman, who was outside the building, bailed up against the glass windows with her back to them. A fellow in a white tunic was kneeling in front of her, displaying all manner of trinkets and knick-knacks on a rug.

Josiah and the children hurried through the crowd towards the exit.

A blast of hot, dry air engulfed them as they left the air-conditioned terminal.

'Boy, it's warmer than I thought it would be for September,' Jacinta said. Millie had been studying her guidebook on the plane and quickly let everyone know that midday temperatures in Cairo at that time of year averaged around thirty-four degrees Celsius. There were other places they were travelling to that would likely be even hotter.

'Excuse me, what are you doing?' Josiah shouted at the man.

'Oh, thank heavens,' Livinia wailed. 'He's been accosting me with his souvenirs and won't leave me alone. I've told him to get going but he's the very definition of persistence.'

'For you, madam,' the tout said, picking up a small metal pyramid that was probably a paper-weight but looked as if it could take an eye out at twenty paces. He held it towards the woman.

'Go away!' Livinia squawked. 'I've told you already I don't want to buy any of your tat. Leave me alone.'

But the fellow was undeterred. He stood up and proffered a bust of Nefertiti, holding it close to the teacher's face as if comparing their profiles.

'Your beauty is like our own Queen Nefertiti,' he smiled, revealing a half-gold tooth second from the front on the left.

Josiah squared up to the man, who was now offering a small sarcophagus in the style of Tut-ankhamun's. 'For you, sir. Very precious. Only one US dollar, but I also take English pounds, Euros, dollars from Australia and New Zealand, and Swiss francs.'

'Please, just disappear, will you!' Josiah ordered.

Millie already had her camera out and was taking photographs of *everything*. After her success in the recent photographic contest held in conjunction with Fayle and Winchesterfield-Downsfordvale, her interest in the art form had increased tenfold. Millie had been thrilled to take out the overall prize for a startling picture of a frill-necked lizard in the Australian outback. Her reward had been a DSLR camera, which she had brought with her on the trip.

'I think security is coming,' Lucas said, spying two uniformed guards running towards them.

Within seconds, the man grabbed his rug and bundled everything up, slipping through the children and running away down the concourse.

'Do not worry. I will see you again soon,' he called back, a huge grin plastered on his face.

'I certainly hope not,' Livinia said with a sigh. She was beginning to feel sick and was desperately in need of a cup of coffee.

'Where's Mr Ferguson?' Millie asked.

'Your guess is as good as mine,' Livinia replied.

Right at that moment, Josiah's phone rang. He answered it and after several minutes relayed the news that there had been a traffic accident near their hotel and Mr Ferguson had been unable to get out with the bus to pick them up. He'd already been to the airport earlier to collect the other participants but unfortunately he was now stuck. The group would have to take taxis to their accommodation.

'Good heavens,' Livinia said, bristling. 'Why did Caroline have to be sick? My head is throbbing.'

'What was that, dear?' Josiah asked, but his wife had already moved on and was rounding up the children.

Alice-Miranda had heard her too, and frowned thoughtfully. She needed to find out exactly what was going on back at school and if there was anything she could do to help.

'Taxi, you need a taxi?' A man appeared in front of them, almost as if he'd arrived in a puff of smoke.

'Hey, aren't you the guy with the trinkets?' Millie asked suspiciously. His clothes were different but there was a strong resemblance in his facial features.

The fellow shook his head. 'No. What trinkets? I do not have trinkets. No, no, no – no trinkets for me.' He waved his hands as if he was about to do a dance.

50

Millie frowned at him, unconvinced.

'Fine,' Miss Reedy said. 'Do. You. Understand. English?' she asked very slowly and deliberately.

'Yes. I. Do,' he parroted her manner back to her, and the children laughed. Miss Reedy clearly hadn't been listening to his conversation with Millie.

'There's no need to be rude about it,' Livinia said, though the children all thought she was the one being insensitive.

'Where are we going, Josiah?' the woman called to her husband, who scurried over.

'The Marriot Mena House, Cairo – it's near the pyramids, apparently,' Mr Plumpton said.

'Yes, of course,' the man replied. 'Beautiful hotel with very fancy public restrooms.'

'Mr Ferguson said we should negotiate the fare now before we leave,' Josiah said, and entered into some hushed discussions with the driver. After a few minutes, the other man nodded his head.

'Well?' Livinia asked. 'What did he charge?'

'More than what Barclay would have agreed to but we don't have a lot of choices at the minute,' her husband replied.

The driver nodded and rushed ahead, turning back every few metres to make sure the group was still following.

He led them across the road to a carpark thronging with black taxis. When they reached his ancient vehicle, everyone gasped. The black Fiat with its white roof rack certainly looked as if it had seen better days.

'We can't all fit in there,' Sep said, wondering what they were going to do now. Perhaps the man was thinking the children could hop up on top.

'I have a friend.' The man was quickly on the telephone, speaking Arabic at a rate of knots. 'He will be here in a minute. Maybe two minutes, but he is very efficient.'

True to his word, in a jiffy another vehicle – equally as old and with nary a straight panel – sped in behind the first one.

'This is going to be interesting,' Millie said, wondering how they were going to squeeze everyone in, and all the luggage too, even with the second car.

But before she could turn around, the bags were on the roof, secured by a tangle of octopus straps, and the children were being ushered into the vehicles.

'One of you will have to sit on a lap,' the first driver said.

'That's not very safe.' Chessie frowned.

'I promise I am very good driver,' the man replied. 'You will be safer than you have ever felt.'

Livinia looked at Josiah. Neither of them was happy about the situation but there didn't seem to be any alternative.

'Well, darling, I think you should go with the first man and I'll hop in with the other chap,' Josiah said. But before he did he raced over and gave his wife a kiss.

'For good luck,' he declared. The children giggled.

Livinia eyed the front seat warily while the four children squeezed into the back. After a little bit of pushing and shoving, Caprice had claimed Lucas's lap. Alice-Miranda sat in the middle and Chessie was on the other side. Jacinta had been relegated to the second car and was wedged in with Sloane, Sep and Millie. Sloane refused to sit on her brother, which left Millie clambering on top of the girl.

'Seatbelts on, everyone,' Livinia said. 'We're not leaving until they are firmly in place.'

She reached up to the pillar only to find that hers was missing. Livinia glared at the driver.

'No seatbelts,' he said. 'But is very safe. More safe than with seatbelts and much more fun.'

Livinia turned to look at the children in the back seat. 'Right, you lot – you must promise me that this is one of those occasions when what happens on tour stays on tour. Do you understand? Miss Grimm and your parents may very well kill me if they find out about this – that is, if we don't die in a car crash on the way.'

'It's all right, Miss Reedy,' Alice-Miranda said. 'We won't tell, will we?'

Caprice's lip wrinkled. 'That depends.'

'You will be safe. Trust me.' The driver turned and smiled, revealing a glint of gold tooth that Alice-Miranda could have sworn was exactly the same as the hawker from outside the terminal.

Chapter 7

The driver turned the ignition several times before the engine fired. When it did, there was a high-pitched whine that didn't do anything to set the children's or Miss Reedy's minds at ease. Fortunately, the man was true to his word and set off slowly from the airport precinct, travelling past barren paddocks of red soil on the outskirts of the city. A few miles down the road, they came upon an army barracks and a stadium before the hotels and housing began to build up.

'Perhaps the traffic isn't as bad as Millie's guidebook predicted,' Alice-Miranda said.

'Famous last words, little girl,' the driver replied as the vehicle came to a grinding halt. All of a sudden there seemed to be thousands of cars and motorbikes on the road, which was lined with shops, flats and houses and filled with crowds of people. The loud and frequent honking of horns reminded Alice-Miranda of New York.

Livinia Reedy stared into the distance, wishing she felt more excited about the trip. If only Ophelia would tell her what was really going on – surely she could help. 'How long will it take to get to the hotel?' she asked. 'I have to make some important calls.'

'Forty-five minutes – maybe less, maybe more. Probably a lot more, but this is Cairo. You must always expect for driving to take long time,' the man replied.

Lucas squirmed as he tried to get comfortable under Caprice's dead weight.

'You don't know a shortcut, do you?' Lucas asked.

'Do I know a shortcut?' the man said, as if the question had instantly given him permission to take it. 'Hold onto your hairstyles.'

The fellow made a sharp left turn. Livinia Reedy gasped as she slammed against the door. In the back the children felt as if they were on a carnival ride.

'Slow down!' Livinia shouted. 'You're driving like a lunatic. Where are my husband and the other children?'

'But you want to get to your hotel quickly,' the driver said. 'You have important calls. And do not worry about the others – they are racing us now to see who will get there first. It will be fun.'

'This is not fun!' Livinia yelled, covering her eyes and gasping.

Lucas, Caprice, Alice-Miranda and Chessie felt as if they were playing a high-stakes game of corners. They knocked against one another every time the man made a turn. Chessie reached up and locked the door and shouted for Lucas to do the same.

'Ow!' Caprice wailed as she was jolted from Lucas's lap into the footwell. Lucas grabbed Alice-Miranda and pulled her onto his knees, holding her tightly around the middle, leaving Caprice to pull herself up next to them. He'd be in far less trouble with Jacinta if his cousin sat on him.

The taxi roared along a wide section of carriageway until a bus pulled up sharply right in front of them. The driver slammed on the brakes, almost sending Livinia through the windscreen and Chessie hurtling into the back of the woman's seat. To everyone's amazement, the bus doors opened and a horde of passengers hopped off, weaving their way in and out of the cars to reach the sides of the road. All the while, new passengers ran the gauntlet of the traffic to get onboard.

'Why aren't they at a bus stop?' Livinia shouted.

The driver shrugged and sped away. 'Is just the way things happen in Cairo. It is busy city.'

He made another sharp turn, this time into an alleyway littered with trash and lined with crumbling buildings that must once have been quite beautiful. There were power lines pinned precariously to the walls, and Livinia was mortified to think that they might end up in some dead end. Thankfully, the driver soon turned back onto another wide road.

'Look, it's the Nile!' he exclaimed, though it was hard to see anything with the barrier railings and the fluffy tops of date palms obscuring the view. The other concerning thing was the lack of line markings on the wide carriageway – and the fact that there seemed to be no rules governing how or where one drove. Using the indicators seemed to be a foreign concept to everyone.

Another taxi sped alongside them and Livinia was relieved to see Josiah and the other children waving frantically, although when a motorcycle crossed the road in front of them, causing both cars to veer sharply left and right, she thought she was going to pass out.

'That is the Egyptian Museum – that browny-pinkish building there – actually perhaps it is best described as salmon-coloured,' the driver said. 'It is where you can see the mummies. But not for much longer. They are constructing a new museum nearer to the pyramids called the Grand Egyptian Museum – it will be huge and has taken many years to complete. It will house all of Egypt's precious antiquities.'

'I think Mr Plumpton said we're going to the Egyptian Museum tomorrow,' Alice-Miranda said. 'I can't wait. Tutankhamun's sarcophagus looks spectacular in photographs – I can only imagine how glorious it is in real life.'

The driver sped up again and turned a corner to head over a bridge across the river, almost colliding with a truck full of men riding in the open tray.

'Look out!' Livinia covered her eyes. Her heart was beating so hard she thought it might expire any second.

But the driver was undeterred from his commentary. 'This part of the city is called Giza. It is very ancient. If you look over there you will see . . .'

'The pyramids!' Chessie shouted. Miss Reedy lowered her hands just in time to see the tip of one of the great structures.

'Wow!' Alice-Miranda gasped. 'They're enormous. But I didn't realise that the city would be so close.'

'You can see the pyramids from your hotel – and if you feel like a pizza there is an American chain restaurant nearby with some of the best views of the Sphinx and the pyramids,' the driver said.

'No. Surely that's not true,' Miss Reedy said.

But the man was emphatic and said that he often dined there himself.

'That's a bit like China. There were fast food restaurants at the base of the Great Wall at Mutianyu,' Alice-Miranda said. 'All the travel brochures make it look as if these ancient sites are in the middle of nowhere, but over thousands of years suburbia has crept up around them.'

'Here we are!' the driver said, turning abruptly into the entrance of the hotel. 'And everyone is alive!' He pulled up with a screech and several porters rushed out to collect the luggage and open the car doors, though no matter how hard one fellow tried – pushing and pulling and huffing and heaving – there was no chance that the rear right door was going to budge. Eventually he gave up. Chessie pushed herself across the seat and literally fell out onto the pavement.

Behind them, in the second vehicle, Jacinta was relieved to see that Alice-Miranda had hopped off Lucas's lap. When she'd spotted Caprice getting cosy with the boy it had been all she could do not to haul the other girl out of there.

The driver pulled a card from his pocket and passed it to Livinia, who was still regaining her composure in the front seat.

'What's this?' She looked at him with disdain and pushed a loose strand of hair behind her ear.

'My number – in case you want reliable taxi while you are in the city,' the man said.

'And I should have introduced myself earlier. I am Ahmed.'

'I can't believe you said that – and with a straight face.' Livinia pushed the card back towards him and jumped out. 'Rest assured we will not be seeking your services again.'

The man looked stung. 'Do not be so sure.'

Alice-Miranda leaned against the open driver's window. 'Please don't be upset, Mr Ahmed. Miss Reedy is just a little bit protective of us,' she said. 'Thank you for an interesting journey. I enjoyed your commentary.'

Barclay Ferguson strode out of the hotel lobby, resplendent in a pale blue linen suit with a white shirt and tartan tie. He'd been sitting inside awaiting the group's arrival and praying that they would make it safely, having had many a hair-raising airport taxi ride himself.

'Hello everyone!' the man crowed. 'All here, safe as houses, I see. Mr Plumpton, Miss Reedy – it's good to see ye both again. Welcome to Cairo.'

Barclay had visited Winchesterfield-Downsfordvale earlier in the year to talk to the staff and students about the exciting new programs that the Queen's Colours program was offering, so he was familiar with the pair.

He shook Mr Plumpton's hand and kissed Miss Reedy's cheek before turning to the children, who were busy gathering their belongings.

'Hello Mr Ferguson,' Alice-Miranda stepped forward and offered her hand.

'Oh me dear girl. How wonderful it is to see ye again. And Millicent and Caprice – yer've grown so tall – and Francesca, ye are nothin' short of a wonder, gettin' through all that work to be able to join yer friends here.' He proceeded to greet all of the children by name, telling them how excited he was to have them on the trip.

'The rest of the children and Mr Pienaar have arrived. We'll be seein' them shortly at dinner. Miss Cranna is inside the foyer with all of yer room keys and a map of the hotel,' the man said. 'There's time to freshen up after yer travels and then we'll meet by the pool – but not in yer togs. There will be no swimmin' tonight.'

'The hotel is beautiful,' Millie said, then pointed towards the pyramids, which were not far away. 'And look at that view.'

'Well, enjoy it, Millicent. We have three nights here, then the rest of the trip we'll be in more modest accommodation in Luxor,' Mr Ferguson said with a smile. 'Although I can promise ye that there will be spectacular sights at every turn, as well as some interestin' *sites* – if you get what I mean. I well remember when I had the opportunity to dig for treasures meself many years ago. It was the most excitin' thing to uncover ancient secrets – even if it was just a tiny oil pot and a cartouche.'

'Do we get to keep the things we find?' Jacinta asked. 'Presuming we find anything, that is.'

Mr Ferguson was about to answer when Millie leapt in, shaking her head. 'No. Every single antiquity is automatically the property of the Egyptian government. You can buy souvenirs, but they won't be real.'

'That's absolutely true, Millicent,' Barclay concurred. 'Unfortunately the Egyptians lost vast amounts of treasures over the years – that's why there are so many artefacts in museums and private collections all around the world. It was only in the mid-nineteenth century that laws were passed to try to prevent the pillagin', but that still doesn't always save them.'

'So even if you're Egyptian and you find something under your own house, you're not allowed to keep it?' Alice-Miranda asked.

'Correct,' Mr Ferguson said as he ushered them into the hotel. 'Ye could even find yerself in prison for that.'

In the foyer, the children were greeted by Morag Cranna, who was looking far more stylish than she had during their Scottish adventure. Today, she was dressed in a pair of navy capri pants, beige sandals and a pretty white blouse with a pale yellow scarf slung stylishly around her shoulders. She was also wearing jewellery – a gold necklace with an amulet featuring Bastet the Egyptian cat goddess.

'You look lovely, Miss Cranna,' Alice-Miranda said. 'And your necklace is gorgeous.'

The woman smiled broadly. 'Thank ye, sweetheart. I bought it today outside the airport – you know me and cats – I couldna resist. And as for me clothes – well, we have a new lass in the office who is very fashionable. When the sweet girl tactfully told me that me wardrobe was channelling her granny – and she's nigh on a hundred – I asked if she'd take me shoppin'. I've had me hair restyled too. I feel like a million pounds, if I do say so meself.'

Alice-Miranda smiled at her. 'I think ten million pounds is more like it.'

While Morag organised the children into their rooms, Alice-Miranda spotted Miss Reedy fidgeting over by the reception desk. She saw one of the hotel staff hand the teacher a note, which Miss Reedy read. Afterwards she looked visibly shaken. Alice-Miranda slipped away to see if the woman was all right.

'Hello Miss Reedy, is anything the matter?' the girl asked.

Livinia slipped the note into her handbag. 'No, I'm fine. Well, apart from that hair-raising taxi ride and a headache that won't give up,' the woman replied, rubbing her temples.

'Did you make your calls?'

The teacher looked at her blankly.

'You said that you needed to make some important calls when we got to the hotel?' Alice-Miranda reminded her.

'Oh, they can wait,' Miss Reedy said, and walked off towards her husband.

Alice-Miranda frowned. The teacher certainly wasn't behaving like her usual self. And then there was the taxi driver, Ahmed, who the girl could have sworn was the same man who had been trying to sell his wares outside the airport – except that fellow's clothes had been different and Ahmed had flatly denied any knowledge of having seen the children before. It was all a bit curious, really.

Chapter 8

Masud kicked away the stone that he'd been chasing around the yard and closed the gate, then carried the bucket into the adjoining stable building. He set it down beside the feed bins and sat nearby to inspect the tack. The boy had not spoken to his father since his outburst but he had done all of his chores regardless. His parents didn't need anything more to worry about.

When he'd headed outside to tend the camels, his father had been at the table checking the itinerary for the week to come and calling his contacts to make sure that everything was in place for the upcoming tour. Akil Salah left nothing to chance; he'd been trained by Masud's grandfather from a young age and was proud of the way he ran his business. Akil's attention to detail accounted for him being one of the most sought-after guides in all of Egypt, and tourist groups paid handsomely for his services (it was still a miserly sum but much more than many of his counterpart received).

Masud had never wanted to be a guide and, while the idea of being a professional football player had crossed his mind many times – as seemed to be the case for most Egyptian boys – his real dream was to be an archaeologist. Like Dr Hassam, who was always on the television showing the world his finds. Masud wasn't keen on the publicity but he loved the idea of uncovering the treasures of the past. He always had his head in a book, and had been the top of his class until a few months ago, when, on his fifteenth birthday, he left school. He had done it for Jabari, so their father wouldn't have to employ anyone else to help with the tours. So they could put the extra money towards his brother's treatment. It wasn't the worst thing.

Being his father's assistant meant he could get practical experience and perhaps one day, when life was normal again, he could go back to his studies.

Tomorrow they would take the new visitors – who included a longtime friend of his father – to the museum and Old Cairo. They would tour the Al Azhar Mosque and the Khan El Khalili – the great souk. Then they would spend the following day at Giza, taking in the Great Pyramid complex and the Sphinx as well as the necropolis of Saqqara, home to the Step Pyramid of Djoser and its mastaba tombs, and the Pyramid of Teti. There would also be sunset photographs with the camels adorned with their splendid saddles and cloths, their beaded headdresses and plaited reins. It was Masud's job to dress the herd – six girls, five of whom had the temperaments of lambs and one, Nenet, who did not.

A loud bellow caused the boy to spin around.

Through the open doorway, Masud could see Nenet biting one of the young camels on the bottom – again.

'Stop that!' Masud called out. The old girl grunted and took off around their small yard, her legs flying as she rounded up the rest of the herd, then came to a shuddering halt by the stables – her left hind leg raised.

'Don't you dare!' Masud called.

But before he could reach her, Nenet kicked out. The camel had recently decided to take her anger out on the ancient building and had worked several stones loose over the course of the past week. This time, she kicked so hard a limestone block on the corner at the base was completely displaced.

'Nenet! You will get both of us into trouble!'

The boy went to make a closer inspection of the destruction. Masud would have to tell his father – he would need help to mix the mortar to fix the block back in place properly – but for now perhaps he could shore it up on his own. His father was likely in no mood for mortar mixing. Nenet leaned down and nibbled the boy's hair.

'Go away!' He turned and swatted at her, but she simply batted her long eyelashes at him, then leaned around and nibbled his cheek.

'Urgh! You really need to brush those teeth of yours, lady,' Masud grimaced at the stench.

She nudged his back and he fell forward, flat on his stomach. Honestly, if the boy didn't know

better he would have sworn that the camel under-
stood every word he said – insults included. She
was certainly a thousand times more cunning than
the other girls, who just did their jobs, ate their
food and kept to themselves.

'Seriously, stop it! I will tell Baba and you
will be in the market making someone else's life a
misery before I can find a whip,' the boy threatened. But they both knew he didn't mean it. Masud
had never hit any of their camels and neither had
his father, who said that his own father had taught
him to respect the animals. No one, not even a
camel, would feel more cooperative after a beating.

Masud was about to get up when he saw a
hole in the base of the foundation, beneath where
the missing block had sat. Something was glinting
inside, but in the setting sun he couldn't see well
enough to tell what it was.

'What's this?' The boy stood up and ran into
the stables, seizing the torch that was hanging on a
hook. He scampered back to where the stone had
been dislodged. Nenet was still there, nosing around.

Masud pushed her out of the way and fell to
his knees, flicking the light on and shining it into
the crevice.

He gasped. 'Nenet, what have you found?'

He was about to run and tell his father when he stopped in his tracks. This was his secret, and the camel's. If this was what Masud thought it was, then perhaps there would be a way to save Jabari after all. Though what he needed more than anything right now, was time. He would return after his family was asleep to make further investigations.

Every one of the cheap plastic chairs in the beige-walled hospital waiting room was full – mostly with officials. Someone had alerted the media, who had descended like vultures. While the majority of the journalists had been ordered to stay outside, several (the ones who curried most favour with the government) had managed to sneak their way into the building. One man had bailed Maryam up, firing question after question, but she refused to say a word – or perhaps it was that she was unable. She didn't think she'd spoken since the paramedics had arrived. Something inside her had shut down while she was processing what had happened. Perhaps it was shock.

As far as Maryam was concerned, performing CPR on her boss was well outside her job description, but her instincts had kicked in. Many years before, when she had lived in a place far from Cairo, Maryam had worked as a lifeguard – a summer job to pay her bills while at university. She had pulled several people from the surf in that time, but none of them had ever been unconscious. Today, when faced with a life-or-death situation, she had been stunned by how much she remembered. What was that acronym? DRS ABCD? She'd checked for danger and a response and that his airways were clear, but he had not been breathing. Mouth-to-mouth resuscitation and chest compressions were required. So many compressions, for what seemed like forever, and all the while she shouted for someone to help her.

Now, Maryam's shoulders were aching and she would have given anything for a cup of coffee. As if by magic, one appeared in front of her. Maryam hadn't even registered that Nour Badawy, Dr Hassam's personal assistant, had left the room, let alone returned with coffee and a chocolate bar. Maryam took both and nodded. Still, she did not speak.

'Miss Moussa,' Nour whispered. 'Would you like to talk about what happened?'

The woman reminded Maryam of her mother. They were both beautiful with ready smiles and a natural kindness, though Nour was far more glamorous – always in silk headscarves matched to her outfit – and the shoes! Maryam thought she had an impressive collection, but she couldn't remember Nour ever wearing the same pair twice.

Maryam didn't think of her mother terribly often, only occasionally allowing herself to wonder what she might be doing, if she was still well, if she was still alive. The woman shook the thoughts from her mind. It wasn't sensible to dwell on the past, particularly when it could not be changed.

Nour sat down in the empty seat beside Maryam. 'Is there anything I can do?' she asked. Nour made Dr Hassam's life much easier than it should have been. She worked in the shadows, a model of quiet efficiency. He, with his overbearing personality and giant ego, took her completely for granted.

Maryam shook her head.

A doctor in a white coat and with a stethoscope slung around his neck stepped into the doorway.

For a fleeting moment, Maryam wondered if she'd walked onto the set of one of those medical dramas she enjoyed so much. Perhaps she would soon rouse and realise that she had simply fallen asleep in front of the television – she could hop up and go to bed. But this was real life.

For several moments there was a tense silence. It felt as if the air had been sucked from the room as everyone held their collective breath.

Finally the doctor spoke. 'Dr Hassam is alive,' he announced, to a loud cheer. The man held up his hands to quieten the crowd. 'But there has been some bleeding on the brain and he is in a coma. We will have to wait and see what the long-term implications will be. I am afraid he is still not out of the woods.'

This time there was no cheer.

The man walked over and stood in front of Maryam. 'Miss Moussa. What you did today – it was very brave. If you hadn't acted so quickly Dr Hassam would not have survived.'

Maryam looked up at the doctor, an unexpected tear falling onto the top of her cheek.

Suddenly there was a flash and Maryam was aware that someone had taken her picture.

'No!' she shouted, then turned away to face the wall. 'Please, I do not want this.'

'Out!' The doctor turned and glared at the man responsible – a journalist with a camera slung around his neck. 'All of you, it is time to leave this poor woman in peace.'

Nour reached over and squeezed Maryam's hand.

The doctor waited until the room was cleared before continuing. 'If you would like, Miss Moussa, I can bring you something for your nerves,' he offered.

Maryam shook her head. 'I will be fine. I just don't like fuss.'

The doctor gave a nod and left.

Nour stood up and walked to the other side of the room.

The two women were silent until Maryam had a thought. 'Who will do the minister's job until he gets well?'

Nour spun around. 'It would usually be Mr Salib, of course, but he is away for some time yet on his honeymoon – unless he returns early. I will telephone him immediately.'

A realisation dawned on Maryam, and she shook her head. 'No, there is no need. He should not be made to change his plans.'

Nour bit her lip. 'Then it is you, Miss Moussa. You are third in the chain of command.'

Maryam raised her eyebrows. 'I suppose I am, aren't I?' she said evenly. It wasn't really a question, given the Ministry had recently issued a chart showing the hierarchy of staff positions.

'I am sure Mr Salib and his lovely wife will be grateful,' Nour said. 'Dr Hassam's calendar is very busy this month – he was due to lead a number of tours and I cannot imagine a young wife would appreciate being separated from her husband so soon. Besides, you are eminently qualified.'

Maryam looked at her quizzically.

'Dr Hassam was well aware that your credentials exceed his. A PhD in Archaeology, a master's degree in Egyptology and an MBA – Dr Hassam has always said that should Mr Salib decide to change direction, you would be his next deputy.'

'Really?' Maryam frowned. She had no idea the man thought anything of her.

'He has always been impressed with your work,' Nour said.

Maryam swallowed hard. He hadn't sounded impressed when he'd come to see her that morning.

Quite the opposite, in fact. She hated to think what it was he had been going to tell her before he collapsed.

The last thing Maryam wanted was to spend days on end playing in the sand, but the position was too good an opportunity to pass up. She would, of course, have to ditch the television crews that followed Dr Hassam around day and night. That kind of coverage was not what she wanted at all. Maryam stood up. Her heart was pounding. Was she dreaming? Was it even possible that she was about to take over one of the most prestigious roles in the entire country? It would be temporary but she would use the time very wisely.

If only she actually deserved it.

Chapter 9

'I'm going to have a shower before dinner,' Alice-Miranda said as soon as she and Millie arrived in their room. The girl unzipped her suitcase and pulled out a change of clothes while Millie flopped onto one of the twin beds and picked up the television remote control on the bedside table.

'I'll jump in after you,' Millie called. She fiddled with the remote for a few seconds before the screen came to life, then flicked through several Arabic news channels until chancing upon

Egypt Can Sing – a franchise that seemed to have exploded all around the world. Millie watched one young girl with a beautiful voice then switched channels when the ads came on. There was a run of English-language news stations that were just as boring as the Arabic ones.

Millie was about to change channels again when the presenter said something that made her ears prick up.

'Up next, we have breaking news on trusted accountant Elias Badger, of the firm Badger and Woodcock, who has allegedly been ripping off clients for years in a complex investment scam . . .'

Badger and Woodcock. Millie had seen that name recently – on several letterheads in Mrs Derby's office when the girls were helping Mrs Parker with the filing.

'Oh no!' She leapt from the bed. 'Alice-Miranda, quickly – you've got to see this!' Millie called out as she charged into the bathroom, shouting over the hissing water. 'You're not going to believe it.'

'What's the matter? Is there a fire?' The other girl wiped the steam from the glass to see what was going on.

'No, it's much worse. Hurry – it's coming up on the news,' Millie urged.

Alice-Miranda snatched the towel her friend was holding out for her and wrapped it around herself before the pair raced into the bedroom, moments after the bulletin had begun.

'Many investors seem unwilling to come forward and fully disclose their losses, making it difficult to assess the scope of the scam. A raft of businesses have also been caught up in the scandal. Early estimates from those who have cooperated with police would suggest that the Ponzi scheme has netted the felon many millions. Mr Badger's associate Simeon Woodcock purports to know nothing about the allegations, telling reporters that he too has lost his entire fortune. Police believe that Mr Badger has fled the country under an assumed name and false passport.'

'There were letters from Badger and Woodcock when we were doing the filing,' Millie said. 'Mrs Parker said they were the school accountants.'

'Oh my word,' Alice-Miranda whispered, nodding. She remembered seeing them too.

'That's got to be it,' Millie said. 'Miss Grimm must have invested with that man and he's taken all the money.'

'Jacinta heard Miss Grimm say it would be even more disastrous if the news became public. At least the reporter didn't mention the school.'

There was a knock on the door. Millie ran to see who it was while Alice-Miranda hurried back into the bathroom to put some clothes on.

'Are you ready to go?' Jacinta asked.

'Not yet, but boy have we got something to tell you,' Millie said, grabbing her arm. Sloane and Chessie filed into the room after Jacinta.

'It's all right,' Jacinta said. 'Chessie knows. I didn't want us four to be having hushed conversations without her.'

'It's so awful – about school closing. I hope we can do something to help,' Chessie said.

Millie closed the door as Alice-Miranda walked out of the bathroom, towel-drying her curls. Together, she and Millie quickly filled the others in on what they'd just seen on the television.

'Does anyone know what a Ponzi scheme is?' Sloane asked.

'I do,' Alice-Miranda nodded.

The girls plonked themselves down on the beds and the sofa while she explained.

'It's where someone like an accountant or a financial planner takes money from people to invest in stocks or shares or other ventures and promises huge returns – much higher interest than they'd ever get from the banks. They make sure that they pay the investors their interest but really what they mostly do is steal the money – spending it on themselves.

'Then the scammer has to keep getting new investors to give them money so they can pay the earlier investors their interest – or all of an investor's money back if they're lucky enough to ask for it. It's illegal, of course, and most schemes come unstuck after a time because it's very complicated to keep up with everything,' Alice-Miranda said.

'So, tell me – how does an eleven-and-a-half-year-old know that?' Jacinta asked. 'Although I probably shouldn't ask as you *always* know way more about the world than the rest of us.'

Alice Miranda grinned. 'That's not true, but years ago, before I was born, Daddy got caught by a scammer in a Ponzi scheme.'

'No way! Millie exclaimed. 'Your father is far too smart for that.'

'He thought so too but this woman was very clever. She knew all the tricks. Fortunately he only gave her a relatively small sum compared to the others who were involved. It turned out she had created a false persona of a highly successful businesswoman and befriended lots of wealthy investors who thought she knew what she was doing. Then one day she disappeared, and all of the money along with her.'

'Did they ever find her?' Chessie asked.

'Never. They have no idea what happened. Daddy said that the police thought she might have met an untimely fate – that perhaps someone caught on to what she was up to – but no one knows for sure. She was a great actress and then she quite literally vanished,' Alice-Miranda said.

'It sounds like Mr Badger has done the same,' Millie said. 'How are we going to get the school's money back? He's probably already spent it.'

'It sounds like Miss Grimm was right. If all the school's money is gone they won't be able to pay the staff and . . .' Jacinta said with a sniff, tears pooling in her eyes.

For a few minutes the girls were silent, contemplating what the future might hold.

'Well, aren't we a bunch of misery guts?' Millie said, rolling over onto her stomach and propping herself on her elbows. 'But I don't see what we can possibly do – not if the money is already gone.'

'We have to think of something,' Chessie said. 'When have we ever just given up?'

'You're right,' Sloane said with a firm nod. 'Look at what we did after the fire. The Fields Festival raised a small fortune for the Abbouds. And we don't even know how much money has been lost. Miss Grimm might be catastrophising – something she's always telling *us* not to do.'

'And we can't let this destroy the trip – I mean, what's the point of even being here if that's the case,' Chessie said.

'Absolutely,' Alice-Miranda agreed. 'Some of our dearest friends have come from all over the world and I've hardly given them a second thought. We need to buck up and enjoy ourselves and I'm sure that over the next few days we'll come up with some ideas.'

The girls stood up and formed a circle.

'We need to make a pact,' Millie said. 'No moping. We'll have a great trip and keep our thinking caps on. Something will work out – it usually does.'

They all placed their hands on top of each other in a circle.

'And whatever happens, if the worst is done, we'll find a way to be together at another school,' Sloane said. Though she wasn't quite sure how, given her fees had been paid upfront by her step-grandmother Henrietta and her parents weren't exactly flush with funds. 'Maybe Fayle will have to become co-ed – although being at school with Sep, well, that's a horrible thought.'

'That's a brilliant idea,' Jacinta said, a huge smile spreading across her face. 'Perhaps we should call Professor Winterbottom and suggest it.'

'You would say that, of course.' Millie rolled her eyes. 'Then you could be with Lucas all the time.'

'Maybe there's another school that can rescue us and take over,' Chessie said.

The girls nodded.

Millie glanced at the clock. 'I need to get changed!' she exclaimed and hurried into the bathroom.

'We'll see you all on the terrace in a few minutes,' Alice-Miranda said.

As the other girls departed, Alice-Miranda stood by the window, running a wide-toothed comb through her unruly curls. She stared at the pyramids in the distance, an idea forming in her mind. There was something her Uncle Lawrence had said while they were in the outback. Maybe the film business could be the answer to their problems, at least for a little while. She'd think on it further, and in the meantime she'd talk to Miss Reedy and see what more the woman knew.

Chapter 10

'Britt!' Alice-Miranda shouted and ran to greet her friend. In the time since they'd been together in Scotland, the girls seemed to have grown even more similar in their features – apart from Britt being blonde and Alice-Miranda brunette. The two girls hugged tightly before Alice-Miranda stepped back.

'Oh my goodness!' Britt exclaimed. 'Look at us.' She realised they were wearing very near the same outfit: baggy harem pants – Alice-Miranda's in white and Britt's in blue – silver sandals and long-sleeved tees with silver sequinned motifs. Alice-Miranda's had a heart on the front, while Britt's boasted smaller swirly patterns.

'Seriously, I think you two really are secret twins,' Millie said, grinning. Britt greeted her with a hug too.

'It is a bit uncanny,' Alice-Miranda said.

Caprice rolled her eyes. 'As if. I bet you two totally planned this and we're all supposed to ooh and ahh over the fact that you're almost identical – as if there's some kind of kooky twin connection. Yeah right.'

'It's lovely to see you too, Caprice,' Britt said, then smiled. 'Your hair is even more beautiful than I remember.'

Caprice's lip quivered. 'I know – it's so shiny at the moment,' she said, then wrinkled her nose, cross at herself for accepting the compliment. She hated that Britt was as sweet as Alice-Miranda and equally accomplished in her disarming behaviour. In that way they were completely alike.

'Excuse me a moment. I've just spotted Neville,' Alice-Miranda said, leaving the other girls to chat.

Their dinner was taking place outside on a two-tiered terrace. Beautiful limestone balustrades with cut-out patterns of stars and circles gave glimpses of the water features and green grass of the gardens beyond. Fairy lights adorning the trees and verandas had begun to twinkle in the low light. In the distance were tall palms and hedges, with two pyramids looming in the background. It was the most enchanting view. Serenading the group was a folk band – musicians dressed in traditional costumes, two with drums and one with an Egyptian lyre called a simsimiyya. They began to play and sing, giving a wonderful atmosphere to the evening.

Alice-Miranda ran down a short flight of steps to the lower terrace and snuck up behind Neville. He was talking to Lucas, Sep and a boy called Vincent Roche, who was from a school in Paris and had been with them in Scotland.

The girl pressed her finger to her lips as Lucas spotted her, then reached up and covered Neville's eyes.

'Guess who?' she whispered.

'Well, that's tricky. Let me think. Maybe some girl who once rescued me from making a complete fool of myself on a ship when I was young and stupid?' Neville said.

The boy spun around and Alice-Miranda hugged him tightly, though for a second Neville didn't seem to know what to do. Vincent frowned at the lad and wrapped his arms around himself, prompting Neville to hug Alice-Miranda back.

'Oh Neville, it's so wonderful to see you. How are you? How are your parents? Have you been enjoying school?' Alice-Miranda prattled. 'Thank you for your letters. I've looked forward to them every month. It's so much fun to have an old-fashioned penpal. It's much more exciting to receive something in the post, don't you think?'

'Do you write to each other?' Sep asked, a frown appearing on his forehead.

The pair nodded.

'For a long time,' Alice-Miranda said.

'Alice-Miranda's letters are wonderful,' Neville said. 'So descriptive and with all the news. I don't know if I'd make it through each month without them. That's how I know a lot about what you've all been up to.'

'And yours are so charming. Last month Neville sent me a collection of origami animals he'd made,' Alice-Miranda said.

Neville's ears began to glow. 'I had to show someone how terrible I was at it – and I hope

92

they've all gone to the bin, where I should have put them in the first place.'

Lucas grinned. 'You two sound like a young soldier and his sweetheart writing to one another during a war.'

Alice-Miranda shook her head. 'Don't be silly, Lucas. We're not in a war.'

Neville grinned, while Alice-Miranda's cheeks suddenly became hot and turned quite pink. She hoped that she hadn't caught anything on the plane.

'Are you all right?' the boy asked. 'You look flushed.'

'Yes, just a bit hot, but I suppose that's to be expected out here in the desert,' she said.

Sep had raced away at the comment, returning with a glass of iced water he'd fetched from one of the tables on the upper terrace where they were going to have their dinner.

'Thought you might need this,' he said as he proffered the drink.

'Oh thank you, Sep – you're very kind,' Alice-Miranda said.

She took it and had a few sips, thinking that perhaps she should sit down. She felt a little bit faint.

Neville had wondered if that was the case and rushed to procure a chair.

'Goodness me, thank you, Neville. Aren't you two the sweetest?' Alice-Miranda said. She didn't notice the glare that passed between the boys, but Millie did. She'd been watching from the upper terrace where she was trapped in conversation by her distant cousin, Madagascar Slewt.

She had desperately hoped that the girl wouldn't be joining them in Egypt, but here she was, pinning Millie down, rabbiting on about how awful everything was and that there was a terrible smell in her room and she had to share with Britt, who she hardly knew even though they'd met in Scotland. Millie was doing her best to get away, looking over the girl's shoulder at the antics happening between the boys and Alice-Miranda.

The PA system squawked like a dying seagull, getting everyone's attention. It squawked once more before Barclay Ferguson gave up and crowed, 'Hello everyone! Welcome to Cairo. It's so wonderful to see ye all. Miss Cranna and I have an exceptional itinerary planned, which be available in yer rooms later this evenin'. Meetin' points and punctuality are key to ensurin' a successful trip so please make sure that you read everythin' carefully and adhere to the guidelines and the times – they are *not* a suggestion. Rest assured we will not be waitin' and chasin'. That's why you're here – because ye've all shown yourselves to have great initiative and resourcefulness.'

'Initiative is an interesting word, isn't it?' Millie said aloud to no one in particular, wondering how her cousin had managed to attain her Queen's Gold award. Chessie, standing beside her, gave a wry nod.

'Durin' our time out here, Miss Cranna and I will be lookin' for students who demonstrate initiative, courage, kindness and a well-developed moral compass – among other things – all of which will be necessary as ye continue workin' towards the achievement of yer Diamond level.'

'That's Caprice and Maddie done for. I don't think either of them have a clue what a moral compass is,' Millie whispered to Chessie. The pair giggled until they noticed Caprice glaring.

'Miss Cranna, do ye have anythin' to add?' the man asked.

Morag stepped forward and offered her own welcome to the children. She then gave some instructions about the buffet meal they were about to enjoy before running through the first part of the itinerary. The group was setting off early in the morning on a tour of Old Cairo. She listed some of the attractions they would be visiting and said that the following day would be spent at the pyramids, and the day after that there would be an early morning flight from Cairo to Luxor. They could read about the rest of the surprises that were taking place when they looked at their itineraries.

There were some excited cheers as the children took it all in.

The woman stepped back.

'Now, I'm wonderin' where Miss Reedy, Mr Plumpton and Mr Pienaar have got to?' Barclay asked.

Hansie Pienaar from Todder House School gave a shout from the lower terrace and Mr Plumpton waved from where he was standing in the corner by the double doors.

'Miss Reedy will be along shortly,' he called, looking around anxiously.

'Ah, very good,' Mr Ferguson said, welcoming the teachers.

The man then invited everyone to line up for the buffet, which was heaving under the weight of a huge variety of traditional Egyptian fare. There was a seemingly endless number of dips including baba ganoush, labneh, beet hummus and a range of flat breads as well as kebabs and kofta. Baked sweet potatoes with sour cream and chives sat alongside delicious vegetables – peppers, zucchini and eggplant stuffed with rice mixed with aromatic herbs – and a dipping sauce. There were platters of meat as well.

Soon the whole group was seated at two long tables. The musicians started up again, playing a loud, upbeat tune. After ten minutes, Alice-Miranda excused herself. She wanted to find Miss Reedy and see if the woman was all right. Mr Plumpton was chatting with Mr Ferguson, though she had seen him keeping an eye on the doorway as he did so.

The girl hurried inside, and made her way to Mr Plumpton and Miss Reedy's room at the end of the hall.

Alice-Miranda knocked gently and waited. On the other side of the door she could hear what sounded like muffled sobs.

'Miss Reedy, are you in there?' she called. 'May I talk to you, please?'

'I'll be out shortly,' the woman replied. The words were followed by some loud sniffs.

'Miss Reedy, please, may I come in?' Alice-Miranda tried again.

There was the sound of shuffling feet and the woman opened the door just a smidge.

'Is it urgent, Alice-Miranda?'

'Miss Reedy, I know there's something wrong at school,' the girl replied. 'And I think that's why you're upset.'

'What are you talking about?' Livinia demanded. She seemed to be debating whether or not to let the child in, then increased the opening just enough for Alice-Miranda to slip through.

'All right. Out with it,' Livinia said, stalking across to the window. She grabbed a tissue from the box on the bench on her way.

'I can't tell you how I know, because it was an innocent accident and I promised, but Miss Grimm said that the school is going to close down,' Alice-Miranda said.

Miss Reedy gasped, her hands flying to her mouth. She spun around. 'Oh heavens, surely it's not that bad?'

Alice-Miranda shrugged. 'And just before we

went to dinner there was something on the English news channel about Badger and Woodcock,' the girl continued.

Livinia's eyes widened as Alice-Miranda explained what was said on the television.

'I had a message to call them,' Livinia said with a sigh. 'When we arrived at the hotel.'

'And did you?' Alice-Miranda asked.

Livinia nodded.

'What did they say?' Alice-Miranda asked.

'It appears that I have done something rather foolish, but . . .'

The English teacher was interrupted by a knock and her husband's voice.

'Livinia, darling, are you all right?' Before she could answer there was the sound of the key card swiping.

'You're not to say a word about any of this, to anyone,' Livinia whispered, eyeballing the girl.

'But, Miss Reedy –' Alice-Miranda started, as Miss Reedy rushed to the bathroom. She was about to tell the teacher that she wasn't the only student who knew when Mr Plumpton opened the door.

'Oh, hello Alice-Miranda,' he said. 'What are you doing here?'

'I wasn't feeling the best and came to ask Miss Reedy for a paracetamol,' the girl replied.

'Yes, we were just coming now,' the woman said, walking back into the room. Her face was much less red and puffy.

It was clear that Miss Reedy wasn't about to tell Alice-Miranda anything more now they had company.

'Yes, well, get a wriggle on. The food is magnificent,' the man said.

Whatever was happening, it was clear that Miss Reedy felt responsible – though why was anyone's guess. Alice-Miranda followed the couple out into the hall, wishing they'd had another minute or two alone.

Chapter 11

The sky was just beginning to lighten when Masud covered the hole with a plank of wood and some straw. He hid the pick and shovel easily, but the dirt and debris was more difficult to get rid of. In the end, he decided the best place for it was the end stall. The stables were mostly used for storage. The camels rarely spent a night inside unless one of them was unwell or injured. His father hardly stepped foot inside the building now that Masud had officially joined the family business. The camels were Masud's responsibility, just as they had been his father's when he was the same age.

The boy looked over the half stable door at the herd gathered together in the corner of the small yard, sound asleep. He was about to make a run for the house when Nenet poked her head inside and puckered her lips, causing Masud to jump.

'Not you again!' he whispered. But he couldn't be too cross. If it wasn't for Nenet and her never-ending tantrums he wouldn't have found the cavity. Masud shooed her back towards the other camels, then turned to make sure that there was no trace of his activities. The sun would soon be up and so would his parents.

Minutes later he climbed silently through his open bedroom window and fell onto his bed, quickly kicking off his sandals and burying himself beneath the covers. His arms were aching and he desperately wanted a drink but he would have to wait. If he was lucky he could still get some sleep before his mother's morning wakeup call. Masud closed his eyes and was soon dreaming of ancient treasures.

★

'Masud!' The boy was suddenly aware of his mother's voice outside his bedroom door, although he had been awake for a little while now, working out exactly what he needed to do. 'You must get up. Your breakfast is ready. The bus will be here to collect you and your father at half past eight.'

But Masud did not move. He had a plan.

His mother called for him once more, then, seconds later, she was in his room, her hand on his shoulder, shaking him gently.

'Masud! Wake up!'

This time he rolled over and groaned, then clutched his stomach.

'What is the matter?' the woman stepped back. 'Are you ill?'

Masud nodded. 'I have a belly ache and I am hot all over.'

Esha put her hand on the boy's forehead, then flinched. 'You're burning up.'

She did not need to know how that feat had been achieved.

'Akil!' Esha called her husband, who appeared in the doorway. 'Masud is unwell. He must stay in bed today.'

Akil looked at the boy. 'What is wrong?'

The pair spoke in hushed tones as they walked out of the room. This made Masud feel genuinely sick. He knew his mother would be concerned that his 'illness' was something serious. The last thing he wanted was to give her more worries than she already had.

He felt bad for his father too. While the man would be fine on his own, it was good for him to have a runner. Masud's role was generally to go ahead and check that entry fees were paid and arrangements were in place while his father entertained the tour group. And entertain he did. Masud had been amazed to see how brilliant he was the first few times he'd accompanied the man to work. Brilliant, and so funny. Then again, Akil used to be funny at home before Jabari got sick. He had always made them laugh. Sadly, laughter wasn't something readily found in the Salah home at the moment. Akil was good at partitioning his personal life and work. Perhaps in those moments when his father was talking to strangers, he allowed himself to believe that things were as they had always been.

Masud's mother returned to his room.

'I will bring some tea before I leave. Your father will work alone today. At least the tour is only in the city. Tomorrow you will be better to help with the camels,' Esha said. 'It is fortunate your father's old friend, Mr Ferguson, is also very familiar with the sights of Cairo, so while they will miss you, I am sure they will cope.'

The woman disappeared and Masud heard his parents talking outside his room again.

'I will go to the hospital very soon. Your mother can watch Masud,' Esha said.

'Very well,' Akil replied. 'I will try to see Jabari this evening.'

Masud was relieved to hear it. His grandmother would not come near his room if that was his request – she would be busy in the kitchen preparing their evening meal, then she would sit in the chair in front of the television and watch her favourite soap operas until she fell asleep. At least that's what happened most days when she stayed at home. He could only hope that today would be no different. Actually, he was counting on it.

Chapter 12

Despite the uncertainty of the previous evening, Alice-Miranda and Millie had both slept well. When the party finished they'd headed back to their room and read the itinerary from start to finish. It was incredibly exciting that they were going to spend a couple of days working on a bona fide archaeological dig site led by none other than the Minister for Antiquities himself, the renowned archaeologist Mustafa Hassam.

'What are we going to do about Miss Reedy and the Ponzi scheme?' Millie asked as she and

Alice-Miranda grabbed their day packs and made sure they had everything they needed.

Alice-Miranda bit her lip. 'I'll try to get some time alone with her today. See what more I can find out.'

'Don't you think it's strange she didn't want Mr Plumpton to know, considering she was going to tell you before you were interrupted,' Millie said.

Although Miss Reedy had asked her not to, Alice-Miranda had told Millie what had happened last night. There was no point keeping the secret, seeing as though there were five of them who were aware of the scam and the possible link to school.

'Perhaps not. I have a feeling that, whatever has happened, Miss Reedy thinks she's to blame,' the girl replied.

Millie grabbed her camera and checked that it was fully charged. She'd already taken loads of great shots and was planning to put together a book of memories from the trip when they got home.

'Has Lawrence called you back yet?' Millie asked. Alice-Miranda had left a message for him last night. He was currently in Russia somewhere quite remote shooting a film. Alice-Miranda had asked him to phone her when he got a chance but hadn't left any details. It wasn't the sort of thing she could explain in a twenty-second message.

'No, not yet. I really don't have any idea if that plan is likely to work, but it's better than nothing,' Alice-Miranda said.

Millie nodded. '*Anything* we can do to help the school is a good idea as far as I'm concerned.'

Alice-Miranda nodded. 'It's the only idea I've had so far,' she said as she stashed a scarf into her pack. The girls had been advised that it was respectful to cover their heads in the mosques. 'We'd better get a move on.'

The pair headed out the door and down the hall for breakfast. The restaurant was already thronging with people. A special area was set aside for the Queen's Colours group. Miss Cranna was directing the children to the buffet, which had a mix of western and traditional Middle Eastern fare. There was French toast and a variety of pastries as well as eggs, sausages, bacon and tomatoes. Ful medames – fava beans served with a boiled egg – sat alongside Beid Bel Basterma – an Egyptian version of bacon and eggs – and there was tea and coffee by the pot-full.

'Good mornin', girls.' Barclay Ferguson was resplendent in a taupe linen suit. He looked as if he'd stepped straight from Lord Carnarvon's 1922 expedition to uncover the treasures of Tutankhamun's tomb.

'Good morning, Mr Ferguson,' the children replied, then scampered off to join the line at the buffet.

Alice-Miranda scanned the room to see if Miss Reedy and Mr Plumpton had joined them yet.

'Hello girls,' Livinia Reedy said tightly as she approached Alice-Miranda and Millie while they were filling their plates.

'You look lovely, Miss Reedy,' Millie said.

The woman was wearing a pair of beige linen pants and a pretty, loose-fitting floral top with tan-coloured sandals.

The compliment seemed to catch the teacher off guard.

'Thank you, Millie,' she said. There was an obvious tension in her voice.

'Are you feeling better today?' Alice-Miranda asked.

'Not especially,' Miss Reedy replied.

'Is there anything we can do?' Millie said.

'I doubt it. These are worries all of my own creation, apparently,' the woman replied somewhat mysteriously.

'There are always solutions to problems, no matter how *big* they seem at the time,' Millie said.

The woman eyeballed the red-haired child.

'And what big problem are you referring to, Millicent?' Miss Reedy asked, a frown puckering her forehead.

'Nothing in particular,' the girl said. 'I just meant problems in general. Nothing to do with jobs or schools or bad accountants or anything like that.'

Alice-Miranda elbowed her friend, willing her to be quiet, while Livinia glared at the girl.

Miss Reedy leaned down close and whispered. 'What do you know?'

Millie shook her head. 'Nothing. Not a thing. I was just talking nonsense – you know I do that all the time.'

'I don't believe you.' The woman narrowed her eyes so that they were barely open. Millie gulped.

She then turned her attention to Alice-Miranda. 'And I thought I told you not to say a word,' she whispered.

'You don't understand, Miss Reedy, I –'

Josiah Plumpton arrived and slid into the line behind his wife.

'Everything all right, dear?' he asked, but Livinia turned and rushed away towards the fresh fruit display.

'Oh dear,' Millie said, pulling a face.

Alice-Miranda frowned and spun around to face the Science teacher.

'How are you this morning, Mr Plumpton?' she asked.

'I'm fine, although Miss Reedy is still very much on edge,' the man said. 'I just wish she'd tell me what's troubling her.'

'I'm sure she will when she's ready,' Alice-Miranda said. 'Oh look, there's Neville,' the girl said, nudging Millie. 'We'll see you later, sir.'

The girls scurried away. 'I'm so sorry,' Millie apologised. 'Seriously, why did I choose now to have the worst case of verbal diarrhoea in my entire life? It's a wonder I didn't just come out and say that we know the school is doomed because of Mr Badger and his Ponzi scheme.'

'Millie!' Alice-Miranda pressed her finger against the girl's lips but it was too late.

'Who's doomed?' Madagascar Slewt demanded. She had been hovering behind a potted palm out of sight.

'No one,' Millie shook her head, hoping that the girl hadn't been paying attention, but that was like hoping Nile crocodiles didn't enjoy munching on the odd villager or two.

'It's nothing to worry about,' Alice-Miranda said.

'I heard what you said. Daddy and Mummy's accountant is called Mr Badger, and Mummy and I laugh about it all the time,' Madagascar said. 'And what's a pansy scheme? Is it something to do with gardening?'

'Yes. My mum is planting a whole new garden of pansies and she's hoping our dog Badger doesn't dig them up,' Millie replied with a smile. She felt quite pleased with that comeback after her previous debacle. 'Look, I think Caprice has saved you a seat over there.'

Madagascar turned to see the copper-haired girl waving at her.

'She is *so* nice. I think we're destined to become best friends. I guess it would have happened in Scotland if we'd been on the same team.

She's going to ask Miss Cranna if it would be all right for Britt to move into Sloane's room and Caprice can swap into mine,' Madagascar said.

'I hope Miss Cranna is agreeable,' Alice-Miranda said. It was a good outcome for everyone.

'Maddie,' Caprice called. 'Would you bring me some breakfast? I'm so tired.'

'Watch this,' Millie whispered to Alice-Miranda, waiting for the ensuing fireworks. No one ordered Madagascar Slewt around. But the girl obviously valued her new friendship with Caprice more than Millie had thought.

Madagascar rushed over to the table. 'Here, have mine and I'll get some more.'

'Wow. That was unexpected,' Millie said.

'I'm glad that they've found one another,' Alice-Miranda said. 'Perhaps that means they'll leave you and Chessie alone.'

'And perhaps pigs will fly,' Millie said. 'Did you hear what Madagascar said? Surely there can't be too many Badgers who are accountants – it would be a ridiculous coincidence.'

'True,' Alice-Miranda replied. 'But not everyone would have invested through the firm. Lots of people have their own brokers and planners.'

'Let's hope so. Madagascar's parents are insufferable and I can't imagine they'd be any nicer if they lost their fortune – though it might be a good lesson,' Millie said. 'Then she wouldn't make fun of me being on a scholarship and having holidays in a caravan.'

The girls took off towards the rest of their friends. There was some competition for where Alice-Miranda would sit, with both Neville and Sep having saved her a chair. In the end the girl chose to position herself between the two lads, opposite Britt, Millie and Chessie. Jacinta and Lucas were at the other end of the table with Sloane, and Alethea and Gretchen, who Alice-Miranda made a mental note to spend some time with. Last night she had barely managed to say hello before it was time for bed.

'Did anyone see the news this morning?' Hansie Pienaar asked. He was perched at the end of the table with Miss Reedy and Mr Plumpton. Mr Ferguson and Miss Cranna had taken charge of the table beside them and were busy quelling a small furore between Vincent Roche and Philippe Le Gall, both French students from Lycée International, who were arguing over who was the greatest Pharaoh of ancient Egypt – not that there was a clear answer.

Alice-Miranda saw Miss Reedy flinch and hoped Mr Pienaar wasn't going to mention anything about Mr Badger and his Ponzi scheme.

'No, Livinia and I never watch television when we're away. What was so interesting?' Mr Plumpton asked.

'The Minister of Antiquities has been temporarily replaced by a woman, Maryam Moussa, for the first time in history,' the man replied.

Millie rolled her eyes. 'In this day and age a woman being put in charge of something shouldn't even be news. It should just *be*.'

Livinia Reedy let out the long breath she'd obviously been holding onto. 'Hear, hear, Millie,' she said, nodding her head.

'Yes, I agree with you both wholeheartedly,' Hansie replied. 'It's just that Dr Hassam was supposed to be joining us during our archaeological dig in the Valley of the Queens,' the man explained. 'He's the most accomplished archaeologist in the whole country, but I imagine his replacement will be extremely knowledgeable too.'

'Oh, I hope so,' Alice-Miranda said. 'Do you know what happened to Dr Hassam?'

'The report says that he had a stroke and Miss Moussa – his replacement – saved his life,' Hansie Pienaar replied.

'How frightening for both of them,' Alice-Miranda said. 'She sounds very brave and definitely someone I'd like to meet.'

Alice-Miranda glanced towards the end of the table where Miss Reedy was sipping her tea. The woman's gaze was transfixed on the phone sitting beside her plate, as if she were expecting bad news to come at any second. The child resolved to talk to her again as soon as she could.

Chapter 13

Miss Cranna finished calling everyone's names and walked down the aisle of the bus, doing her final headcount. It seemed that while Mr Ferguson had told the students that they wouldn't be chased to be in the right place, Miss Cranna had other ideas about that – at least for now.

'Good mornin' again, everyone.' Barclay Ferguson had the microphone. 'We're just goin' to make a quick stop in a few minutes to collect our tour guide, Mr Salah, and his son, Masud. Then we'll be on our way to the city.'

The bus roared to life and lurched from the hotel portico onto the long driveway.

Britt Fox spun around and knelt on her seat, peering at Millie and Alice-Miranda, who were sitting behind her.

'I was reading this morning that the authorities believe there are hundreds, if not thousands, of tombs here in Egypt that have still never been found. Imagine if we stumbled upon something – wouldn't that be incredible?' Britt said.

'It certainly would,' Millie agreed. 'Though I suspect pretty much every tourist who visits probably thinks the same. It must be such hot and dusty work on the dig sites. A bit like a day's mustering on an outback cattle station.'

The girls told Britt about their most recent travels to Hope Springs Station in South Australia and the exciting treasure hunt they had found themselves part of while there.

'I would love to do something like that,' Britt said. 'Perhaps when we finish school we can go on a gap year together around the world and have many adventures?'

Alice-Miranda nodded. 'I can just imagine it. We could ask Jacinta and Sloane and Chessie and

Lucinda to join us too – although Mr Finkelstein might send a chaperone, knowing how protective he is of Lucinda.'

Britt pulled her itinerary out of her day pack and looked at the first page. 'It says we're going to have a couple of hours in the souk later. Apparently Khan El Khalili is the most important bazaar in the country – perhaps in the entire Middle East. I can't wait to see all the fabrics and the jewels. My mother told me that it's one of her favourite places in the city. Last time she was in Cairo she spent two whole days there.'

'It sounds fabulous,' Alice-Miranda agreed, while Millie said that she was on the lookout for rare treasures. She'd read in her guidebook that tourists sometimes got lucky and found something valuable for a relative bargain.

'Britt, dear, please sit down properly,' Morag Cranna asked from where she was sitting a few rows down on the opposite side. 'I'm afraid I get a wee bit nervous in the traffic here, although our driver seems to be a sensible man so far.'

Britt nodded and spun back around.

'Unlike that insane taxi driver from yesterday,' Millie said. 'The one who looked so much like that fellow selling the trinkets outside the terminal.'

'Yes, I thought so too,' Alice-Miranda said.

The girls were soon caught up chatting and pointing at this and that as the bus wound its way through the streets.

Alice-Miranda felt a tap on her shoulder. She turned to see Neville leaning forward to speak to her in the gap between the seat and the window.

'Hello,' she said.

'What are you most looking forward to seeing today?' he asked.

Sep piped up before she could answer. 'I think the King Tut exhibit is going to be amazing.' He was sitting beside Neville. 'And I can't wait to see some genuine mummies. Although some of them might be daddies.' The boy laughed at his own dad joke but the others just groaned.

On the opposite side of the aisle, Sloane nudged Chessie. 'Do you think my brother is acting weird at the moment? I mean, weirder than usual?'

Chessie looked across at the boy. He and Neville were both tapping Alice-Miranda on the shoulders, vying for her attention.

Sloane leaned across to Millie. 'What's up with those two?' she whispered.

'Hormones, I suspect,' the girl replied rolling her eyes.

'Eww, poor Alice-Miranda,' Sloane quipped. 'I mean, Neville is cute, but Sep . . .' She grimaced.

'Is adorable,' Millie said under her breath.

'What was that?' Sloane asked.

'Is deplorable,' Millie said.

'Got that in one.' Sloane giggled as they passed some donkeys who were hee-hawing so loudly they could be heard inside the bus.

The vehicle turned a corner and slowed down, coming to a stop outside a stone house with a flat roof. Giant steel rods protruded skyward and it looked as if some of the windows didn't actually have any glass in them. A man dressed in a long linen tunic with a grey cotton scarf around his neck and a turban wound loosely on his head was standing at the gate.

'Why is that guy in a dress?' Madagascar blurted.

Sloane looked at her. 'Seriously? Have you not noticed anything people have been wearing?'

'Why should I?' Madagascar replied rolling her eyes.

'Because we're here to learn about the culture and you'd do well to show some respect,' Millie said. She couldn't help herself. That cousin of hers was a nightmare.

'It's called a galabiya,' Britt said. 'It's a tra-ditional outfit for men. Some wear it and others prefer western-style clothing. I imagine that must be Mr Salah, our guide.'

'Whatever,' Madagascar said, then whispered something to Caprice and the pair sniggered behind their hands.

'I hope Mr Ferguson and Miss Cranna are a wake-up to those two,' Millie said, wondering why the girls always felt the need to be mean.

Mr Salah's house had more land around it than many of the others nearby, with fences out the back and a smaller stone building beyond the house. The yard was dusty, without a blade of grass in sight. Unlike the hotel with its emerald lawns, beautiful palm trees and water features – a veritable oasis in the desert – this was just desert.

'Look, they have camels,' Chessie called out. She was pointing and grinning.

'Poo! Camels stink,' Caprice griped. 'I hope we're not going near any of the ghastly beasts.'

'You do realise that this is Egypt, Caprice,' Millie said. 'There are camels everywhere – though interestingly there are a lot more in outback Australia.'

'Of course I know that – and as long as "everywhere" is nowhere near me, that's fine,' the girl retorted, then poked out her tongue.

'Clearly she hasn't read her itinerary properly. We're spending a whole day helping at an animal rescue charity later. I imagine there will be plenty of camels there,' Lucas said.

The children watched as Mr Ferguson stepped off the bus. He greeted Mr Salah with a hearty hug before the two men spoke for a few moments. Mr Ferguson's cheerful look was quickly replaced with a much more serious one.

Alice-Miranda wondered if there was something amiss.

Soon, Mr Ferguson was hopping back onto the bus, Mr Salah behind him.

'Everyone, this is me dear friend Akil Salah. He once saved me life – and I am sure that he will regale ye all with that story at some point on the tour. Like his father before him, who was also a dear friend and involved in the aforementioned lifesavin' incident, Mr Salah is an expert on everythin' Egyptian and he will be joining us not only today in the museum and Old Cairo but for the rest of the tour. Unfortunately Akil's son

Masud is not feelin' well, but we hope that ye will meet him tomorrow when Masud brings the family's camel train to the pyramids. It is a bit of cliché I know, camels – the ships of the desert – in front of the pyramids, but I want ye to have the opportunity for some fabulous photographs. And Masud will give ye a lesson in camel husbandry.'

'Urgh, I *hate* camels,' Caprice said, poking out her tongue.

'It is all right, miss, I can assure you that our girls are extremely well behaved. Except perhaps Nenet, and I am afraid she has very bad breath,' Akil said, to a titter of laughter. 'You do not want to get too close to her. She adores kissing our guests and her slobber is very sticky and stinky.'

'That's disgusting,' Caprice grizzled.

'Yes, I can only agree. Last time she kissed me I had to gargle an entire bottle of Minty Mint and paint some on my face just to get rid of the smell.' Akil received great guffaws of laughter from the rest of the children at that.

He slipped into the seat behind the driver and took charge of the microphone as they drove off, pointing out places of interest on the way to their first stop at the Hanging Church. The man was a font of information and the children were all keen to ask questions.

'Excuse me, Mr Salah,' Chessie called out. 'Would you be able to tell us why so many of the houses have those steel rods sticking out of the roof, and no glass in the windows like your house did?'

Akil nodded and raised one hand in the air, twirling it around. 'Yes, of course. The reason that sometimes the windows are not finished is that we get taxed on them once they are. As it is mostly quite hot here, the breeze is refreshing – except in the winter when it is actually freezing. And as for those steel rods – in Egypt, when a man gets married he does not usually leave home. Instead we just build another storey to accommodate the new family – or an extension out the back as was the case with my parents. It is quite normal for three or four generations to live together.

'Here in the Middle East we believe that family is the most important thing. I can give you an example of our closeness. My mother said to me just the other day, *You know your cousin twice removed and his wife have sadly lost their cat, Akil – you must telephone and give them your condolences* – which is exactly what I did. All family, no matter how distantly related – including their cats or dogs or donkeys or camels or mules – are important, and parents are very good at reminding their children to keep in touch.'

It turned out that Akil Salah wasn't just a wonderful guide – he was also a brilliant and funny storyteller. By the time the group arrived at their destination, everyone felt as if they'd just heard a great show, and the best thing was, there was so much more to come.

Chapter 14

Masud felt the vibration beneath his pillow as the bus left. He was about to get up when he heard his grandmother's footsteps. He quickly rolled over to face the wall and closed his eyes as she entered the room. She had brought his favourite breakfast, Beid Bel Basterma, and a cup of black tea. He could smell it. There was a gentle clunk as she set it down on the small table beside his bed. He could have happily wolfed down the entire plate, but today he would have to take things slowly, lest she suspect anything.

'How are you feeling, my darling boy?' she asked.

Masud pretended that she had just woken him. He let out a small gaspy shudder then rolled over and looked at her. 'Teta, my stomach hurts.' He grimaced as if he had a cramp.

The woman's arthritis-ridden fingers curled to grip the handles of the tray.

'No,' the boy said. 'Please leave it. Just in case I feel well enough to eat something later. It would be a shame to let it go to waste.'

His grandmother smiled at him and left the tray where it was. She studied his face and sat down beside him on the bed, touching his cheek then feeling his forehead.

She stared into his dark brown eyes. 'What are you really up to?'

Masud frowned.

'You might be able to fool your parents, Masud, but not me,' the woman said. 'Remember, I raised three children of my own – including your father, who was my naughtiest by far. I saw you this morning from my window. You were in the stables before dawn and I know that you are not one who enjoys getting up in the dark hours. I hardly think you were grooming the camels.'

Masud's face crumpled. 'Teta, please do not tell them. What I am doing, it is for Jabari. So that he can be well again.'

'For Jabari, you say?'

He hoped she wasn't after details. They would only put her in a very difficult position.

'If it is for your brother, then all I ask is that you be careful and if you need help you come to me,' she said. 'Now eat your breakfast. I will make a start on dinner and watch my shows and ignore you completely.' She reached out and held his hand. 'You are a good boy. And I know that you love your brother very much.' Her brown eyes glistened and Masud wiped tears from his own.

'Thank you, Teta. I love you,' he said.

'I love you too, Masud. Now eat – before my delicious eggs are cold,' she scolded, then left the room.

Masud had spent hours last night chipping away at the opening revealed during Nenet's rampage. It was now large enough for him to wriggle through the hole and into the cavity below. What he'd found in there had literally taken his breath away.

He pushed himself back up into the stables and set the torch down on the straw alongside the growing collection of shabti-like figures. He reached into his pockets and pulled out the last two. The most beautiful of them was gold with a simple hieroglyph. That must have been the glinting he saw when he first found the chamber. The other figures looked to be a mixture of clay and timber, but they had similar markings. In total, Masud had found twelve of the small figurines that ancient Egyptians traditionally placed with the dead. It was their purpose to work for the deceased in the afterlife. From Masud's research, he knew that they were usually assigned a spell from the Book of the Dead to help them with their chores. These figures did not have those markings, though, which could mean they were even older than he had first thought. Funerary figures from the Old or the early Middle Kingdom.

There was no evidence of a tomb nearby, but Masud had spent enough time with his father in the souk and the museum to know that these pieces were real. He would have to check the hiero-glyphs, though. They were not his forte yet. Masud wondered how the figurines had come to be buried in a compartment beneath his family's ancient stable block. He would probably never know for sure. The stables were at least one hundred and fifty years old and very close to the pyramid complex at Giza, but it was also possible the figurines had come from a tomb far away. Perhaps a grave robber had hidden them here and met an untimely fate before he could return to collect his ill-gotten gains. A good theory, Masud thought, but mere speculation.

Masud sat beside his haul and picked up the finely crafted gold statue. He studied it carefully. The figure was no doubt created in the image of someone very important. 'Who are you?' he whispered.

He knew that the answer would influence what someone would pay for the precious dolls. Which brought him to the biggest problem of all. If the authorities found out about his find, the treasure would be confiscated at once. It hardly seemed fair, given his family needed the money so badly and the figurines were found on his father's property – a piece of land that had been theirs for many generations.

Masud had heard rumours of dealers who paid princely sums for antiquities that were smuggled out of Egypt and sold to collectors. There was a story about a diplomat's wife who spent her days trawling archaeological digs and souveniring her finds. It was highly illegal, but the woman had been in a powerful position with immunity on her side. There were tales, too, of those who didn't have political protection. A man who lived just a few kilometres away from the Salahs had discovered a tomb beneath his house. The artefacts he had unearthed – six engraved statues on the walls and a damaged pot – were nothing compared to what Masud had found. The man had tried to sell the goods but was arrested and the treasures confiscated by the Ministry for Antiquities. There had been whispers that he had gone to prison.

Masud did not have time for gaol. These little dolls, thousands of years old, were the key to his brother's fate. If he could find a buyer and make enough money to fly Jabari to the hospital in America, then hopefully the boy could be cured. Eventually Masud would have to tell his parents what he had done, but by then it would not matter. They would be so overjoyed that Jabari could be well again that the treasure would remain their secret forever. He just needed to find someone who would make a deal, but how he could contact such a person was a mystery.

Masud wrapped the dolls individually, taking great care, before placing them in an old timber box he had found near the feed bins and covering them with a chaff bag. He would hide the box under the straw in the third stall for now.

His best chance to find the person he was looking for would be when they were away later in the week. Archaeological dig sites attracted all manner of characters. There was one man who sprang to mind. A fellow who had spoken with his father the last time they were in the Valley of the Queens. His father had brushed the man off and told Masud that he was not to be trusted. That was just the sort of person Masud needed to find.

Chapter 15

Mr Salah led the children as they spilled out of the bus and onto the street. They soon found themselves at their first destination – the famed Hanging Church, which dated from the seventh century AD.

As they walked through the forecourt lined with beautiful frescos and up the twenty-nine steps to the door, Mr Salah continued his commentary. 'This is the oldest and most important church in all of Egypt. It is called the Hanging Church because part of it hung over a passage on the southern gate of the Roman fortress that was part of Cairo long after the Pharaohs had disappeared into the annals of history. It is a Coptic Orthodox place of worship,' Mr Salah said. Millie noticed that he had reached into his pocket and pulled out a long rope, which he was now turning over and over in his hands.

'What does that mean?' Sep asked.

'Around ten percent of Egyptians, including my own family, are Coptic Orthodox, which is a Christian religion. We're a bit like Catholics in that we practise the sacraments, baptism and confirmation, and we believe in the Ten Commandments, but we do not believe in purgatory or that the Pope is infallible. Coptic priests are also allowed to marry,' the man explained.

'What's purgatory?' Caprice asked.

'Sharing a room with you,' Sloane muttered, to chuckles from all around.

Akil Salah grinned. 'She must be a very bad housemate.'

'I am not!' Caprice retorted, glowering at the man. 'She's the one who makes my life hell.'

'Girls!' Miss Reedy admonished the pair, but Mr Salah ignored the fracas.

'And there is your answer, miss. Purgatory is sort of like hell – the place that many Christians think they will spend time to amend for their ill doings on earth before they ascend to heaven,' the man said. 'Let us move on and look at some of the artefacts.'

The group followed Mr Salah while he explained the significance of the wooden screens and several icons including one of Saint Mark, who was the first Patriarch of the Coptic Orthodox Church.

Jacinta was standing beside Lucas in front of the altar. She felt his fingers gently brush against hers but resisted the urge to grab his hand.

'Are you rehearsing?' Millie asked, facing the pair.

'What are you talking about?' Lucas replied.

'Da, da, da-da, da, da, da-da . . .' the girl sang, to the tune of Wagner's Wedding March.

'As if!' Jacinta huffed, her cheeks turning bright pink. 'We're way too young for that.'

Lucas looked at her. 'So you *don't* see something like this in our future?' He smiled at Millie and turned to find Sep and Neville, standing either side of Alice-Miranda like bodyguards, admiring the marble pulpit.

'Wait, Lucas, what did you say?' Jacinta wore a puzzled look. 'Did he . . .?'

Millie chuckled. 'I think in a roundabout sort of a way, Lucas just asked if you thought you might get married one day.'

'Oh,' Jacinta mumbled, her heart pounding. She tried to speak but the words wouldn't come out, almost as if her tongue were tied in a knot. The two of them had been getting on better than ever since their trip to the outback and to Lucas's mother's wedding, but the last thing she wanted to do was jinx things, so perhaps it was best she was rendered mute.

'Children, we must be moving please,' Mr Salah instructed the group. 'We are off to the museum.'

Brendan Fourie and Henry Yan let out synchronised squeals of delight, but quietened down when they found themselves on the receiving end of a death stare from Miss Reedy, who was not impressed by their overt enthusiasm.

'Boys, you will do well to remember where you are,' the woman snapped.

'Yay!' the lads whispered, waving their arms in the air.

Mr Salah grinned at them. 'I agree, boys. There are many sights to make you squeal in the museum, but I hope you are not squeamish. Sometimes on television from America I have heard the phrase – how do you say – yummy mummies? These ones you are about to see are not so much.'

'Oh, Akil, I think ye've got the wrong end of the stick there.' Barclay Ferguson slapped his friend on the back and chuckled. 'I can explain that sayin'. Yummy mummies are . . .'

Josiah steered his wife to a quiet corner. 'Livinia, the children were just excited. I am too and I really hoped that once we got here you would be as well.' He touched her arm but she batted him away.

'I'm sorry, Josiah – it's just that I've got other things on my mind. Please leave me to my thoughts and go and enjoy yourself,' Livinia said, and turned to join the group filing outside.

Alice-Miranda, having watched the entire exchange, was more worried about the woman than ever.

A man approached the children as they left the church courtyard. He had a long grey beard and wore a white galabiya with a kaftan – a type of coat – over the top. He had a huge turban on his head. Alice-Miranda thought it was so high he could likely hide things underneath it.

'Would you like to purchase a keyring?' the man asked, opening his coat to reveal rows and rows of trinkets inside. 'I have every icon from inside the Hanging Church – one hundred and ten of them – and also some larger items like the altar, the screens, the baptismal font. For you, only ten American dollars, or something different if you have other money. But we can negotiate because that is the kind of guy I am.'

Millie looked at the fellow. There was something familiar about him but she couldn't put her finger on it.

'Please go away – we are not interested in your wares,' Livinia Reedy rebutted, then forged ahead to gather some of the students who were wandering close to the road.

But the man was undeterred and rushed up to Caprice. 'Hello, miss. Please may I say that you have the most beautiful hair that I have ever seen? It is like the sunshine has been spun into threads – or perhaps not threads but shiny copper wire – if you understand what I am saying.'

'I know exactly what you mean.' Caprice sighed and flicked her long tresses. 'My hair is lovely, isn't it?'

The man thought he was on a winner.

'And your skin, miss, it is like goat's milk – good goat's milk. Not the lumpy kind that I found in the back of my refrigerator last night.' He smiled broadly, revealing a gold tooth.

'Eww, that sounds disgusting,' Caprice grimaced.

'It was, but never mind my poor housekeeping habits. May I interest you in this beautiful keyring? It shows the baptismal font – though I must say this one looks a little bit like the toilet in my brother's outhouse.' He quickly put the trinket away and pulled out another; this one was flat faced and in the image of the church itself.

'No thank you,' Caprice said. 'I'm saving my money for the souk.' At the mention of the bazaar the man's eyes lit up. He was just about to target one of the boys when he caught sight of Akil Salah and scurried away.

'I could have sworn I've seen that man before,' Millie said to Alice-Miranda as they lined up so that Miss Cranna could do a head count. 'He had a gold tooth.'

'Oh, really,' the girl replied. 'Don't you remember the man in the airport had a gold tooth? So did the taxi driver, but when I asked him if he was the same person he was emphatic that he had no idea what I was talking about. Perhaps gold teeth are a fashion trend here.'

'Maybe,' Millie said with a shrug as the girls boarded the bus and found their seats.

Chapter 16

Maryam heard a gentle knock on the door before Nour poked her head around.

'Excuse me, Miss Moussa. You are due to meet the children from the Queen's Colours program in the museum in thirty minutes. They will be in the Tutankhamun exhibit.'

Maryam looked up from her computer. She had been busy reading everything there was to know about the Pharaoh and his treasures, but not much had sunk in. She quickly closed the website.

'I imagine you're looking forward to having more opportunities to share your knowledge. It must be difficult to have advanced degrees in archaeology and Pharaonic history and be confined to a desk as you have been,' Nour said with a smile.

'Yes, of course,' Maryam replied, feeling somewhat sick at the thought. She changed the subject. 'Is there any word on Dr Hassam's condition?'

'I'm afraid there is no change,' Nour said. She placed a delicate china cup of Turkish coffee on Maryam's desk, and two fresh dates beside it.

'A journalist would like to interview you this afternoon for the newspaper,' Nour said.

Maryam shook her head. 'Absolutely not. I refuse to participate in any publicity. I am only here for the shortest of times and it's really not my thing at all.'

Nour bit her lip. This particular reporter would be difficult to fob off, and he had important connections to other government officials.

Maryam leaned forward and stretched her spine. 'You have to stop bringing me treats too – they're not good for my waistline.'

Nour smiled and Maryam knew that the other woman had no intention of doing anything of the sort. So far this morning her new assistant had been in with three coffees, all accompanied by a sweet titbit. Nour had turned to leave when Maryam remembered something.

'Hang on, before you go, could you tell me what's in the bottom drawer of the filing cabinet over there?' she asked. 'It has its own separate lock system and I cannot find the code anywhere among Dr Hassam's things.'

Nour glanced at the cabinet in question. Like the rest of the furniture in the room, it had been made especially for Dr Hassam when he took up his position.

'I'm afraid that I have no idea. Dr Hassam has never told me and I have not had reason to ask,' Nour replied.

Maryam frowned. If she was supposed to do the man's job she needed to know everything. Given the lack of a handover – obviously impossible with Dr Hassam in a coma – Maryam felt as if she were running through a pitch-black tomb, hoping not to fall down an open shaft.

'Very well, thank you,' she said, giving Nour permission to leave.

So far this morning Maryam had read through the physical files in the upper drawers and accessed what she could on the computer. She wondered if there was another user and password she was unaware of – she should have asked Nour about that too. The hard drive was clogged with recordings of Dr Hassam's expeditions as documented by the television crews that seemed to follow his every move. But as to the paperwork outlining budgets and the like, well, that information was negligible. The only other thing Dr Hassam seemed to have in abundance were newspaper clippings of his remarkable achievements while on dig sites in the desert.

Going by Dr Hassam's calendar, the most important parts of his job were public relations – generally involving meeting tour groups and telling them how amazing he was, as well as getting his face on television. Maryam was sure that most of the real work was done by Fadil Salib, the man's deputy. Perhaps it was his computer that she needed access to.

Maryam stood up. Her back was aching. Dr Hassam's ornate chair was the most uncomfortable she'd ever sat in and would have to go, or at least be put into storage until he returned. She leaned over to take a closer look at it and had a terrible thought. Surely it wasn't a real throne from a tomb? She wouldn't have put it past him – his ego was that big. Maryam was about to take a look on the underside of the seat when a muffled buzzing diverted her attention. It sounded like a telephone, but it wasn't the landline on her desk or her mobile. She wondered if it was coming from Nour's office, but the noise faded as she walked to the door to check. The sound was coming from inside Dr Hassam's office somewhere. She was sure of it.

Maryam hovered next to the long glass cabinet that took up the whole of one wall. It was filled with ancient treasures – death masks, shabti and mummified scarab beetles sat alongside reliefs of hieroglyphics and Canopic jars. She hated the idea that some ancient Pharaoh's innards were being stored within a few metres of where she ate her lunch. It didn't matter that they were thousands of years old – guts were guts in Maryam's book. But the sound was further away.

She hurried around the room, hoping that the caller didn't give up too quickly, and soon identified that the buzzing was coming from the filing cabinet. She wrenched open the top drawer, then the second and third but to no avail. Maryam knelt down on the floor and pressed her ear to the bottom drawer. There it was. The phone buzzed a final time – loudly – then stopped.

'Miss Moussa, are you all right?' Nour had returned, carrying some paperwork. Maryam jumped. The woman had a habit of knocking intermittently and it was getting on Maryam's nerves.

She fiddled with her left ear. 'Yes, I'm fine. I just dropped the back of my earring on the carpet.'

'Did you find it?' Nour asked. 'You have the most beautiful jewellery, Miss Moussa – those diamonds are quite breathtaking.'

'They're not real,' Maryam lied, batting her hand.

Her mind was still on the mysterious phone. 'Do you know if Dr Hassam had his cell phone with him when he was taken to hospital?'

'Yes,' the woman nodded. 'It was in his suit jacket. I took the charger in so that if he . . . I mean *when* he wakes up he will be able to use it.'

'I see. Did Dr Hassam have a second phone?' Maryam asked.

'Not to my knowledge, Miss Moussa,' Nour replied, the cool look on her face belying her curiosity about the odd question. 'Is there something I can help you with?'

'Just let me know when the tour group arrives. I want to be prompt, given they're probably on a tight schedule,' Maryam said. At least that's what she was hoping. Surely a bunch of children ranging in age from eleven to fifteen couldn't ask too many hard questions.

Nour left the room while Maryam sat at the desk, her mind whirling. The mystery of the locked file drawer had just intensified. Tonight, after Nour had gone home, Maryam would do whatever it took to get inside and see what secrets Dr Hassam was hiding.

Chapter 17

The children stood outside the salmon-coloured Egyptian Museum while Mr Salah gave a quick overview of its history.

'This museum was the first building in the Middle East specifically designed for the purpose of displaying collections of antiquities. It was opened in 1902, and houses over 120,000 artefacts dating from prehistoric times through the Roman periods. Although when the Grand Egyptian Museum is opened it will dwarf this place and much of what is here will be moved.'

The group followed the man inside. He excused himself to attend to some paperwork and suggested that Mr Ferguson, Miss Cranna and the other teachers should take the children to the ground floor's main pavilion where there was plenty to see.

'It's magestic,' Alice-Miranda said, her eyes everywhere.

'I know,' Millie gasped. 'I'm just going to take some pictures,' she said, removing the lens cap from her camera and scampering away.

The vast space boasted an open gallery above, though according to the map there were many smaller rooms and long hallways to explore too. The group had naturally split up into pairs and trios, or some students wandered alone, marvelling at the wondrous variety of artefacts.

Alice-Miranda found herself standing beside Miss Reedy. The girl looked up and gasped. 'That must be Amenhotep the Third, his wife Tiye and their three daughters.' She pointed at the colossal statues at the end of the room.

'Goodness me, Alice-Miranda, how did you know that?' Miss Reedy said. For the first time since they'd arrived in the country, the woman seemed to be just as mesmerised by her surroundings as everyone else.

'When I found out that we were coming to Egypt I read as much as I could and I watched a number of documentaries as well. Dr Hassam, the Minister for Antiquities, has been in a lot of shows over the years. I was really looking forward to meeting him – he's such a knowledgeable man.' The pair stood admiring the figures in silence for a few seconds before the child continued. 'It's fascinating to think what an advanced civilisation the Egyptians had thousands of years ago.'

'Indeed,' the teacher replied. 'But countries tend to rise and fall, don't they? If you consider the empires that have existed over thousands of years around the world you'll find so many have had their moments of glory and then faded into obscurity.'

'It's strange, isn't it – to be incredibly progressive and then it all stops. I was looking out of the hotel window this morning, thinking about how the ancient Egyptians could have built the pyramids and all of the other monuments with such primitive tools,' Alice-Miranda said. 'I imagine manpower was the main resource.'

'Yes, sheer hard work,' Miss Reedy said. 'Though sometimes it doesn't matter how diligently one applies oneself, the odds can still be stacked against you.'

Alice-Miranda nodded, wondering if that last comment had more to do with what was happening at school rather than the rise and fall of the Egyptian empire.

She looked up at the woman. 'You know, Miss Reedy, a problem shared is a problem halved,' the child said. 'At least that's what my granny has always told me and I dare say she's right. Whenever I've got something bothering me I try to talk to Millie or one of the other girls or Miss Grimm. I've found her to be the most wonderful listener over the years – even if our relationship didn't start out that way.'

'Yes, I thought so too,' Livinia replied, her shoulders sagging. 'If only she would talk to me now.'

Alice-Miranda frowned. She hated seeing Miss Reedy so obviously deflated, but she couldn't pass up such a perfect opportunity to ask the woman more about what she knew.

'Last night, you were going to tell me something and then we were interrupted by Mr Plumpton. What was it?'

Livinia sighed. 'I really shouldn't have mentioned anything. It's not for you to worry about, Alice-Miranda. Apparently I got us into this mess and so I will have to work out how to get us out of it.'

'By "us" do you mean the school?' the girl said.

Livinia shuddered as she let out a long breath. 'Yes.'

'What's going on, Miss Reedy?' Alice-Miranda asked.

'I really don't know the extent of it,' the woman replied, just as her telephone rang in her handbag. She pulled it out and looked at the screen. 'It's Miss Grimm,' she said, before answering.

Alice-Miranda took that as her cue to leave and wandered further away to give the woman some privacy, only for Miss Reedy's loud gasp to give the clearest indication yet that what Jacinta had overheard two days earlier was true.

Alice-Miranda turned at the sound of her name being called across the room. Alethea, Gretchen and Millie were standing in front of a huge stone sarcophagus. She hurried towards them.

'Do you think there's a mummy in there?' Alethea asked.

Alice-Miranda shrugged. 'I'm not sure. Perhaps we can ask Mr Salah when he comes back.'

The girls nodded. It seemed Alethea and Gretchen were in the middle of a spirited debate about whether the archaeologists would leave mummies inside the coffins where they were found, or risk the old mummy's curse by removing them.

'I think that's only in movies,' Millie said.

Alice-Miranda disagreed. She told the girls that lots of people believed it – especially after Lord Carnarvon died not long after Tutankhamun's tomb was opened, killed by blood poisoning from an infected mosquito bite, of all things.

'How was your parents' wedding?' Alice-Miranda asked, changing the subject. She'd hardly had any time to catch up with the pair so far, and was keen to find out how things were after Alethea's mother had recently married Gretchen's father. Alethea and Gretchen had both been flower girls.

'Amazing – but the wedding wasn't the best part,' Gretchen said.

Millie looked at her curiously.

'The best part is that my *best friend* is now my *sister*,' Gretchen clarified, leaning over to give Alethea a hug around the middle.

Millie shook her head. 'Who knew?'

'Right?' Alethea said. 'I know what you're referring to and I cannot agree more. I was the most horrid child in the world before we moved to New York. Spoilt and monstrous. I still can't believe that I was so awful to you, Alice-Miranda, when you first arrived at school. I burn with shame every time I think about the things I did, although your revenge with the mineral water was pretty spectacular and unexpected.'

Alice-Miranda looked at the girl. She felt an unexpected stinging in her eyes.

'Oh, I'm sorry,' Alethea said. 'I've just brought up all those terrible memories again. I didn't mean to make you cry.'

'That's not it at all, Alethea,' Alice-Miranda said, throwing her arms around the girl. 'I'm just really proud of you.'

Millie choked up, and Gretchen too, and before long all four girls had tears rolling down their cheeks.

'Oh gosh, look at us – bawling like a bunch of babies,' Millie said, wiping her eyes. The others followed suit.

'We still want to come back and do an exchange at Winchesterfield-Downsfordvale,' Alethea said. 'If Miss Grimm will have us – or me, rather. I'm sure that she'll adore Gretchen.'

'I can't wait,' Gretchen said. 'Our parents want to take an extended belated honeymoon at the beginning of the next school year, so they'll drop us off and then collect us on their way home.'

'Maybe you should try to come sooner – like next term,' Millie said, exchanging glances with Alice-Miranda.

'That won't work,' Alethea said, shaking her head. 'I've signed on for the musical and Gretchen is a year group leader. We can't bunk out on our responsibilities at Mrs Kimmel's.'

'Well, you might miss your exchange then,' Millie mumbled.

Alice-Miranda gave her a nudge.

'I'll have a chat to Miss Reedy and she can talk to Miss Grimm too. I'm sure they'll have you back next year,' Alice-Miranda said, before the pairs parted company.

'What did you say that for?' Millie asked once the others had gone.

'We don't know for sure if the school is going to close so we have to stay positive. That's always been the best way to approach things,' Alice-Miranda replied. 'And I dearly want everyone at Winchesterfield-Downsfordvale to see just how much Alethea has changed.'

Mr Salah called everyone over to explain that they were going straight to the Tutankhamun exhibit, where they would meet with Miss Moussa, the Acting Minister for Antiquities. She was going to give them an in-depth, behind-the-scenes look at some of the pieces.

He led the children upstairs and down a long hallway to the back of the building, where a woman in a smart red suit with matching heels and sparkling diamond earrings was waiting for them. Her long dark hair was pulled into an elegant chignon and she had the most exquisite green eyes. She introduced herself as Maryam Moussa and said hello to Mr Salah and the other staff before asking the children to gather inside the exhibit.

'I'm sure that you must be eager to see the rest of the museum,' Maryam said, 'so I won't take up too much of your time.'

'We have allocated an hour with you, Miss Moussa,' Akil Salah said.

The woman pursed her lips and looked at her watch.

'But, of course, if you have more important things to do, we understand. It's just that Dr Hassam was always so keen to show children the exhibit. He loved their questions, and I must say that he was never stumped by the most obscure of enquiries, not once.'

'He is an amazing man,' Maryam said, smiling tightly and hoping that she had done enough study to get through the morning.

Alice-Miranda put up her hand. 'Excuse me, Miss Moussa, could you tell me if it's true that Tutankhamun's beard was accidentally broken off?'

Maryam looked at the gold sarcophagus beneath the glass.

'I'm afraid that is not something I am able to talk about,' the woman said, dismissing the girl. 'But perhaps you'd like to know how Tutankhamun came to be found by Mr Howard Carter and his patron, Lord Carnarvon?'

The woman spoke about the expeditions and the unlikelihood of finding a tomb intact with its treasures, given that many like it had fallen victim to grave robbers over the years.

'I don't mean to be disrespectful, Miss Moussa, but we've already studied much of what you're telling us,' Vincent Roche said in his thick French accent. 'I would really like to hear some of the lesser-known facts about the boy king.'

Maryam gulped. This was just what she had been afraid of.

'Well, um.' She looked around the room. 'Ah,' she faltered again. 'He liked to hunt. There is a strong possibility that he was killed – or at the very least injured – whilst on an expedition.'

The boy nodded. This was more like it. 'What sort of animals did he go after?'

Maryam glanced at her watch. How was it possible they had only been in the room for twenty minutes?

'Um,' she said again. 'Ah.'

Millie raised her camera to take a photograph.

'No pictures, please!' Maryam demanded.

The children looked at one another. For someone who was meant to be an expert, Miss Moussa seemed completely out of her depth – and obviously unaware it was perfectly acceptable for tourists to take photos inside the museum.

Millie lowered her camera back down. 'I hope she's more confident in the field,' she whispered to Sloane, who nodded.

'And less snappy,' Sloane replied.

Fortunately, Mr Salah saved the woman. 'It is believed that Tutankhamun enjoyed hunting ostriches in particular.' The man then beckoned the children to another glass display case. 'This ostrich feather fan was found close to his body. It is thought that perhaps he sustained fatal injuries while hunting the beasts. It could also have been a hippo that did him in – they are renowned for being particularly vicious.'

'Thank you, Mr Salah. I'm afraid I have far too many things on my mind at the moment,' Maryam said. Her face was red as she glanced at her watch for at least the third time in as many minutes.

'Can you tell us about the coffins?' Gretchen asked. 'And the sarcophagus?'

Maryam eyeballed the child. 'What exactly would you like to know?'

'Why were there two of them?' the child said.

The woman hesitated again.

'There were three,' Brendan Fourie said, 'resting inside one another like a set of Russian dolls.

But the carpenters didn't do a great job because the middle one was too big for the outer one to be able to close properly, so they trimmed part of the feet. The wood shavings were found by Howard Carter three thousand years later. Tutankhamun was also found with one hundred and thirty walking sticks, and he wore orthopaedic sandals with the faces of his enemies on the soles – so he could trample them.'

Maryam looked at Akil Salah, who nodded.

'You are indeed correct, my friend,' the man said. 'The young Pharaoh had a club foot, which made walking difficult without the aid of a cane.'

'Yes,' Maryam agreed, plastering a stiff smile on her face. She reached into her jacket pocket and pulled out her phone. 'Excuse me a moment,' she said, then hurried to the other side of the room, her heart beating so loudly it was a wonder the children couldn't hear it.

'Oh, I see,' she exclaimed. 'Yes. It is a pity but I am sure they will understand.'

She finished the call and put the phone away before hurrying back to the children.

'Please forgive me, Mr Salah, but I must leave you. Something important has come up and I am needed elsewhere,' Maryam said.

'Of course,' the man replied. 'It is fortunate I have done this tour many times myself. We look forward to seeing you the day after next on the dig site in the Valley of the Queens.'

Maryam nodded. 'Yes, until then.' She turned and walked quickly from the room.

Alice-Miranda bit her lip. She'd been standing next to the woman and, unless Miss Moussa's phone had the most silent vibration ever invented, she was almost certain that there had been no call.

'Well, children, we will have a little more time here but then we will head to the mummies. They are one of my favourite exhibits,' Akil Salah said.

'Oh yes, mine too,' Barclay Ferguson chimed in. 'I hope that funny old monkey mummy is still here.'

A little while later, the children were perusing the mummified remains of all manner of creatures, from cats and primates to birds and crocodiles, in addition to the human mummies too.

'Miss Moussa is a bit weird, don't you think?' Sloane said to Millie, Neville and Alice-Miranda, who were all gawking at the mummified remains of a baboon.

None of them replied as Millie was reading the details of the exhibit. 'Although not native to

Egypt, the baboon was revered by ancient Egyptians and is often found mummified in tombs. Thoth – the supreme being of the moon and wisdom – is sometimes depicted in hieroglyphs as a baboon but is also represented with the head of an ibis.'

'I wonder where the baboons came from,' Neville said. 'The Egyptians must have been great travellers.'

'We'll have to investigate,' Alice-Miranda said. 'And to answer your question, Sloane, I suspect that Miss Moussa was anxious. I suppose it would be only natural to feel that way – stepping into the shoes of a man like Dr Hassam, given that he's one of the most revered archaeologists in the world.'

Sloane shrugged. 'I suppose, but Mr Salah seemed to know everything she didn't.'

'She probably had a mental blank,' Millie said. 'I'm hopeless when someone asks me to spell a word out loud off the top of my head and yet I'm fine when I write it down. I remember Miss Crowley asked me to spell "serendipitous" a while back and I just stood there looking like a gormless idiot with my mouth open.' Millie gave a demonstration, which made the others laugh.

'Hopefully Miss Moussa will feel more comfortable on the dig site,' Neville said. 'Mr Salah did say that she is an accomplished archaeologist.'

But Alice-Miranda wasn't confident that would be the case. There was something about the woman that gave her a strange feeling. Hopefully in a couple of days she'd find out exactly why that was.

Chapter 18

The children finished their tour of the museum and were soon on their way to the souk for lunch and the opportunity for some shopping. Mr Salah was adamant they stay together in their allocated group – and with the adult assigned to them – at all times. It wasn't that the souk was an especially dangerous place, but there were a lot of interesting characters about and he didn't want anyone feeling intimidated or uncomfortable. Mr Salah would move between them all and keep an eye on things.

Alice-Miranda, Millie, Neville and Sep would be together with Miss Cranna, while Miss Reedy was looking after Britt, Chessie and the two French boys, Vincent and Philippe. Jacinta and Lucas were with Caprice and Madagascar with Mr Plumpton in charge, and Mr Ferguson was taking care of Gretchen, Alethea, Sloane and Hunter Martin – who had come from St Odo's School in New Zealand. The remaining four boys, Brendan and Junior from South Africa, Aidan from Ireland and Henry from Hong Kong, were under the supervision of Mr Pienaar.

The bus pulled up at the main entrance to the ancient Khan El Khalili just as a loud chant began to ring out across the city. 'We have reached our destination,' Mr Salah announced.

'What's that noise?' Madagascar blurted.

'It is the adhan – the Islamic call to prayer,' the man replied. 'You will hear it many times in Egypt. In Cairo there has been a unification of the call – previously hundreds of mosques would broadcast their own versions and it was a little bit hard on the ears. Now we have one lovely melodious version.'

'Melodious? You are kidding?' Madagascar said, rolling her eyes.

Caprice glared at her. 'It's an important part of the culture here,' she whispered, garnering herself a glare. 'It's rude to make fun.'

Sloane nudged Millie. 'Wow, did you hear that?'

Millie nodded. 'Imagine being told to be considerate of others by Caprice, of all people.'

Mr Salah continued his commentary. 'In a few moments you will be inside one of the oldest marketplaces in the world. I can guarantee it will be colourful and exciting and there will be sights and smells that perhaps you have not experienced before. But please – and this is for the girls – if anyone proposes marriage you must say that you are already spoken for. Even if they offer five camels to your father, you cannot accept. And, Miss Cranna – I have a ring for you to wear which will make things easier for you.'

'Really,' Caprice scoffed. 'I'm worth a lot more than five stinky camels.'

'I don't know about that,' Sep mumbled, to chortles of laughter from those nearby.

'Yes, of course you are,' Mr Salah said. 'Perhaps someone will offer five camels, three goats and ten chickens. Then I would consider the offer.'

Caprice's jaw dropped. 'Are you joking?'

Akil Salah nodded. 'Yes. People haven't offered camels for a dowry for hundreds of years – cash is king these days. You must remember that this is a marketplace and while the attentions of the shopkeepers are intended to be flattering, there is a reason for their flirtations. They are actually focused on getting you to part with your money – not marrying you.'

There was a burst of laughter around the bus.

'But in all seriousness, do not pay full price for anything. It is customary to haggle. Think of it as a sport and enjoy it. The vendors certainly will.'

The children all nodded.

'But first, we eat!' Akil said, directing everyone to hop off and wait by the bus.

Minutes later – having wound their way along a number of alleys, past shops boasting all manner of brightly coloured wares – the group arrived at a cafe called El Fishawi. The place was adorned with beautiful old arabesque furniture, dark wood panelling and yellow ochre walls. There were copper chandeliers hanging from the ceiling and mirrors everywhere, creating an illusion of space. Some of the cafe's patrons were smoking strange pipes called shishas, which emitted a sweet smell a bit like apples. When Lucas asked Mr Salah if they had a bad effect on people's health like cigarettes, the man told the children that under no circumstances should they ever try one as these were just as likely to cause cancer in the long run.

'This is one of the oldest cafes in all of Cairo – established in 1797, a year before Napoleon Bonaparte invaded Egypt,' Mr Salah informed the group as he led them towards a thickset man with bristly dark hair. 'Meet Mr Akram el-Fishawy, the owner and seventh generation in his family to run this place. It is a true fact that I cannot remember a time when he has not been here to greet my tour groups, no matter if it is morning, noon or night.'

The man welcomed the group with a huge smile and directed them to their seats. A fat tabby cat had made itself at home in the corner and refused to vacate, so Chessie picked the creature up and sat it on her lap where it purred contentedly.

The menu had been prearranged and consisted of a variety of teas and falafel with a yoghurt dip. It was generally agreed that lunch was delicious, though Madagascar whined that her tea tasted weird and the air smelt spicy. It was true that the souk had an abundance of aromas, and not all of them were pleasant.

Afterwards the children split into their groups and wandered among the treasures. Millie was keen to make a deal, purchasing a beautiful piece of papyrus with hand-painted hieroglyphs at half of what the man was asking.

Mr Salah had been right about the flattering remarks. Despite the fake ring, Miss Cranna still managed to garner the attentions of three men before the group had made it to the end of the first laneway. Millie was stunned to be singled out too, by a young lad who couldn't have been much more than sixteen. He commented on her beautiful freckles then asked if she was in need of a husband.

'I'm his,' Millie blurted, and grabbed hold of Sep's arm. The boy was obviously taken aback by her declaration, though he was happy enough to play along.

'Well done, Millie,' Neville said. 'And might I say that the two of you do make a very cute couple.'

Sep glowered while Millie's cheeks lit up. Neville grinned and winked at Alice-Miranda, who linked arms with the boy. Neville turned and gave Sep a smug look.

All the while, Mr Salah dashed here and there, helping the children with their shopping.

In Miss Reedy's group, Britt had found a store that sold the most beautiful fabric and scarves. She held up several of them, suggesting that the teacher might like one, but the woman wasn't remotely interested. She'd been brooding ever since the museum and Alice-Miranda noticed several times that she was short with Mr Plumpton too. Fortunately, Britt had better luck helping Chessie and the French boys select gifts for their mothers.

Miss Cranna's group was keen to see an antique stall towards the exit. Neville had spied it on the way in and pointed out some of the interesting pieces, like death masks and Canopic jars.

'Aren't those scarabs gorgeous?' Alice-Miranda exclaimed, eyeing the small bronze amulets. Their undersides were covered in hieroglyphs.

'I think I'd like to get one,' Neville said. 'I love the symbolism of those little beetles pushing the sun across the sky to protect their owners.'

Millie glanced around, wondering where the shopkeeper had got to, when suddenly a man appeared in front of them. He had a long black beard and wore a brightly coloured tunic as well as a skull cap in the same material.

'Hello my friends,' he smiled, revealing a gold tooth.

Millie and Alice-Miranda's eyes widened. They looked at one another then back at the man.

'You again?' Millie said.

'I am sorry, miss, but I am certain this is the first time I have made your acquaintance,' the man replied, a glint in his dark brown eyes.

Millie shook her head. 'You were at the church before, and I'm sure that you were our crazy taxi driver *and* that you were trying to sell trinkets to Miss Reedy at the airport.'

'No, miss. No, no, no. I think you have me confused with someone else,' the fellow said. 'But this Miss Reedy – what does she look like?'

'Tall, thin,' Millie said, glancing about. 'That's her over there.' She pointed across the passageway to where the teacher was standing with her group. 'Why?'

'Oh, no reason,' the man replied.

172

'And you're sure we've never seen you before?' Millie said.

'Absolutely not,' he said, shaking his head.

'Fine,' Millie said, wondering if she was losing her mind. 'My friend would like to buy a scarab beetle and I would like one of those little blue dolls and that one there – the gold one.'

'They are not dolls to play with, miss. They are shabti. They work for their owner in the after-life. This one was found in none other than the boy king's tomb, and this one is from King Khufu who built the Great Pyramid.'

'As if,' Sep said. 'We might be kids but we didn't come down in the last shower. They're replicas, right – like everything else in here?'

'Okay, you got me. But they are splendid wares and I can guarantee that they are made right here in Egypt and there is not one thing from China,' the man replied.

Sep raised his eyebrows.

'Okay, perhaps one or two things from China, but I promise that I will not sell them to you as you are very smart children,' the man replied.

The group finished their transactions and turned to leave. Millie was very pleased with her purchases, though she hoped that perhaps someone could tell her a little more about the shabti and what the inscriptions on them meant. Maybe she would ask Mr Salah.

'I will see you again,' the shopkeeper called.

Somehow Millie and Alice-Miranda thought that might very well be the case.

Chapter 19

Heading to the exit and their designated meeting place, the children could hear Mr Salah somewhere behind them calling the rest of the group to hurry up. Their next stop was the Al Hussein Mosque, which was within walking distance, and then the Citadel of Saladin, two Islamic icons of the city.

As they were passing a tiny kiosk, Alice-Miranda faltered, shocked.

'Look.' She nudged Millie. There, among the local newspapers, was a selection of western head-lines – one of which had caught her eye.

Millie gasped and raced over to pick up the paper that read 'World's Biggest Ponzi Schemes – there's a new one to add to the list'.

'That can't be a coincidence, right?' Millie said to Alice-Miranda, who shook her head and dug into her pocket for some coins. She quickly paid the stall owner.

Millie folded the newspaper in half and stuffed it into her backpack. 'We'll have a proper look later.'

Alice-Miranda nodded.

'Girls, what are ye doin' over there?' Miss Cranna called. Fortunately, she and the boys had been distracted watching a young lad spinning a top. *Un*fortunately, none of them had realised that the young fellow would be expecting payment for his demonstration. They were about to leave when a tall man approached from the shadows.

'*Fooloos!*' he said emphatically, and held out his hand.

Miss Cranna looked at the boys. Neville pulled out some change and handed it to the lad who had performed, appeasing the agitated fellow.

'I think maybe it's a good idea to assume that you have to pay everyone here,' Sep said as the children and teachers assembled outside. Touting and tipping appeared to be common practice.

The heat had intensified since they'd arrived at the souk and the group was beginning to fade. Mr Salah promised that where they were going would be cooler, with the added enticement that he'd have them back at the hotel by five so they could have a swim before dinner.

The tours of the mosque and citadel were extremely interesting, with another call to prayer punctuating the end of their visit. To Caprice's displeasure, Madagascar had covered her ears and scowled. The time flew and soon the children were on the bus heading back to the hotel. Millie and Alice-Miranda were both bursting to read their newspaper, to see if the article had anything to do with Mr Badger.

Unable to wait a moment longer, Millie pulled out the paper and turned quickly to the article as soon as they sat down. Alice-Miranda scanned it alongside her.

The feature detailed numerous scandalous Ponzi schemes over the years, some affecting thousands of people and costing multiple millions of dollars, and the new player the headline mentioned was Mr Elias Badger from Badger and Woodcock Accountants. Everything the girls had seen on the television the previous night was repeated, but the story also contained information about other scams, including a scheme involving a woman called Gianna Morsey, whose victims comprised several high-profile individuals – one of whom was a very close friend of Alice-Miranda's parents.

'I'm almost certain that's the woman Daddy was tricked by,' the girl said. 'I'm quite glad that his name is not listed as one of her victims, but I remember he told me that Uncle Harold had recommended her and his name is there. I wonder where she is now.'

Millie made a hmming sound, deep in thought.

Sloane reached around and tapped Millie on the shoulder. 'What are you two looking at?'

She and Chessie had been watching the pair through the gap in the seat in front of them. Millie quickly explained and passed them the paper. A minute later the girls were gasping and gahing, horrified by what they read.

'They don't mention the school,' Chessie said. 'So maybe that's not the problem.'

'It's too big a coincidence – that Miss Reedy was given that message to call Mr Woodcock when we arrived,' Alice-Miranda said.

'I think it's time we knew for sure,' Sloane said. 'We have to ask outright, or there won't be time to help fix things. I can't imagine Winchesterfield-Downsfordvale closing down – it's too awful for words. We need to say something about it, even if Jacinta might get into a little bit of trouble.'

'She couldn't help that she needed to pee,' Chessie said. 'It's hardly her fault that she was there, and she didn't mean to eavesdrop.'

'Miss Reedy knows what's going on,' Alice-Miranda said. She quickly filled Sloane and Chessie in on what had happened the previous night and then the call at the museum, which was news to Millie too as there hadn't been a chance for Alice-Miranda to update her until now. 'For some reason, she's blaming herself.'

'That can't be right – she's not in charge of the school. Isn't it far more likely to be Miss Grimm's fault?' Sloane said.

'It's not fair to Mr Plumpton either. Did you see them at the citadel? He whispered something to Miss Reedy and she almost bit his head off,' Chessie said. 'The poor man looked as if he was going to cry.'

'I think the five of us need to talk to Miss Reedy – together. I tried to say last night that it wasn't just me who knew but she cut me off. She's so stressed. It can't be good for her health,' Alice-Miranda said, 'and it's certainly not good for her marriage.'

'Mr Plumpton should be there too,' Millie said. 'She's more likely to tell the truth in front of him, don't you think? And besides, I pretty much let her know that I knew too at breakfast this morning.'

The other girls agreed. Once they were off the bus, Alice-Miranda would ask if she and Millie could speak to Miss Reedy and Mr Plumpton privately before they headed off to the pool. The plan was to have the teachers visit their room where Sloane and Chessie, and Jacinta too, would be waiting.

Chapter 20

Maryam Moussa had spent the remainder of the afternoon with her head in the history books. The morning's museum visit had been nothing short of a disaster and she feared it would only get worse. But it wasn't the only thing on her mind.

She glanced at the clock to see it was almost five. Nour would be leaving shortly – but there was something she needed from the woman first. Maryam pressed the intercom button on her phone and asked the woman to step inside for a moment.

'Yes, Miss Moussa?' Nour said, appearing in the doorway. Maryam couldn't help noticing that the woman's hair and makeup was as immaculate as it had been when she arrived at work that morning. She was stunning, even for someone who must have been nudging sixty. Maryam suddenly felt self-conscious, wishing she'd bothered to reapply her lipstick after lunch.

'Could you give me a quick lesson on the office's internal security system, please?' Maryam asked.

Nour's perfectly plucked eyebrows jumped up. 'What do you mean, Miss Moussa?' she said.

'I assume there is an alarm for this room, given what's here,' Maryam said, glancing at the treasure-filled glass cabinets that lined the walls behind the desk and to Maryam's right. 'That is a camera up there in the corner, isn't it? I gather it's only turned on after hours?' She certainly hoped so, given her extensive investigations of the room.

'Yes, I usually activate it all when I leave,' Nour replied.

'But what if Dr Hassam is working late? Surely he knows how to do it,' Maryam said.

Nour nodded. 'Of course.'

'Then I need you to teach me. I've got a lot to do. I'm planning to work back tonight and get in early tomorrow,' Maryam said.

Nour smiled. 'I can stay late with you. My husband is overseas on business this week and I do not mind missing my French class as I have not done my homework.'

'That's not fair,' Maryam said. 'It's my choice to work after hours and I hadn't asked you, so please – just show me how to set the alarm and the camera and you can go home.'

Nour nodded, though Maryam got the feeling the woman was reluctant to share the information. Perhaps she was just being protective of Dr Hassam, though heaven knew the man didn't deserve it.

'The keypad is inside the second drawer of your desk on the left, at the very back. It looks like a calculator you cannot remove,' Nour explained.

Maryam pulled the drawer open.

'Ingenious,' she said. 'Now I need you to write a list of instructions, including the code, and I will make sure that I commit it all to memory before I leave. I won't do anything stupid like put the notes in my handbag.'

Nour grinned.

'Did I say something funny?' Maryam asked.

'I picked up one of Dr Hassam's suits from the drycleaners when the system was first installed, and the shopkeeper handed me a piece of paper that he had found in Dr Hassam's pants pocket with the code on it,' Nour said.

Maryam laughed. 'That makes me feel better about a few things.'

Nour left the room and returned a few minutes later with a typed page outlining the procedures.

'Thank you,' Maryam said.

'May I organise something for you to eat, or some tea?' Nour asked, but Maryam shook her head. The sooner the woman was off the premises the sooner she could get to work.

'Please, go home. You have been so helpful to me and honestly I will be fine. I promise I won't stay too late,' Maryam said, lying through her teeth. She was staying as long it took to get into that locked drawer.

Nour nodded and left the room. Maryam waited until quarter past five, then wandered out to check that the woman had actually left before calling down to reception to ask if Miss Badawy had signed out. Confident the coast was clear, Maryam locked her office door and walked to the filing cabinet. She knelt down and punched the numbers for the security system into the keypad, to no avail. Entering the same digits backwards didn't work either.

What if the system only allowed her a limited number of attempts before she was locked out for good? Her mind was in overdrive. What else might the man use? His birthday, perhaps? Unlikely, but she would give it a try. Without really knowing Dr Hassam, it was difficult to think what other numbers could be of significance. Maryam picked up a pen and jotted some ideas.

His birthday, home address, phone number, perhaps the anniversary of when he took up the position as Minister? None of them worked. What if it was something to do with his work? The date that Tutankhamun's tomb was discovered or, even better, the day that it was opened? It was his particular specialisation, after all. Maryam had studied that information just this afternoon. It had been 2 pm on 17 February 1923 that the seal of the tomb had been broken. Maryam flew back to the filing cabinet and punched in 21721923.

There was a long beep and, to Maryam's great delight, the drawer clicked. She took a deep breath and pulled it open, eager to see what treasures lay inside, but was disappointed to find a stack of old archaeology magazines. Her shoulders slumped. Maryam lifted them out and flicked through. 'You have to be kidding. Dr Hassam, does your vanity have no bounds?' the woman muttered. Every cover had a picture of her boss on it.

She was about to put them back when the buzzing started again – the same as she'd heard earlier in the day.

'Where is that phone?' Maryam said. She pulled the drawer out as far as it would go and looked for a false bottom, only to come up empty. Feeling the underside of the drawer above, she finally found what she was looking for. Maryam struggled to pull the device out. A magnet on the back had been holding it in place.

There were two missed calls and several text messages. Maryam swiped the screen and was asked for a passcode. Maybe Dr Hassam used the same one that had got her into the drawer. She tried it and was successful.

The messages had all come from the same

unknown number. Although the sender's identity was unclear, their intentions were not.

'Dear me, Dr Hassam – what on earth have you been up to?' Maryam whispered. Tomorrow she would investigate for herself. Fortunately, the excavation the last text message had mentioned was only at Saqqara – just near the Step Pyramid on the outskirts of Giza.

Maryam hurried over to her computer and found the file related to the dig. There was nothing of particular significance in the catalogue of artefacts found thus far. Although perhaps that wasn't the truth of it. Maryam needed to find out who was working there – this was perfect. She couldn't believe that Dr Hassam himself would provide her with everything she needed and more.

Chapter 21

'Girls, this is an outrage!' Miss Reedy said as she paced the floor back and forth to the window. She stopped and stared at the pyramids in the distance, for a moment allowing herself to wonder what it would have been like to have lived here thousands of years ago – perhaps that would have been preferable to her current situation.

Josiah Plumpton was sitting on the couch, Millie perched on the arm beside him. Jacinta was on the other cushion. Sloane and Chessie were cross legged on Alice-Miranda's bed while the girl herself was seated on the desk chair turned around to face everyone.

The newspaper Millie had bought at the souk lay open on the desk – Mr Badger's name clear in the headline.

Josiah Plumpton's lip quivered. 'Well, at least it all makes sense now, darling. I just wish you had confided in me. Surely I could have helped.'

'I didn't actually know the extent of it myself until Alice-Miranda told me last night. Ophelia phoned to confirm the bad news while we were at the museum,' Livinia said.

'I'm sorry, Miss Reedy,' Jacinta apologised. 'I promise I didn't mean to listen to Miss Grimm and Mr Grump's conversation, but I couldn't help it. I really needed to go to the loo and by the time I knew what was going on it was too late.'

The woman spun around and stared at the girl. 'Who else knows?'

Jacinta bit her lip. 'Just the five of us. I swear we didn't say a word to anyone. Especially not Myrtle Parker, though she probably did wonder why we were so keen to help her tidy the office.'

Livinia frowned. 'What was Myrtle Parker doing in the office?'

The girls looked at each other.

'You haven't heard?' Millie said.

Livinia glared at her husband, who raised his eyebrows in confusion.

'Mrs Parker is Miss Grimm's assistant until Mrs Derby returns from her maternity leave,' Sloane said.

'What!' Livinia gasped. 'There's a disaster waiting to happen. Once *she* finds out what's going on, everyone will know what I've done.' The woman blinked back the tears that had been threatening for a while now, but she couldn't hold them off any longer.

'Oh Livinia, darling!' Josiah exclaimed. The man leapt up to comfort her and Sloane grabbed a tissue from the box on the bedside table.

'But Miss Reedy, you're not in charge of the school,' Millie said. 'I mean, you're the second-in-charge with Miss Wall, but it's Miss Grimm who makes the big decisions, isn't it? It can't be *all* your fault.'

Livinia wiped her eyes while Chessie quickly opened a bottle of water from the mini bar and poured her a glass.

'I'm afraid that while you're right about Miss Grimm having ultimate responsibility for the school, this particular disaster was my doing. She explained it all to me this morning. You see, when Miss Grimm was on maternity leave and I was acting headmistress, Mr Badger sent some paperwork to the school. It was while Ophelia and Mr Grump had taken baby Aggie for a short break to the seaside. I should have waited for her to return, but Mr Badger was most insistent that the documents be signed that day. As Miss Grimm's nominated replacement I had been approved to sign for everything. I thought it was just confirmation to roll over some term deposits, but I was so busy and there was no time to read it all. Mrs Derby wasn't there either – she had gone to an appointment. I now know that she would usually go through this type of thing and check the fine print.

'Mr Badger called three times to chase the documents, so I signed them, and in doing so apparently gave authorisation to that scoundrel to take charge of all the school's funds. I can't believe I gave him the original deeds to the school too – Ophelia says he came in personally to collect them, though I don't recall that happening at all. With those in hand, the monster took out several large mortgages on our behalf. Not only have we lost the funds we had, we're up to our eyeballs in debt. It's my signature on the documents, so ultimately it's *my* responsibility,' Livinia explained. 'Although I honestly can't remember exactly what I signed – it's such a blur.'

'Oh dear,' Josiah said, a tremble in his voice.

'I'm sure that Miss Grimm doesn't blame you,' Millie said, garnering herself an 'are you kidding?' look from Miss Reedy.

'And now it's headline news,' Livinia wailed.

'At least the school's name hasn't been mentioned,' Chessie said. 'So no one has to know.'

Livinia straightened her back.

'Everyone will know! The school has *no* money. We will be closed by Christmas and even then we still won't be able to pay the staff properly. Someone will join the dots and then Winchesterfield-Downsfordvale will be splashed all over the papers too. It won't take long before someone lets on that it happened while I was in charge. My name will be mud. I will be unemployable. The school will be sold and you'll all have to go somewhere new,' the woman said, before breaking down and sobbing inconsolably.

'Yes,' Mr Plumpton whispered as he wrapped his arms around the woman. 'It does seem rather desperate.'

Sloane shook her head. 'It can't be the end. There has to be something we can do.'

'Fundraisers,' Millie said. 'We're good at those. We can have another Fields Festival – call it a different name.'

'And some cake stalls and a walkathon,' Chessie chimed in.

'Alice-Miranda, couldn't your parents just buy the school?' Sloane said. 'You could at least ask them.'

The girl shook her head. 'I don't think so. Daddy mentioned that the grocery business has been under a lot of pressure lately and Mummy and Aunt Charlotte are in the middle of a huge expansion with Highton's. Buying a school wouldn't be part of their mission statement – unless it was for disadvantaged children and we're hardly that. Besides, my parents are away at the moment in Alaska looking at sustainable energy options for off-grid settlements. They want to get a better understanding of the ways people in the region live and can't be contacted for at least another couple of weeks.'

'Girls, please stop,' Livinia said, freeing herself from her husband's grasp. 'I know you have good intentions, but I'm afraid that none of that would raise anywhere near what we've lost. Quite honestly it takes a fortune to run Winchesterfield-Downsfordvale, with all the salaries and maintenance and food and teaching supplies and everything else.' Livinia pointed at the newspaper. 'If what's printed there is true then we are never likely to see a cent of that money back.'

'Unless we find something like King Tut's tomb,' Josiah said with a tight grin.

'This is Egypt, sir. We wouldn't be allowed to keep the treasure anyway,' Sloane said.

'Yes of course,' the man replied. 'I was just trying to lighten the mood.'

While Josiah had been stunned by the girls' revelations, there was a part of him that was relieved. At least he now knew why his wife had been so busy and distant the past few weeks. And if they could get through this together, he was certain they could get through anything.

He guided Livinia to the couch.

'Are you going to tell Miss Grimm that we know?' Jacinta asked.

Miss Reedy shook her head. 'What's to be gained from that? Ophelia was on the cusp of a nervous breakdown before I left. She must be beside herself now that it's out in the press.'

'What are we going to do then?' Millie said.

Livinia looked around the room, eyeballing each of the girls.

'Nothing. You are to do nothing and say nothing,' the woman said, a stern look on her face. 'You will enjoy this trip and make the most of every minute, and then we will go home and face the music.'

'But that's awful,' Jacinta said.

'Yes, I agree. Nevertheless, that is the plan,' Livinia said.

Alice-Miranda's mind was ticking. 'Miss Reedy, have you seen these documents that you signed since all of this has come to light?' the girl asked.

The woman shook her head. 'No. Miss Grimm says that the police have taken everything from Mr Badger's office as evidence.'

'What about copies? Surely there must be copies somewhere at the school?' the child said.

Livinia shrugged. 'I certainly don't remember them. I can ask Miss Grimm, if it's important. What are you getting at?'

'I just think you should be able to see what it is that you supposedly signed, that's all,' Alice-Miranda said.

'I couldn't agree more.' Josiah Plumpton gave a nod. 'We need to call Ophelia and ask her to look for them.'

Alice-Miranda was still pondering as she picked up the newspaper. There was a photograph of Mr Badger and his associate, Mr Woodcock – though the latter wasn't believed to have had anything to do with the scam. There was also a picture of Gianna Morsey among the other scam artists. She was very glamorous, despite a slightly prominent Roman nose, with a tumble of long dark hair and almond-shaped eyes. There was a beauty spot just above her lip on the right side. Alice-Miranda wondered if she would ever be found – though given she'd been missing for more than ten years it didn't seem likely. But there was something about her that was absolutely intriguing. Where on earth had she gone?

'It says here that the police believe they might have a lead on Mr Badger,' Alice-Miranda said. 'If they could find him, he could help with their enquiries.'

'Yes,' Mr Plumpton said. 'But if that woman in the article is anything to go by, there's also every chance that he's vanished into thin air.'

Chapter 22

Myrtle Parker's eyes felt like lead sinkers. She was doing her best to keep them open, but after a cup of tea and two of Mrs Smith's delicious date scones she was finding it hard to stay awake.

The woman stood up and stretched her arms above her head, then executed a couple of quick star jumps. When she was a girl, her grandmother had told her they were the best thing for an on-the-spot pick-me-up, and her grandmother had never been wrong about anything – much like Myrtle herself, who took after the woman in almost every way.

Except for her granny's love of dogs. On that front they were polar opposites. Myrtle had found the school hound, Fudge, trying to nose his way into her office earlier and had promptly sent him packing. The last thing she needed was another furry creature running amok – she'd still not located the mouse that had got away on Saturday.

Myrtle could understand why the personal assistant role had been challenging for poor Mrs Derby, especially in her condition. She herself hadn't stopped since she arrived on Monday morning. The demands of both staff and students were never-ending, though Myrtle had thus far managed to solve all problems without anyone setting foot inside the headmistress's office – apart from that haughty Maths teacher, Caroline Clinch, who had snuck past when she'd popped out to the loo. She had only discovered the problem when the woman was making her exit. Myrtle had glowered so hard that her face had begun to ache. She was sure Caroline wouldn't make that mistake again.

Granted, not everyone had left with a smile, but it was impossible to please all of the people all of the time and besides, Myrtle's primary objective was to look after Miss Grimm – and that meant shielding her from as much nonsense as possible. Really – did the headmistress need to be asked about a change to the timetable or permission to organise an excursion? She certainly wasn't required to decide whether or not a child should move classes. How hard was it to read a report and work that one out? Myrtle had wondered what these teachers were paid for. Miss Grimm was looking after the big picture, not the minutiae.

The woman had seemed particularly stressed this week, and even more so after Myrtle had delivered the newspapers this morning. She'd asked if there was a problem but Ophelia had shaken her head. Clearly that was a lie, but Myrtle didn't have time to follow up given everything else on her plate. It was a hectic business, running the school.

Myrtle had just sat down when the intercom buzzed.

'Yes, Headmistress?' she said.

'Mrs Parker, would you please bring me a new student enrolment form and a copy of the prospectus?' Ophelia asked.

'Certainly, Miss Grimm. I shan't be a moment,' Myrtle said. She stood up and walked to the filing cabinet, looking under S for student but was surprised that the form wasn't there. She had asked those girls to file everything according to alphabetical order. Thankfully Myrtle found prospectus under P, then tried E for enrolment. She pulled out the form and tsked to herself – it was the *student* enrolment form and therefore should have been under S. She pulled out the other copies and found the right place, dropping them into the file.

Myrtle closed the drawer and walked to the headmistress's door, knocked, then entered.

'Good heavens, Miss Grimm, whatever is the matter?' Myrtle hurried to the woman's desk, where Ophelia had just pulled out a tissue and was loudly blowing her nose.

The headmistress swiftly wiped her eyes and pushed her shoulders back against the chair.

'Oh it's nothing, Mrs Parker,' Ophelia replied, shaking her head. 'I was just reading a letter from a parent telling me what a wonderful job we're doing with her daughter. It made me feel a bit emotional, that's all. Given we're in the business of shaping young lives, it's a privilege to be able to . . .' Miss Grimm's face crumpled and she burst into tears, this time accompanied by racking sobs.

Myrtle Parker swallowed hard. Children were important, but good heavens – they were nothing to get worked up about. She placed the documents the woman had requested down on the desk.

'I'll get Mrs Smith to bring you some tea and scones. You'll feel much better after that,' Myrtle said. And while she was making the call she might as well organise another round of afternoon tea for herself too.

Myrtle turned and left the room, closing the door behind her.

She couldn't help but think how fortunate it was that she had taken over Mrs Derby's role. Ophelia Grimm was in a fragile state at the moment. It was just as well Myrtle was there to protect her – and a good thing Mrs Derby had left a step-by-step list of instructions detailing how to divert all telephone calls to the main office too. No one was getting to Miss Grimm without her say-so.

Chapter 23

'Oh, wow, look at that!' Millie exclaimed as the first rays of daylight flooded the horizon. 'It's gorgeous.'

'Take yer photographs quickly,' Barclay Ferguson urged. 'Sunrise here is a fast-movin' event. It's quite literally all over in a few blinks of the eye.'

The students snapped away. Millie got some particularly stunning images.

'It's breathtakin'.' Morag Cranna could barely speak.

'Indeed, Miss Cranna. I've witnessed this sight more times than I can remember, and it still gets me here,' Barclay banged on his chest, 'every time.'

'Mr Ferguson's right, Miss Cranna,' Hansie Pienaar remarked. 'The magnificence really makes you think about your tiny place in this world.'

The sunrise expedition to the pyramids had been offered to the children as an optional excursion this morning. It required a twenty-minute walk from the hotel before breakfast and their tour with Mr Salah.

Barclay had been thrilled to see eighteen of the group appear at 5 am. Sadly, Madagascar and Caprice had chosen not to join them and, while the outing wasn't compulsory, he felt that it showed some fortitude on the part of the students who had forsaken a lie-in for this wondrous sight. He was surprised that Miss Reedy and Mr Plumpton had stayed behind too, though he noted last night that the woman had been in a better mood at dinner.

'So beautiful,' Neville breathed, but he wasn't looking at the sunrise. Alice-Miranda was standing beside him, focused on the horizon while he focused on her.

'It is,' she said. 'But I don't want to see it through a lens – I just want to watch with my own eyes.'

Neville's heart swelled inside his chest and he let his hand brush against hers. A spark of static electricity passed between their fingers and they both jumped and giggled. But the moment was soon extinguished with the arrival of Sep, who forced his way between the pair.

'What do you think, Alice-Miranda?' the boy asked. Neville glared. Sep's timing was horrible, and he had a feeling that it was intentional.

'Oh it's perfect,' she said, giving Sep a smile. 'I hope you got a lot of pictures, because I didn't take any.'

As Mr Ferguson had predicted, it was all over within minutes. Alice-Miranda offered to take a photo of Sep and Neville with the Great Pyramid behind them but neither seemed particularly keen. She took one anyway and wondered what it was that had upset the pair. They'd always got along so well before, but there was some strange tension between them on this trip. She'd talk to Sloane and Millie and see if they had any ideas.

'Let's head back for breakfast. And make sure to slop on yer sunscreen before the tour, and wear loose clothin' and a hat and bring at least two bottles of water. It feels like it's goin' to be a bit warmer today,' Barclay instructed.

'There's a lot happenin',' he continued. 'First up we're on the bus to the Step Pyramid and Saqqara necropolis, where Mr Salah has organised exclusive access to a new archaeological site. Ye'll be given some lessons in excavation in preparation for our visit to the Valley of the Queens in a couple of days. Then we're back here by mid-afternoon to tour the pyramids and Sphinx and take pictures with Mr Salah's camels.'

'Caprice hates camels,' Millie said with a chuckle.

'Yes, thank ye, Millicent, we're all very aware of that,' Mr Ferguson replied.

'I just thought I'd remind you seeing that she's not here – in the unlikely event you might have forgotten,' the child said.

'I don' think there's any chance we'll ever forget Caprice,' Barclay said. 'She's one of a kind, that girl.'

'That's a very nice way of putting it,' Millie said with a cheeky grin. Barclay chuckled too.

✯

Masud walked through the back door into the kitchen and washed his hands at the sink, having just finished feeding the camels and checking that all of the tack was prepared for today's outing. He nodded at his grandmother, who was stirring a pot on the stove.

His father looked up from the newspaper he was reading at the end of the green laminate table.

'You are feeling better, Masud?' Akil asked.

'Yes, Baba,' the boy replied. 'Teta looked after me very well.'

The woman turned and gave the boy a wry smile.

'Good morning, Masud,' Esha greeted her son as she poured some tea into a cup and carried it to the table. 'You have made a miraculous recovery. I am so pleased.'

'Yes, Mama,' he replied, sitting down in front of the empty place setting. 'What time are we leaving today, Baba?'

Akil Salah raised his eyebrows. 'I will need you to have the camels ready by two. In the meantime, I have scored something of a coup. We are visiting the new dig site at the Saqqara necropolis.'

'I thought you said that site was off limits to tour groups,' Esha said. 'Didn't you try to get another party in there recently?'

'I talked to a fellow who talked to another fellow who talked to someone else,' Akil said with a sly wink.

Masud chuckled. It was good to see his father smile.

'And Mr Ferguson was prepared to pay handsomely for the experience, which helped considerably,' Akil said.

Masud bit his lip. 'May I come too, Baba?'

Akil and Esha exchanged frowns. 'Your mother and I thought you could visit Jabari this morning. The doctors have changed his medications and he is feeling stronger,' his father replied.

'Is Jabari getting better?' Masud asked.

His parents looked at one another.

'Your brother is stable. We must say our prayers and hope that God will answer them,' Akil replied.

Masud sat quietly for a moment. Stable did not mean better – it simply meant not getting any worse. Jabari still needed to have the bone-marrow transplant – although his parents had spared the little boy that news. Last night, Masud had been on his computer researching as usual, but this time he had done something more. He had written to the hospital in the United States and asked how to go about finding a donor. His parents would be upset if they knew, but he couldn't just sit back and do nothing.

'Will there be archaeologists at the site?' the boy asked.

'Yes, of course,' his father said. 'The place will be crawling with them.'

Masud's grandmother placed a plate of taameya on the table. Similar to a falafel but larger in size and made from fava beans, this was Masud's second-favourite breakfast dish. His grandmother made them perfectly, with just the right combination of crunchy and soft textures. He reached out and put one on his plate.

'I would like to come with you, Baba,' the boy said, much to his parents' surprise.

'But you have not seen Jabari since the weekend,' Esha said. 'He was asking after you yesterday – though I said that you would not be able to return until you were feeling better. And today you are better.'

Masud felt a tightness in his tummy. He wanted more than anything to spend the morning with his little brother. He'd learned a new card trick to show him. But if he could have time with real archaeologists, then perhaps he could learn more about the funerary figures he had found. He needed to know how old they might be and get an idea of their worth. If he was going to sell them, this information was vital. Of course he could not take the pieces with him – he would simply appear to be asking out of curiosity.

Masud nodded. 'Yes, but what if my sickness is still a little contagious?'

'Then you should not be going anywhere,' his mother said. 'We do not want you spreading an illness to the children on the tour.'

It was his grandmother who came to Masud's aid.

'Esha, dear. I think Masud is right that perhaps it is taking too big a risk for him to visit Jabari today. The boy's immune system is very weak and, though Masud is obviously much better, while ever there is even the slightest chance of germs he should stay away. I will go with you. Masud can accompany Akil,' the woman said. 'He can surely keep a distance from the others at a dig. Those areas are vast.'

Masud smiled at his grandmother. 'I wrote Jabari a letter yesterday, Mama,' the boy said, pushing his chair out and running to his bedroom, quickly returning with the envelope. 'Tell him I will be there as soon as Baba and I are back from the tour at the end of the week.'

The envelope was decorated with a picture of camels and two boys smiling. In the background, a camel with the name Nenet on her blanket was biting another one's bottom. The biting camel looked as if she were laughing.

Esha turned it over in her hand and smiled. 'It is very good, Masud. Your brother will love this.'

Akil looked at his son. 'We will need to leave in half an hour. There will still be time to prepare the camels when we return. I can take the tour group to the pyramids and you can walk the girls up a little later.'

'Yes, Baba,' Masud replied. Today he would learn as much as he could – his little brother's life depended on it.

Chapter 24

Cars and tour buses clogged the streets of Giza as they drove south, Mr Salah pointing out various places of interest during their journey. They were en route to the Saqqara necropolis, but would see the Step Pyramid of Djoser first. With an age of 4700 years, it was the oldest in Egypt.

Mr Ferguson had introduced Masud Salah to the group before they set off, but the boy hadn't made eye contact with anyone and immediately sat down right behind the driver.

'You will notice that traffic is a never-ending problem for us Egyptians,' Akil said over the microphone. 'Though if you are ever driving a car here I must warn you, do not take on a determined pedestrian – they will always win.'

'They're either very brave or absolutely mad the way they just walk out,' Millie said, watching as a mother with five small children in tow charged across three lanes, waving her hands in the air. Vehicles screeched to a halt while the family made their way safely to the wide island in the centre of the road. They still had another three lanes to negotiate before they arrived on the other side.

'I assume that you are all familiar with the word "necropolis",' Mr Salah said.

'It's a cemetery, isn't it?' Lucas called out.

'Yes.' The man nodded. 'And that is where we are joining the team of archaeologists on their dig.'

'We're digging up a cemetery?' Madagascar said, aghast at the thought. 'Well, that's disgusting.'

'She obviously didn't get the memo that we're studying ancient Egyptian culture while we're here, and that means a lot of mummies and tombs and dead things,' Sloane whispered to Chessie, who giggled.

'You will also be having a lesson in Egyptology and excavation,' Mr Salah added. 'The necropolis contains the remains of Egyptians who lived thousands of years ago. We like to say hello to our elders when we can find them.'

The forty-five-minute bus ride took the group through miles of residential and commercial areas before the buildings thinned out and emerald green farmland stretched as far as the eye could see to their left. But not for long – they were soon back in suburbia. To the right, the desert was never far away.

The bus pulled up in the carpark, and within a couple of minutes the students and staff were headed to the Step Pyramid, where they were led inside to see the remains of the sarcophagus and burial tomb of the King known as Djoser – on display once more after a fourteen-year renovation.

'This pyramid was designed by Imhotep, who was reputed to be the world's first architect,' Mr Salah said. 'There is a museum here dedicated to his honour.'

'It's really plain,' Neville said. 'I thought there would be hieroglyphs.'

'Not here,' Mr Salah said. 'The Great Pyramid is also devoid of decoration. Later today you will see the mastaba of Queen Meresankh the Third, which has beautiful paintings. It is at the Valley of the Kings and the Valley of the Queens, though, that you will see the true artistic skills of our forebears.'

The children remarked that it was quite a lot cooler in the chamber.

'Aye, it is usually twenty degrees inside the pyramids,' Mr Ferguson said. 'Although I'm not a big fan of the air quality – it always smells musty to me.'

'A bit like damp socks,' Lucas said.

'Or ancient bandages,' Millie quipped. 'Are there any actual mummies here?'

Mr Salah reassured her that Djoser had disappeared long before the tomb was opened by modern treasure hunters.

Alice-Miranda noticed Masud standing at the back of the group and went to introduce herself.

'Hello,' she said. 'My name is Alice-Miranda Highton-Smith-Kennington-Jones. It's very nice to meet you. It's Masud, isn't it?' She didn't offer her hand. Alice-Miranda wasn't sure if it was culturally acceptable for boys to shake hands with girls and she didn't want to put Masud in an uncomfortable position.

'Yes, hello,' the boy replied. He didn't look up.

'Your father is an amazing guide – he's so smart,' Alice-Miranda said. 'And funny. I imagine your house must be full of laughter.'

'He is very knowledgeable,' the boy agreed, but their home had not been a place of joy for some time. Masud found himself thinking back to the days before Jabari got sick and how their father was always playing tricks on them and they on him. Their grandmother liked to join in too. Their home had been the happiest place he knew. But not anymore.

Alice-Miranda noticed the faraway look in Masud's eyes.

'Are you all right?' she asked, wondering if she had said something offensive.

The boy nodded. 'Yes, of course.'

'Have you worked with your father for long?' she asked.

Masud shook his head. 'I have only just started a little while ago.'

Alice-Miranda glanced around the tomb, taking in the scale of things. It was difficult to imagine how the pyramids were constructed thousands of years ago.

'It must be terribly exciting – to travel all over the country and visit places like this and learn about archaeology. What a thrill it must be to find treasures from thousands of years ago. I can't even imagine,' the child prattled.

'Neither can I,' Masud said, although that was a lie. The excitement he had felt yesterday when he uncovered the funerary figures had made him want to leap in the air and shout to the heavens. Thankfully he had resisted that urge.

'Your father said that you have camels. We're looking forward to meeting them – well, except for Caprice. She's not a big camel fan,' Alice-Miranda said.

'She will definitely not like Nenet,' the boy said.

'Nenet?' Alice-Miranda queried.

'She is the boss of the herd and has a big personality,' Masud replied.

'Caprice has a big personality too. Maybe they'll get on better than we think,' Alice-Miranda said with a smile.

Masud nodded as he spied Akil beckoning him. 'It is unlikely. Excuse me, miss, I must help my father.'

'Oh yes, of course,' the child said. 'Sorry to have kept you. I do tend to talk a lot.'

The boy disappeared. Soon, the other children were ushered from the tomb to follow Mr Salah cross-country to the burial grounds that were currently under excavation.

Sep hurried to catch up to Alice-Miranda and Neville. Millie, Chessie and Sloane walked behind the pair.

'Would you like a date?' Sep offered.

'Did my brother just ask Alice-Miranda on a date?' Sloane asked, a cringey look on her face.

Millie grimaced. 'No, I think he offered her food.'

The children were introduced to the woman in charge of the dig – Dr Louisa Brooks, a professor of archaeology from the United States. They followed her to a roped-off area in various stages of excavation. Dr Brooks told them that it would take months, if not years, to fully uncover the treasures that lay beneath the surface. She then showed the children the range of tools used onsite, including shovels, mattocks, trowels, brushes and sieves. It was a painstaking business, but one that could have rich rewards – both materially and in terms of understanding the past.

Miss Cranna had already split the children into groups of four. They were heading off to work with an archaeologist each for the next ninety minutes. She warned them not to expect too much and that the chances of finding something were slim at best, but this was an opportunity for real, experiential learning. The best kind of education, as far as she was concerned.

Alice-Miranda found herself with Britt and the two French boys, although Neville and Sep both told Morag they'd be happy to swap groups. Instead, the lads had been placed with Alethea and Gretchen. The woman flatly denied their request. It was important the children worked with everyone over the course of the week.

Millie had just learned that she was to be with Madagascar, Lucas and Aidan – the Scottish boy who had proven himself lots of fun on their last trip. He was an excellent bagpiper, so the musicians had given him a go on some of their instruments the previous night, though the sounds he created hadn't been the most appealing.

Madagascar looked across at Caprice and rolled her eyes, clearly unimpressed with the way things had been organised. Caprice, who was set to work with Henry, Hunter and Jacinta, wasn't best pleased either.

'Watch this,' Madagascar mouthed to her friend. Clearly she thought no one else had noticed but Millie had seen it. She wondered what the girl was up to this time.

'Miss Cranna, I'm not feeling well,' Madagascar moaned. She raised her hand to her forehead dramatically and stumbled as if she were about to faint. 'It's heat stroke, I'm sure of it.'

'As if,' Millie said, rolling her eyes.

'Oh dear,' Morag grabbed the girl's arm. 'Miss Reedy, could you please give me a hand here?'

The teacher sped to the woman's aid. She felt the child's forehead with the back of her hand and while Madagascar didn't seem especially hot, they decided they couldn't risk it.

'I'm afraid that you'll have to sit this activity out, Madagascar,' Livinia said to the girl, who looked at Caprice and gave her a wink. Caprice pulled a face, clearly unimpressed that she hadn't thought to feign illness first.

'Oh, that's a pity,' Dr Brooks said. 'I really wanted you to work in pairs.'

Millie spied Masud standing by his father. 'What about Masud? He could join our team.'

Akil Salah had kept one ear on what was happening with the children. 'My son would be happy to step in,' he said, though he wasn't sure it was entirely true. Masud was naturally very shy and Akil wondered if he should have volunteered the boy without asking him first.

Millie proceeded to introduce herself, Lucas and Aidan to Masud, who smiled broadly.

The children were each allocated an archaeologist, who took them to one of five different areas that had been marked out but not yet excavated. They were given a brief lesson in how to use the tools and shown the sorts of things they were likely to find on the site – mostly broken pieces of pottery, as this area was believed to have been used for preparing bodies for mummification. From tests done on the fragments they had uncovered so far, it seemed that the containers would have held fluids used in the embalming process. The archaeologists had already detected a variety of concoctions, hinting at the fact that the process wasn't always the same. Perhaps it had to do with the materials that were available to the priests at the time.

'That is so gross,' Caprice said, wondering if she might suddenly develop heat stroke too, though given Madagascar was now sitting right beside Miss Reedy in a shady spot and doing nothing, the idea didn't appeal quite as much.

Millie's group was with an Egyptian man called Harry, who told them that he had been working on digs all over the country ever since graduating from university almost twenty years ago.

Harry finished his explanations and allocated the children their tools. While Lucas and Aidan loosened the ground with the mattocks, Millie had a thought.

'Excuse me, Harry, yesterday when I was in the souk I bought two shabtis. I was wondering if you could tell me more about them?' the girl asked. She pulled the figurines from her backpack and passed them over.

'This is a replica of a piece found in Tutankhamun's tomb. There were four hundred and thirteen shabti found there – the most ever. This inscription here,' the man pointed at the hieroglyphs carved onto the body, 'is spell four hundred and seventy-two from the Coffin Texts. It decrees that this fellow was to spend part of each year engaging in public works. This here,' he pointed at another line of inscription, 'is the name of the boy king.'

'Wow, that's amazing,' Millie said, looking at the piece with new-found admiration. 'I can't believe that you can read all of that – it looks so complicated. And this one?'

The man turned it over in his hand studying the hieroglyphs. 'Can you see these symbols here?'

Millie nodded. 'That looks like a sun maybe, and a worm or a snake or a snail without a home and a chicken perhaps?'

The man grinned. 'Not bad. The first is a sieve representing a placenta and meaning one who belongs to kh – an infant – and the letters KH, the chick is U, the viper – though I agree he does look a little like a snail missing his shell – is F and then lastly another chick for U.'

Millie thought about the spelling. 'It says Khufu. Isn't he the Pharaoh who built the Great Pyramid at Giza?'

'Yes,' Harry replied. 'But I am afraid that this shabti is pure poetic licence. None of the treasures from his tomb have ever been found, and there is but one statue of the Pharaoh known to exist. Ironically the man who built the biggest pyramid has the smallest tribute. He also would not have had shabti – they weren't around until the eleventh dynasty and must be inscribed with the Book of the Dead. His would have been funerary figures and marked perhaps only with his name.'

Masud was listening to the chatter. 'May I see please?' he asked.

Harry passed him the statue. It didn't look anything like the ones he had found, but the hieroglyph . . . he was almost certain that it was the same, or nearly so. He would check it against the symbols he had copied into his notebook before he had hidden the pieces again.

'So there were no treasures found in the Great Pyramid at all?' Masud asked.

The man shook his head. 'Khufu's tomb had been pillaged long before the modern-day raiders came to Egypt.'

'Perhaps one day something will turn up,' Masud said. 'The desert is always revealing things that have been hidden for thousands of years.'

'Well, Masud, if you ever find anything with that hieroglyph – that wasn't bought in the souk – then you must let me know. To unearth pieces associated with Khufu, the builder of the Great Pyramid . . . that would be a discovery like no other,' Harry said.

Masud nodded.

'What would it be worth?' Millie asked. 'Something that had belonged to Khufu?'

Harry grinned. 'Well, it would automatically become the property of the government, but there are black-market dealers who would pay tens of millions – perhaps even hundreds of millions – of dollars for that sort of thing.'

'Really?' Millie said, her eyebrows jumping up. 'So it's true that people sell antiquities even though it's against the law.'

'I am afraid so, Millie. There are dealers willing to take the risk. There are whispers that even government officials may be involved. But it is a dangerous business – I have heard of people disappearing along with their treasures.'

'I can imagine,' Millie said. 'There are some evil individuals in the world who wouldn't be opposed to double crossing someone for that kind of money.'

'Have you had experience with this sort of thing?' Harry asked.

'Not exactly, but we were in outback Australia not too long ago and met some bad guys who were highly motivated by treasure and the money it would bring them. Some of my friends and I were trapped down a mine,' Millie explained.

'It sounds as if you and your friends are very adventurous,' Harry said with a grin.

'We've had more than our share of exciting experiences,' Millie said.

While Masud had been interested in Millie's stories, he really wanted to know more about the black-market dealers. He couldn't help himself.

'And where do you find these people? The ones who operate in the shadows?' the boy asked.

'I believe that if you ask the right questions, there is always someone who will tell you the right answers,' Harry said mysteriously.

Masud wondered what the right questions were, exactly. Millie did too.

The boy was about to say something else when Lucas called out for some help. Millie quickly took the second shabti from Masud and put the pair back into her bag before she scurried away to lend a hand, remembering why they were there. For a moment, though, Masud was lost in his thoughts. Could it be true? Was there even a chance that the funerary figures hidden in the stables had belonged to the man who had built the most impressive pyramid in all of Egypt? The boy's heart pounded. It would be hours before he could go home and check if he was right, but working out what to do next would be the most important thing he had ever done in his life.

Chapter 25

Maryam Moussa arrived at the dig site just after ten. The drive had taken far longer than she had anticipated, not helped by a truck that had lost its load of watermelons on the freeway ramp. A squally wind whipped across the desert, creating a veil of hot sand that stuck to everything. She could feel the grit in her eyes and on her skin.

Maryam was looking for Dr Brooks. Surely the woman could furnish her with a list detailing the people who had been working on the site.

Determining who it was that Dr Hassam had been dealing with would be a process of elimination, though entirely worth it. Nothing would bring her more satisfaction than facilitating the great man's fall from grace – which would be spectacular and, as far as Maryam was concerned, well deserved.

Earlier in the morning she had telephoned the hospital to check on the man's condition and was told it remained unchanged. While she hoped that he recovered, of course, having enough time to investigate things for herself was crucial.

Maryam hopped out of her car and immediately stumbled on a rock, almost losing her shoe. She spread her map of the area on the bonnet and worked out where the dig was then set off, trekking across the sand until she spotted a woman wearing beige dungarees and a matching shirt with a fedora on her head. She was crouched down beside a boy as the pair examined something closely.

'Hello! Dr Brooks?' Maryam called. She'd looked the archaeologist up before she left the office.

The woman gave a wave and Maryam walked closer. Other adults and children were spread across the area too.

'Oh hello Miss Moussa,' a girl said, looking up. She had long brunette curls and a huge smile, with a straw hat on her head. A few metres away stood a blonde girl, almost identically dressed and almost identical-looking but for the fairness of her features.

Maryam flinched, recognising the children from the museum the previous day. She scanned the site to realise it was the same tour group – the youngsters from the Queen's Colours with their enthusiastic leader Mr Ferguson and their know-all guide Mr Salah.

The idea that she was to spend two days with these children in the Valley of the Queens was horrendous. Between thinking about Dr Hassam and what he'd been up to and wondering how she was going to study all of the information she needed to know, she was desperate to find an excuse not to attend. There was work to do. Being away from the office would only make things more difficult.

'We're learning some of the basics of archaeology,' the brunette child said. 'But we're looking forward to you sharing your expertise with us later in the week.'

The blonde one piped up. 'It's so thrilling – the idea that right here there could be something thousands of years old that will give us a glimpse into the past.'

'Yes, thrilling,' Maryam said with a tight smile. 'Dr Brooks!' she called again. The woman stood up. A boy had just found a piece of pottery and she had been showing him how to clean it with one of the brushes. He was clearly elated about his discovery, chatting animatedly to the other boy beside him in French, but Maryam couldn't see that there was anything to get excited about. Bits of broken pottery were a dime a dozen in Egypt.

'Hello, how may I help you?' the woman said.

Maryam introduced herself and offered her hand.

'The pleasure is all mine,' said Dr Brooks. 'I wondered when you would stop by the site. Such a dreadful business with Dr Hassam. I heard he owes his life to your quick actions. It's strange not having him here, actually.'

'How often was he on the dig?' Maryam asked.

'Frequently, when he wasn't touring the country working on other sites and educating the next generation of treasure hunters. We've been blessed to have a man in his position who has played such a hands-on role,' Dr Brooks replied.

That was an understatement. The man was *hands on* and then some. Maryam thought that was the end of the woman's appraisal, but it seemed Dr Brooks was only getting started.

'His knowledge is beyond compare, although I read in an email from the Ministry that your qualifications exceed his and Deputy Fadil's. You've certainly been hiding your light under a bushel, Miss Moussa. Or should I say Dr Moussa?'

Maryam smiled tightly again, wondering why she hadn't seen that particular communication. She'd have to ask Nour for it when she returned to the office. 'One doesn't like to brag, and I've always considered the prefix "doctor" should be reserved for those in medicine – no disrespect intended,' she said. 'I certainly wouldn't invite any comparison with the extraordinary Dr Mustafa Hassam. The man is a wonder.' She forced the words out of her mouth.

'Oh indeed, Miss Moussa. And I am sure that he would be very grateful that you are looking after things while he recovers. How may I help you today?' Dr Brooks asked.

'Actually, I would like to have a list of all of the people who've been working here since you started the excavation,' Maryam said.

'May I know why?' the woman asked.

'I'm interested in compiling a database of archaeologists and excavators currently offering their services throughout the country,' Maryam replied, glad she had thought of that on the drive out.

Dr Brooks frowned. 'I can give you what I have, but I'm afraid there have been many volunteers over the past months and our record-keeping is a little scratchy – there are always students of archaeology and Egyptology who come and go, as well as our qualified staff. I must stay here with the children now but I can get it for you after they go. Perhaps you'd like to join us?'

'Oh yes, please do, Miss Moussa.' The child with the brown curls jumped up and proffered Maryam a trowel, showering the woman with sand in the process.

'Watch out!' Maryam snapped, shaking the grit from her suit. She could feel sand on her face and absently wiped the skin above her lip, then rubbed her left eye.

'I'm terribly sorry,' Alice-Miranda apologised, then peered more closely at the woman, realising that one of her previously bright green eyes was now brown. 'I was wondering if you could tell us what sort of techniques are used to differentiate between a proper artefact and something modern.'

Maryam looked at the child. 'Sorry?'

She repeated the question.

'And you could show us how to use these tools more effectively,' the blonde girl said. 'I think I'm digging too aggressively. I don't want to break anything.'

Maryam swallowed hard. Something about carbon dating entered her mind but she wasn't in any position to explain it. 'Dr Brooks, look, I really have to go, so if you could forward me that list as soon as you're back in the office I'd appreciate it.'

And with that Maryam turned on her heel and fled. The last thing she needed was that pesky brunette making a fool of her for the second time in as many days.

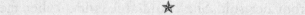

Alice-Miranda and Britt watched Miss Moussa trudge across the sand.

'I don't think she likes us very much,' Britt said.

'Perhaps she's just overwhelmed. From what I've seen and read, Dr Hassam is one of the most revered men in the country. Taking over his role even in a temporary capacity would probably be daunting,' Alice-Miranda said. 'But I do agree that Miss Moussa hasn't exactly seemed excited by the prospect of spending time with us.'

'She needs to think about what she wears out here,' Britt said. 'Suits and the desert are not a good combination, and heels on the sand is just asking for trouble.'

Alice-Miranda grinned. 'Perhaps you can give her some wardrobe tips.'

'I wouldn't dare. I think she would tear my head off,' Britt said. 'Did you see the scar above her lip? I only noticed it after she rubbed her face and her makeup came off.'

Alice-Miranda nodded. She'd seen it as well and wondered what it was from. 'I think she wears coloured contact lenses too. Yesterday I couldn't help notice her bright green eyes, but then today after her accidental sand shower her left eye was brown.'

The girl thought for a moment. There was something about Miss Moussa that seemed out of place, and not just the fact that she was so reluctant to share her knowledge. From what Alice-Miranda had watched of Dr Hassam's documentaries, the man approached his work with the enthusiasm of a small child waiting to open presents on Christmas Day. Even the smallest discovery had him jumping for joy. In contrast, Miss Moussa looked as if she'd rather be doing the washing up in a sink full of asps than showing off the treasures of Egypt.

Chapter 26

'Would you like some help with the camels?' Akil Salah asked his son.

Masud shook his head. 'No, Baba, I will be fine. I have everything ready.'

The pair had been dropped at their gate while the rest of the tour group was returning to the hotel for lunch and a rest. They would all meet up again to visit the pyramids mid-afternoon. Trudging about in the desert in the midday sun was ill-advised.

'You did well this morning,' Akil said. He slapped his son on the back as the pair walked to the house. 'Thank you for stepping up and being part of that group. I know that the other children appreciated it.'

Masud turned and smiled at his father. It was nice to hear words of praise. They did not come often, but when they did he knew he had earned them.

'I will see what your mother and grandmother have left us for our lunch,' Akil said, heading to the kitchen.

Masud scurried to his room to thumb through his notebook. He was looking for the symbols he had copied from the figures under the barn.

His heart was pounding as he saw the sieve and the chick and the viper and the second chick. Could it be true? Was it possible that he had found the treasures of Khufu right here in their own backyard?

'Masud, lunch is ready,' his father called from the kitchen.

There were falafel with tahini sauce and a salad of fresh tomatoes and rocket. Masud had barely sat down before his meal was gone. He took several large gulps of tea and slammed the cup on the table.

'My goodness, were you starving?' Akil asked, frowning at the boy. He had hardly taken his first bite and the boy was already finished.

'Sorry, Baba,' Masud lowered his eyes. 'I think archaeology is a hungry business – and I am a teenage boy. Mama said that I have grown two inches in the past month.'

His father chuckled. 'I remember the same thing happened to me when I was your age. Your grandfather was always complaining that I was eating them out of house and home, and you can imagine with another two brothers after me, my mother was forever at the stove,' Akil said. 'You must eat – you are a growing boy. We should be thankful that we have good jobs so that we can provide for the family and pay for your brother's medicine.'

'Even if it is not enough?' Masud muttered.

'What did you say, Masud?' Akil narrowed his eyes, but the boy was not interested in an argument.

Masud shook his head. 'Nothing, Baba. May I be excused?' He was keen to get the camels sorted so that he could take another look at the funerary figures. He could still feel his heart beating faster than it should have been.

If he was right about their origin, surely he would make more than enough money to pay for Jabari's treatment. Then his brother could likely get the best care anywhere in the world. But he had to ask the right questions and hear the right answers. He was entering dangerous territory – on so many fronts. Masud could not afford to make mistakes. His parents would not be happy if he was found dead in a ditch.

The Queen's Colours group had had lunch and a swim before setting out again just after two o'clock. They were meeting Mr Salah for a tour of the Great Pyramid, followed by a visit to the mastaba of Queen Meresankh the Third.

Alice-Miranda and Millie were walking with Miss Reedy and Mr Plumpton.

'Miss Reedy, have you managed to get hold of Miss Grimm today?' Alice-Miranda asked.

'I got through to the office three times but I think Mrs Parker must be screening the calls.

She said Miss Grimm was terribly busy and as long as everyone on the tour was all right, there was no need for me to call again. Honestly, you'd think she was in charge of the school,' Livinia replied. 'I never even got a chance to ask her to convey a message about trying to find copies of those documents.'

'Told you she'd turn into a tyrant,' Millie said, glancing across at Alice-Miranda.

'I'm sure Mrs Parker means well,' the girl replied. 'Though sometimes her good intentions might be lost in translation.'

Alice-Miranda resolved to phone the school as soon as they returned from their outing. She had an idea and she might as well get Mrs Parker started while she reached out to her uncle.

The children arrived at the Great Pyramid and found Mr Salah. The place was heaving with tourists and touts and horse-drawn carriages that were ferrying visitors about.

'I expected more camels,' Millie said. 'There are so many horses – and donkeys and mules.' The girl couldn't help thinking that a lot of the animals did not look to be in top shape.

She gasped as the sight of a skinny beast with a long red gash on its side. 'Oh my goodness, the poor thing.'

Alice-Miranda shuddered. The thought of Bony or Chops being injured like that, and still having to work so hard, was beyond comprehension.

Akil Salah saw the looks of concern on the girls' faces.

'I am afraid that life is difficult here in Egypt. Many of these men are working for a pittance. They can barely afford to feed their families, let alone their livestock,' he said.

'But that horse needs to see a vet! The wound could become infected and then the horse will get very sick and likely die,' Millie said.

Mr Salah shook his head. 'They cannot afford to pay for the medical attention unless they find an animal shelter that is able to provide treatment for free.'

'Aren't we visiting somewhere like that?' Alice-Miranda asked. 'In Luxor?'

'Yes. The woman who runs it is passionate about saving all the animals she meets, but I fear her heart has been almost broken by some of the things she has seen,' Akil said.

'I think mine might break too,' Millie said.

Alice-Miranda could only agree. 'There's nothing worse than seeing animals or children in pain.'

Akil Salah stared into the distance, suddenly overcome with emotion. He reached into his tunic pocket, pulled out the rope the girls had seen him fiddling with before and turned it over and over. The man hurriedly wiped tears from his eyes, but not before Alice-Miranda had seen them.

'Are you all right, Mr Salah?' the girl asked.

He looked at her and smiled. 'Yes of course. Sometimes thinking of the animals makes me sad too.'

The man regained his composure and hurriedly gathered the group together before Alice-Miranda could say anything else, but she wondered if there was something more going on.

'Welcome to the Great Pyramid of Giza, built by the Pharaoh Khufu, who was otherwise known as Cheops. It is the only remaining Ancient Wonder of the World and a proud monument to our forebears. Today, thanks to the work of men like our own Dr Hassam, we have a great deal of information about how it was constructed and the workers who toiled here.

'For a long time it was thought that these giant structures had been built by slaves, who were a key part of ancient Egyptian life. More recently we have discovered that the twenty-five thousand men who toiled here had great skills and came willingly to work in Cairo during the annual flooding of the Nile. We know this because their burial place has recently been unearthed. Slaves would not have been interned within view of the Pharaoh – therefore these were workers he respected. When it was built, the Great Pyramid was almost one hundred and fifty metres tall.'

The entire group was awestruck.

'I feel so small,' Chessie said.

'Really?' Caprice replied. 'Just looking at it makes me feel powerful. If I'd have lived here in ancient times I'm sure I would have been a princess.'

'Of course you would,' Millie said, rolling her eyes. 'And you would know that because?'

'You really have to ask? I mean, princesses were beautiful and had gorgeous hair, like mine, and they were talented and adored. I think I would have been Cleopatra. She was stunning, wasn't she?'

Mr Salah was listening to the children. He looked at Caprice and shook his head. 'I am afraid that Cleopatra's beauty appears to have been over-stated – there are coins that depict her with a very large hooked nose. Though she was a cunning strategist and revered for her intellect, she married two of her younger brothers and had both of them killed, along with her sister as well – so perhaps she wasn't someone to aspire to.'

Caprice wrinkled her nose. 'Then I'd be Nefertiti – she was lovely, wasn't she?'

Mr Salah nodded. 'A much better choice for you. And you are right about the significance our ancient forebears placed on hair. It was highly prized, and hairdressers were revered. One named Ty has a large tomb in Saqqara with very beautiful artwork – a sign of his importance.'

'I told you, Millie,' Caprice glared. 'Did you see the way all those boys in the souk looked at me yesterday? And that man with the keyrings. He told me that my hair was like spun sunbeams.'

'You do realise that he was trying to sell you something,' Millie said.

'Yes.' Madagascar leapt to her new friend's defence. 'Who do you think you would have been in ancient times, Millie? A servant? A goat herd?'

'Well, considering it's all sheer speculation, I think I would have liked to be the Vizier,' Millie replied.

'Good choice,' Sep said.

'What's that?' Caprice asked.

'The Vizier was in charge of everything. The most powerful person in the whole country other than the King or Queen – and probably having way more fun,' Sep said.

'I'd have kicked princess butt,' Millie said, narrowing her eyes at Caprice.

'Whatever,' the girl scoffed.

Mr Salah chuckled at the children, then continued his explanation. 'The Great Pyramid was truly something to behold. It took only fourteen years to construct. There are more than two million stones, some weighing up to two and a half tonnes each. And the outside was lined with granite, though it is all gone now – pillaged to build modern Cairo. You can still see some at the very top of the Khafre pyramid over there.'

The children remained silent for quite a while, mesmerised not only by the pyramid itself but by Mr Salah's extensive knowledge. He showed them the points on the ground that were used by the ancient Egyptians to do their mathematical calculations as well as the survey lines. The precision of the structure was incredible. It was no wonder that for many years people believed that it had been built by aliens. He also spoke about why the pyramid was built and how it served as a burial chamber for the Pharaoh, and what the ancient Egyptians believed about gods and the afterlife.

'It's intriguing – the whole idea that the civilisation was so sophisticated,' Neville said, shaking his head. 'I think I'd like to study Egyptology at university.'

'It's very appealing, isn't it?' Alice-Miranda agreed.

'We could study together,' Neville said, raising his eyebrows.

Alice-Miranda could feel her cheeks getting hotter and wondered if she needed to reapply her sunscreen. Millie, watching the exchange, giggled. Her friend might have been the smartest person she knew, but when it came to being the object of not one, but two boys' affections, Alice-Miranda was clueless and then some.

Chapter 27

The children spent the next hour or so inside the Great Pyramid, then headed over to see the tomb of Queen Meresankh the Third and its beautiful artwork depicting scenes of huntsmen and various craftspeople intended to provide for her in the afterlife. Next it was time for a drinks break before meeting up with Masud and the camels near the Sphinx. Everyone had packed iced water and an afternoon snack from the hotel before they'd left. Dinner was to be a relatively late affair following their sunset photo opportunities, but Mr Ferguson said he had something very special planned.

'There's Masud,' Millie called, pointing at a boy leading six camels – all tied together in a train – towards them. The animals were beautifully adorned in saddles, coloured cloths, decorative reins and headdresses befitting princesses.

'Urgh, camels,' Caprice griped, yet again.

'Really, Caprice? They're not your favourite animal? Who knew?' Millie said, to a chortle of laughter from the others.

'You do know that sarcasm is the lowest form of wit,' Caprice retorted.

'Of course I do – it's your go-to response.' Millie waved her hand dismissively.

As the boy drew closer it was clear that this herd was well cared for. Their eyes were brighter and their coats shinier than any other animals the group had seen around the pyramids.

Masud stopped in front of the children and turned to the camels, who were now lined up in front of the Sphinx. He lowered his hand and together the six of them bowed their heads, much to the delight of the onlookers.

'Bravo, Masud,' Mr Ferguson clapped. 'And bravo, girls – they are all girls, aren't they, Akil?'

Mr Salah nodded while the rest of the tour group clapped.

The boy then lowered his hand and the camels clambered to the ground, sitting on their haunches. They were definitely not the most elegant of animals, but considering the length of their legs and the load on their backs it was a wonder they got down at all.

'Masud works hard with our herd. And now, as promised, he is going to share some facts about these beasts of burden,' Akil said, nodding at his son.

Caprice yawned widely, waving her hand over her mouth.

Madagascar mimicked her friend while Miss Cranna gave the pair of them the hairy eyeball.

Masud walked closer to the children. This was only the second time he had addressed a tour group. On the first occasion, he had been so nervous it felt as if he'd swallowed a handful of sand. Today was a little better – though only just. The girl he'd met on the dig called Millie looked at him and gave a thumbs up. Masud smiled at her. He had enjoyed her company much more than he'd expected. She was fun for a girl – not that he'd had much to do with many of them, other than his mother and grandmother and some neighbourhood kids.

'There are two types of camels,' the boy began. 'Here in Egypt and throughout the Middle East you will find camels with one hump, known as dromedaries. The camels with two humps are called Bactrian camels, and they come from South-East Asia. Contrary to popular belief, camels do not store water in their humps but fat, which they can convert to food or water if necessary.'

'Urgh, that's gross,' Madagascar said. 'Imagine having a big fatty lump on your back.'

'I don't know,' Aidan said. 'Some people have one on their shoulders – going by the stupid things they say.'

Madagascar frowned, unsure whether that comment was directed at her. He'd cop it later if it was.

Chessie raised her hand. 'How much water can camels drink?'

'Up to forty litres at a time, which helps them to survive in the heat. We humans only have to lose fifteen per cent water from our bodies to become dehydrated, but camels can lose up to twenty-five per cent before they are in trouble,' Masud explained.

Millie was watching one camel tilt her head to and fro, as if she were listening and understanding everything that was being said. The name Nenet was embroidered on her blanket in English along with some Arabic lettering. The girl photographed a few portraits of the beast before taking some wider angles of the rest of the train. She couldn't wait to take a look at her snaps later.

'I wish I had eyelashes as long as theirs,' Sloane said.

'Oh no you don't, Miss Sloane. Their mascara bills are outrageous,' Mr Salah said.

Caprice wrinkled her nose. 'What are you talking about? Camels don't wear makeup. Do they?' She sounded less sure of herself now.

Masud grinned at his father. 'Baba is joking. Camels have two rows of eyelashes and three sets of eyelids to keep the sand out, so it would be an expensive exercise if it were true.'

'Haha,' Caprice said. 'I still say they're ugly. Look at that one there – her lips are all weird and twisty and what's that frothy stuff in her mouth? She's gro–'

Before the girl had time to finish what she was saying, the camel in question fired a great gob of spit that landed with a loud splat on Caprice's forehead. For several seconds nobody moved. Caprice began to shake, her face contorted and she let out a bloodcurdling scream. Madagascar ducked in behind her, not wanting to be the beast's second target, while Alice-Miranda and Britt rushed to Caprice's side, begging her to calm down. Alice-Miranda pulled a small packet of wet wipes from her backpack and set to cleaning Caprice's face. The girl was fidgeting and fussing so much that the goop dropped down onto her nose and dribbled onto her lips. Who knew that one camel could produce so much sticky saliva?

The rest of the children were laughing hysterically while the camel began to roar and looked as if she were laughing too, flapping her head up and down.

'Oh, Miss Caprice, please never tell a camel she's ugly,' Mr Salah said. 'The word camel comes from the word for beauty in Arabic. I'm afraid that Nenet does not take kindly to having her looks assessed in such a manner.'

'Nenet's beastly. And you can all stop laughing!' Caprice ordered, still wiping the muck from her face and almost heaving at the smell. 'It's not funny!'

'It is from where we're standing,' Philippe said with a chuckle.

Millie had taken so many photographs that there were bound to be a few absolute crackers. She quickly reviewed some and held the camera out for Sep to see. 'Oh, Caprice is going to kill you for that one,' he said, grinning widely.

Millie shrugged. 'Probably.'

Caprice had finally calmed down enough to interrogate Madagascar as to why she hadn't leapt in and helped her. True to form, Maddie protested that she had tried but Alice-Miranda and Britt – those goody-two-shoes – had pushed her out of the way and Caprice was so upset she hadn't noticed.

Millie heard her and shook her head. Honestly, her cousin was reprehensible.

Meanwhile, Mr Salah decided that those who were keen for a ride should head off so that there was still time for photographs with the animals as the sun was starting to set in front of the pyramids.

Mr Ferguson organised the first twelve riders who would be doubling on the six camels. Sloane and Chessie paired up, while Jacinta and Lucas volunteered to ride Nenet – which some of the others thought very brave. The boys from France went together, as did the lads from South Africa and Alethea and Gretchen. Mr Plumpton managed to cajole Miss Reedy into taking a spin too. The other ten children, Miss Cranna, Mr Pienaar and Mr Ferguson would wait until the next round, though Caprice had said there was no way she was getting on any of those ghastly beasts' backs. Madagascar was doing her best to change her friend's mind. She really wanted a go.

Alice-Miranda was keen to get a closer look at the Sphinx, given they were so near to the monument. Neville and Sep offered to join her, and Mr Salah as well. He was confident that Masud could look after the camels and their riders, though Miss Cranna would have been happier had the man stayed with his son.

Soon they were standing at the sculpture. 'I wonder if Napoleon really used the poor fellow's face for target practice?' Neville asked.

'I read that it was destroyed much earlier than that, after peasants made offerings to the Great Sphinx to control the Nile floods. When it didn't work, a Muslim man was so outraged by their devotion to the old gods he destroyed the statue's face. He was apparently in big trouble for vandalism, though there's no verification of that story either,' Alice-Miranda said.

The children were walking around to the other side of the monolith when Neville suddenly stopped.

'Isn't that Miss Moussa over there?' the boy said.

The others peered where he was pointing. It certainly looked like her from a distance.

The woman was standing in an alcove talking to a man wearing western-style clothing. Miss Moussa was looking around and, if her body language was anything to go by, she wasn't entirely comfortable with the situation.

'Do you think she's all right?' Alice-Miranda asked.

Akil Salah frowned. 'I am not impressed by the company she is keeping.'

'Do you know that man?' Sep asked.

'Unfortunately I know of him and that is enough. There have long been whispers that he and his associates deal antiquities on the black market. There is a network of some men who work on the dig sites and others that find the buyers – mostly foreign collectors who are willing to pay a fortune. It is a huge problem here in Egypt although our government says that it is not. Dr Hassam has been fighting the war on these thieves for years,' the man said.

'Why would Miss Moussa be meeting with him?' Millie asked. 'Perhaps she has some intelligence from Dr Hassam and she's luring him into a trap? That would be exciting, but it's probably not the best idea for her to be out here alone. Do you think we should let her know we're here? Just in case.'

But before Akil could answer, Maryam Moussa and the man parted ways. He disappeared around the end of the Sphinx as she headed towards the carpark.

Akil Salah nodded. 'If you are right, Miss Millie, then she should not be putting herself in danger like that. These are bad people – they will do anything to make money. We will see her the day after tomorrow in The Valley of the Queens. I will warn her then.'

The group continued walking around the Sphinx. As they did, Mr Salah shared the widely accepted theory that the monument was built facing the sunrise by the Pharaoh Khafre, the son of Khufu, to protect the precious pyramids and tombs of Giza.

It was when they turned the final corner of the Sphinx to head back to their group that they saw the man who had been speaking to Miss Moussa now talking with several other men on horseback. The men were laughing and carrying on until one of them made a disturbing gesture, running his finger across his throat. Alice-Miranda shivered. She didn't like the look of that one little bit.

Millie laughed as Nenet bellowed loudly and tried to chew Masud's hair, then turned her attention to their surroundings. From her vantage point on high, with Alice-Miranda seated behind her, the girl was amazed by how much they could see.

They hadn't walked terribly far. Nenet wasn't being particularly cooperative and, as leader of the camel train, the length of the journey seemed to be dictated by her mood. The first group of riders had travelled much further but clearly the camel had decided that this time she'd had enough. The animal nibbled the boy's collar.

'Nenet, stop that!' Masud ordered, turning to

scold her, only to be hit in the face by the camel's long tongue. 'Urgh! You are disgusting.'

'I agree,' Millie said, then giggled. Alice-Miranda quickly took some wet wipes from her backpack and offered them to the boy, but he had already cleaned his face with his sleeve.

'It is not the first time I have been on the receiving end of her affections – though her breath is getting stinkier by the day!' the boy said with a grin.

Millie, having already taken loads of photographs, twisted around to see if she could capture some of the other riders behind them.

'I wonder what Miss Moussa was doing with that man? Especially given what Mr Salah said about him being part of the black market,' Alice-Miranda said, ducking down low so that Millie could get her shots.

Masud's ears pricked up. 'May I ask what my father said?'

Millie turned back to face the front and let her camera rest on the strap around her neck while Alice-Miranda explained what they had seen.

The boy listened carefully.

'That's him over there,' Millie said. She pointed at the group of fellows in the shade of the Sphinx.

It looked as if they were sharing some drinks. 'He's the one in the blue shirt and beige pants.'

Masud stared at the men, then turned back to the girls. Nenet had stopped walking and no amount of pulling on her lead was going to entice her to move another step.

'I am afraid that our ride has come to an end,' the boy said. He motioned for the camels to sit, which they all did – apart from Nenet, who refused to go down until Masud produced an apple from his pocket. She gobbled it greedily, then finally did as she was asked.

Alice-Miranda and Millie slid from the saddle and re-joined the group.

'We will walk the camels up towards the Great Pyramid and you can take some photographs,' Mr Salah informed them.

A few minutes later, with some members of the party bemoaning their sore bottoms, the children snapped away, taking pictures of the camels in the setting sun with the pyramids behind them. There were so many fantastic angles, Millie found herself running around trying to take as many shots as possible. The students positioned them-selves with the camels here and there, and finally

Mr Ferguson asked that they assemble for one group picture.

'That, me friends, was pure magic,' Mr Ferguson said, his eyes welling with tears as he turned full circle and took in the magnificence of the site. 'But I'm afraid that this very special time has come to an end and we need to get back to the hotel quick smart. Ye'll only have about fifteen minutes to freshen up before we head out to dinner – which I promise will be like nothing ye've ever experienced before.'

'But I want to wash my hair and scrub that camel spit off properly,' Caprice complained.

'Well, you'll have to be quick, Caprice,' Mr Plumpton said.

The children farewelled Masud and the camels before following Mr Salah back towards the path that led to the hotel. He would accompany them there before returning home.

As they walked, Neville showed Alice-Miranda some photographs he'd taken of her and Millie during the camel ride. Sep was doing the same, though his weren't quite as good given his tandem position behind the other lad. Both boys jostled for the girl's attention.

Jacinta and Lucas had fallen behind the rest of the group. Miss Reedy asked Millie to run back and tell the pair to hurry up.

The red-haired girl reached them, chuckling when they immediately let go of each other's hands.

'Don't stress, it's only me. Miss Reedy said to get a move on,' Millie said. 'And while I don't care if you're holding hands, you do realise that public displays of affection are unacceptable in Egypt – even from clueless tourists who don't know any better.'

'Killjoy,' Lucas said with a cheeky grin.

The light was fading quickly as Millie spotted Masud with the camels in the distance. They were a lot for a young boy to be responsible for, but clearly he'd been well trained and, despite Nenet being difficult, he handled the herd with great skill. Millie raised her hand to give the boy a wave when she noticed him tie Nenet's lead rope to a low fence and scamper away towards the Sphinx.

Millie followed him with her eyes and was surprised to see that he headed towards the group of men the children had been watching earlier. She picked up her camera and zoomed in, scoping the boy through the lens. Masud said something to the man Miss Moussa had been talking to. The fellow nodded and Millie thought he smiled. One of the other men was pouring drinks from an old-fashioned coffee pot and another was passing around a container from which the rest were taking some sort of food. Millie pressed the shutter button, snapping several pictures in quick succession.

'Millie! Hurry up!' Chessie shouted. Miss Cranna had just done a head count and realised the girl was missing.

'Coming!' Millie called out.

She turned back towards the Sphinx a final time, but Masud and the man were gone.

Chapter 28

'Any luck getting hold of your uncle?' Millie said. She had just emerged from the bathroom in record time. The shower couldn't have run for more than a minute. Alice-Miranda had already had a lightning-speed wash and was dressed.

She put the phone down, but it wasn't Lawrence she'd been speaking to. 'No. He's still not answering and neither is Aunt Charlotte. I was speaking to Mrs Parker,' Alice-Miranda replied.

Millie's eyes widened. 'What did you tell her?'

'Nothing that I shouldn't have. I had an idea,' the girl replied, then quickly explained what she was thinking while applying some pale pink gloss to her lips. 'I felt a bit mean, appealing to her vanity like that – especially when Uncle Lawrence hasn't even agreed to the project – but I knew she'd get to work collecting all the things I suggested he might need straight away.'

'It's genius, if you ask me,' Millie said with a smile. 'Myrtle is obsessed with Lawrence. The idea that she could be an extra on one of his movies or his PA on set . . . she must have been practically frothing.'

'Yes, well, Mrs Parker was telling me how well she was looking after Miss Grimm, protecting her from everyone – which is probably why Miss Reedy can't get through. When we get back after dinner I'm going to call Magdalena in LA and see if she has a copy of Uncle Lawrence and Aunt Charlotte's itinerary – hopefully she's at home but I have a fleeting memory that Aunt Charlotte mentioned she might take some time off while they were away to visit her family in Mexico,' Alice-Miranda said, then glanced at the clock beside her bed and jumped up. 'We have to go!'

'I need to tell you something about Masud too,' Millie said as Alice-Miranda grabbed their key card off the desk and the pair walked out the door. 'Actually I can show you.' Millie reached into her day pack to realise she'd left her camera charging inside the room. 'Oh blow – I'll be back in a tick.'

'Hurry, girls,' Miss Cranna called from the end of the hallway. 'The bus leaves in two minutes.'

'You go,' Millie said. 'I'll be there in time.'

She took the key card from Alice-Miranda and dashed back inside.

Mr Ferguson's surprise for the evening had turned out to be a Nile River city cruise with dinner and a show. 'You look lovely tonight, Miss Reedy,' Alice-Miranda said with a smile as the pair walked side by side up the gangplank onto the boat.

Neville was walking behind them, thinking the very same thing about Alice-Miranda in her sparkly white leggings and long pink tunic.

'Thank you, Alice-Miranda,' Miss Reedy said, her voice catching in her throat.

'Are you all right?' Alice-Miranda asked. They stopped when they reached the deck and stood to the side, letting everyone else go ahead of them.

It was obvious that something had happened in the past hour. Miss Reedy and Mr Plumpton had been all smiles on their camel ride. 'Did Miss Grimm call?'

Livinia shook her head and took a deep breath. 'No, but Mr Woodcock did just as we arrived back from the pyramids. He was rather curt. The bank has decided to foreclose on all of the loans Mr Badger took out against the school. The entire property is to be sold immediately and Winchesterfield-Downsfordvale closed. Apparently Miss Grimm has already met with some prospective buyers.'

Alice-Miranda's eyes widened. 'Surely they can't do that. Don't they have to wait and see whether Mr Badger can be found and if the money can be recovered first?'

'That's what I said, but he assured me that the bank can do whatever they like – particularly as Mr Badger has fled the country and taken all the money with him,' the woman replied.

'That's terrible,' Alice-Miranda whispered. The very idea that their lovely school was going to be sold was just about the worst thing she could imagine.

'I get the feeling Mr Woodcock thinks I have something to do with the missing money – not just that I signed the papers,' Livinia said, raising her hand dramatically to her forehead.

'Well, that's ridiculous,' Alice-Miranda replied.

Livinia swallowed hard. 'If only Ophelia would return my calls. I just feel so helpless being here.'

Alice-Miranda looked at the teacher, then hugged her tightly around the middle.

Livinia's hands hovered for a second before she grabbed the girl and hugged her back, squeezing her eyes shut and willing the tears to stay away. Finally, they stepped apart. Alice-Miranda was about to say something when Livinia pressed her finger against the girl's lip. 'Not another word, miss. Let's just get through tonight, shall we? If I start crying I fear I'll never stop.'

Alice-Miranda nodded as the teacher dashed away to find her husband, but the girl's brain was in overdrive. She had to get hold of her uncle – tonight if possible – or it seemed that their lovely school would be lost forever.

★

'What was that about?' Millie asked as Alice-Miranda joined her on the rear deck. She'd been watching the exchange from there.

'I'll tell you later,' the girl replied. 'Come on, let's go and find a table.'

'Somewhere quiet,' Millie said. 'So I can show you what I wanted to before, about Masud.'

The girls still hadn't had a chance to talk. Millie had been thwarted on the bus ride by Neville as he'd saved Alice-Miranda a seat and she couldn't very well tell him to move.

'So what's up?' Alice-Miranda said, but Millie's reply was interrupted by Sep waving his arms and calling that he'd saved them a table.

'Seriously!' Millie rolled her eyes. 'It'll have to wait – again.'

Alice-Miranda smiled and waved back. 'Thank you, Sep. You didn't have to. And please don't feel as if you must sit with Millie and me. I thought you might like to spend time with some of the other boys.'

Sep shook his head. 'Why would I want to do that?'

Sloane and Chessie were watching from the other side of the room. 'I cannot believe that she still has no idea how besotted he is,' Sloane said. 'And he's such a dork.'

'What about Neville?' Chessie said, then spotted the boy hurrying to the table with a plate of dips and breads. 'Speak of the devil.' Somehow Neville managed to end up beside Alice-Miranda, and Sep was relegated to the end of the table, which he didn't look remotely happy about.

Soon a man stood on a small plinth beside the dance floor and called their attention. 'Good evening, everyone, my name is Captain El Mazry and I will be in charge of this vessel tonight,' he said, outlining the safety procedures before entreating everyone to enjoy their evening. 'As you may have noticed, the buffet is set up on the rear deck.' He glared at Neville. 'Our wait staff will let you know when it is time to eat.' The boy blushed and leaned forward, trying to hide the plate of food he'd already collected.

The crowd had not long found their seats when a man walked onto the dance floor playing a traditional arghul flute. The instrument sounded a bit like a clarinet, though it had two pipes and was made from a light-coloured wood. It produced a loud, high-pitched sound. A few minutes later a band of drummers joined him, followed by a beautiful woman dressed in gold harem pants and a matching crop top with tinkly bells hanging from the seams. She had a veil over her face and looked as if she'd just stepped from the pages of *The Arabian Nights*. Her dark hair tumbled in waves down to the small of her back and her fingernails and lips were painted bright red.

'She's gorgeous,' Gretchen gasped, clearly mesmerised. She wasn't alone in her adoration, given the stares from other guests.

The woman's hips wriggled and sashayed in time with the music and, while she was an adept belly dancer, her stomach was so flat there was no way she could have got even the slightest jiggle from that part of her anatomy. A fact Millie thought a little disappointing as she'd watched a few videos of belly dancers with more ample proportions and their movements were far more interesting to watch.

Some of the other diners began to clap in time with the music. The spectacle continued for far longer than Barclay Ferguson thought necessary – though he could appreciate the woman's talent. He would have to explain to the children later, though, that traditional Egyptian belly dancers usually wore modest, covered costumes. This display was more Hollywood movie than cultural Cairo.

When it was all over, the performers left the floor and the diners were directed to the buffet, where a spectacular selection of traditional Egyptian fare was on offer – everything from falafel and dips to ful medames, shish kabab and kofta as well as a wide selection of meat dishes.

Caprice pointed at a plate lined with what looked like miniature barbecued chooks. 'Is that chicken?' she asked loudly to no one in particular.

'No, Caprice, it's squab,' Mr Ferguson replied.

'What's that?'

'Pigeon,' the man said.

Caprice pretended to gag. 'Eww – as in the rats of the sky? That's disgusting.' The girl wrinkled her nose and made a dive for the platter beside it. 'But this lamb looks delicious.'

The man smiled and nodded. He didn't have the heart to tell her that it was camel.

Everyone had just sat down again when the second round of entertainment commenced. The music started, and a man dressed in a long white robe and a rainbow-coloured jacket over the top literally spun onto the dance floor. He twirled and twirled, faster and faster, his tunic flaring at the bottom as he did so, giving him the appearance of a colourful spinning top.

'Whoa,' Neville gasped. 'That's amazing!'

The crowd clapped and cheered and two more dancers joined in; one of them was highly skilled, spinning and spinning, but the other looked to be off-kilter soon after he started. The man crashed into a table, then flew across the room and almost landed head first in Miss Reedy's lap.

'Get off me!' the woman squawked.

'Sorry!' The man smiled, revealing a gold tooth.

Livinia's jaw dropped. That tooth – hadn't she seen it somewhere before?

The man stumbled to his feet and started spinning again – this time in the opposite direction, but it didn't help. Seconds later the audience was in hysterics as he careened out of control from one table to the next like a human pinball. Finally he crashed to the floor while the other two men spun around him. When the music stopped, the man rolled on his side and propped himself up on one elbow, beaming at the audience as the other two took their bows.

'Please thank our most excellent and talented Tanoura dancers,' said the captain. 'Mostly excellent . . . but perhaps not equally talented.' He glared at the fellow on the floor.

'Millie, does that chap in the middle there look familiar to you?' Alice-Miranda asked. She smiled at him, hoping that he would return the gesture.

'There! That tooth!' Alice-Miranda exclaimed as the man grinned.

'You're right! It's the man from the bazaar. I'm sure he was at the Hanging Church and driving our taxi. Now he's a dancer?' Millie cried. 'What's with this guy? Do you think he's following us?'

Alice-Miranda shrugged. 'There's one way to find out.' She jumped up and scurried across the dance floor. The man was still catching his breath and sweating profusely. The other dancers had already left. 'Excuse me, sir, but haven't we seen you before?' Alice-Miranda asked.

The man rolled over and pushed himself to his feet.

'No, miss, I have never in my life set eyes on you,' the fellow said.

Millie scoffed, arriving in time to hear his

reply. 'Oh, please. Do you really think we came down in the last shower?' she said.

Alice-Miranda took a gentler approach. 'Sir, didn't you try to sell us things at the Hanging Church and at the souk yesterday?'

The man shook his head. 'No, no, no. I am not a salesman, miss. I am a dancer.'

'No, you're not,' Millie said.

'Yes, I am,' he replied.

'Well, you're a very bad one,' Millie said. 'Almost as bad as your taxi driving.'

'No, no, no. No taxi driving for me,' the man said, shaking his head. 'I have never even done a driving test.'

'That's *not* a surprise,' Millie said. 'You have a beaten-up old Fiat about the same age as the pyramids.'

'That was not me,' the man said. 'I can assure you.'

'Well, there is something weird going on. If you turn up in Luxor or the Valley of the Queens, we'll know that you're following us,' the girl said.

'Luxor, you say? The Valley of the Queens? They are very beautiful places but I am here in Cairo, dancing, dancing, dancing,' the man replied.

He raised his arms and clapped his hands as if to emphasise the point. 'And your teachers, they are looking after you well?' He glanced at Miss Reedy and Mr Plumpton.

Millie and Alice-Miranda exchanged curious looks. That seemed a strange thing for him to say.

'Yes, of course,' Alice-Miranda said. 'Our teachers are wonderful.'

'Even that cranky lady there?' he said.

'Miss Reedy's not cranky,' Alice-Miranda said.

'She's just been a bit upset, that's all,' Millie said, wondering why she'd told him that. It was really none of his business.

'Oh, okay,' he said. The man's brow was still dripping with perspiration and there were large sweat stains on his robe under his arms and across his chest.

'Perhaps you should get a drink,' Alice-Miranda said.

'Yes, miss. Dancing is a very thirsty business,' the man said. He adjusted his cap. 'Goodbye, young ladies. Perhaps I will see you again.'

Millie glowered. 'Really?'

'When you are next in Cairo, of course,' he said, grinning broadly.

But Millie and Alice-Miranda both got the feeling that might not be the only place he popped up.

Livinia Reedy caught sight of the fellow leaving. He turned and smiled at her, but she didn't repay the favour. There was something about him that made her very uncomfortable and, after this evening's update from home, her anxiety was already through the roof. The last thing she needed was the feeling that she was being followed.

Chapter 29

Alice-Miranda hung up the phone. Magdalena wasn't answering. She'd tried her uncle and aunt again too with no luck.

'How are we ever going to get hold of Lawrence in time?' Millie said.

Alice-Miranda bit her lip. She was out of ideas.

The girls were supposed to be asleep. When Miss Cranna had checked on them a little while ago, they had both been in bed, but now Alice-Miranda was up and the pair was wide awake.

They were also expecting Jacinta, Sloane and Chessie any minute, having made plans to meet after lights out. There simply hadn't been any time to talk on the cruise and Alice-Miranda thought they needed to more than ever. A sharp knock announced the girls' arrival. Millie hopped up from where she was sitting cross-legged in bed and opened the door. Sloane, Chessie, Jacinta and Britt hurried through.

'Sorry. I couldn't very well sneak out and leave Britt behind,' Sloane said. 'Besides, you know she won't tell anyone else.'

Britt nodded. 'Oh my goodness, I cannot believe it. What a disaster for your school and for all of you.'

Alice-Miranda waited until the girls were sitting down before explaining what Miss Reedy had said about the bank and the loans. This wasn't the kind of news to hear while standing up.

'What?' Jacinta blurted, quickly covering her mouth as she realised that her exclamation had been louder than she intended. 'How is that possible?'

'The school must be in a huge amount of debt,' Millie said, then bit down on her thumbnail.

'It's even worse than we first thought,' Jacinta said. 'I really wish I hadn't been in that toilet. Then we could just be here having a good time and none the wiser.'

Millie unscrewed the lid of her water bottle, taking a swig as she walked over to the window. She turned around to face her friends. 'So that would mean we'd just go home and find a big "SOLD" sticker over the "FOR SALE" sign out the front? I think that would be worse. Anyway, Alice-Miranda has an idea.'

'It might not save us completely, but it could stave things off for a while – at least until we find a better solution,' Alice-Miranda said. 'It relies on Uncle Lawrence and at the moment he's somewhere in deepest, darkest Russia shooting a film and Aunt Charlotte and the twins are there too – I've called and left messages with no luck so far. But if he could make his next movie at Winchesterfield-Downsfordvale, the school might earn enough money to stay open a little while longer. He has a script that he told me about when we were in the outback – he wants to direct the film and star in it too. I know that producers pay a lot for the right location and Winchesterfield-Downsfordvale would be perfect.'

'That sounds amazing,' Chessie said. 'Can't we just tell Miss Grimm that it's all organised and then cross our fingers that Lawrence agrees?'

Alice-Miranda stood up. 'I had thought about that, but there's a chance he'll say no. I can't make him feel as if he has to do it just for us. Anyway, I've got Mrs Parker working on something too.'

'Myrtle!' Jacinta blurted loudly for the second time, then looked around, hoping that the teachers down the hall didn't wake up.

'Yes. Under the guise of the movie idea, I've asked her to search out the school plans and any papers relating to its history. I also told her that Miss Reedy needed her to find any documents she'd signed recently. I sort of glossed over that one, but I'm hoping that she locates copies of the papers so we know exactly what powers Mr Badger had. I don't know if it's any use but I feel like Miss Reedy should be able to see what she consented to. Apparently Miss Grimm said that the originals have been taken by the police investigating the case.'

'That's as good a plan as any, seeing the rest of us don't have one,' Chessie said. She lay back against Millie's pillow.

'So what do we do now?' Sloane said.

'Wish on a star,' Millie replied, looking into the sky outside, 'and hope that Lawrence gets Alice-Miranda's message before it's too late.'

The girls had stood up to leave when Britt noticed the newspaper on the desk, still open at the page with the photos of the Ponzi schemers, including Gianna Morsey.

She stopped and studied it more closely, covering the bottom half of Gianna's face with her palm. 'That woman there looks a bit like Miss Moussa,' Britt said. 'Except she has a much bigger nose.'

Alice-Miranda and Chessie peered at the page.

'I can't see it,' Chessie said, but the comment had piqued Alice-Miranda's attention.

'You're right. She does a bit – especially her eyes,' the girl said. Miss Moussa didn't wear her makeup the same and this woman had a large mole above her lip, but there was a certain resemblance. 'Don't they say we all have a doppelganger out there somewhere?'

'Except that yours is standing beside you,' Jacinta said.

Alice-Miranda smiled at Britt, who grinned back. Considering everyone said that Britt was the blonde version of Alice-Miranda and Alice-Miranda the brunette version of Britt, that notion certainly rang true.

Chapter 30

Ophelia Grimm opened her office door and peered out.

'Mrs Parker, have you heard from Miss Reedy at all?' she asked, a row of frown lines creasing her forehead.

'Yes, yes, everything's fine on the tour. They're having a lovely time. No need for you to call her – she said that she's terribly busy,' Myrtle replied. It wasn't entirely true, but given Livinia hadn't pestered her again, Myrtle felt she could make that assumption. 'Would you like me to organise you some tea?' she asked. Myrtle rather fancied a brew herself.

The headmistress glanced at her watch and then at the clock on the wall.

'Are you expecting someone?' Myrtle clucked. There was nothing in the diary and she'd be cross if Ophelia had gone and made an appointment without her knowledge. That wasn't how their relationship was supposed to work. It was Myrtle's responsibility to know exactly what was going on at all times.

At least she had that pet project of Alice-Miranda's to work on. The child wanted it to be a surprise and had sworn her to secrecy, saying that not even Miss Grimm knew what was happening. If Myrtle could help, the rewards would be huge – not just for her but for the whole school. She couldn't wait to tell her friends that she was working with Lawrence Ridley. They'd be green with envy.

Ophelia frowned. 'Are you all right, Mrs Parker?'

'I'm fine,' Myrtle said, then realised the woman hadn't replied to her earlier question. 'But you didn't answer me. Are you expecting guests?'

'Yes, please show them in when they arrive,' Miss Grimm replied tightly. 'And if you could organise tea for three, that would be lovely.'

'May I ask who your visitors are?' Myrtle said.

Ophelia shook her head, her lips pursed. 'No, Mrs Parker, you may not. And I will thank you not to ask them for their names either. This is confidential school business, and none of yours!'

'Really!' Myrtle let out a small gasp, stunned by the rebuke. Fortunately the telephone rang, interrupting the potential explosion. Myrtle waited three rings, then picked it up. She didn't like whoever was calling to think she wasn't busy.

She listened and nodded and clicked her tongue, then looked at Ophelia, who was still standing in the doorway.

'No, I'm afraid not,' Myrtle said. There was another long pause and the woman spoke again.

'I'll let her know, Mr Woodcock.' At the mention of the man's name, Ophelia raced towards the desk.

'Put him through – now!' The headmistress ordered, but Myrtle placed the phone back into its cradle, a smile playing on her lips. That would teach Ophelia Grimm to keep things from her.

'I'm afraid he hung up,' Myrtle said.

'Why didn't you tell him I was standing right here? What did he say?' Ophelia demanded.

'He said to tell you that there was still no news on Mr Badger,' the woman said. 'But things were progressing as discussed.'

'You should have put him through to me immediately, Mrs Parker,' Ophelia said.

Myrtle glanced across at the open newspaper on her desk. Ophelia followed the woman's eyeline and realised what she was looking at – a double-page spread about the underhand dealings of Elias Badger of Badger and Woodcock Accountants.

'Is there a problem, Miss Grimm?' Myrtle asked, motioning towards the page. 'You haven't got the school into trouble have you?'

'I have done nothing of the sort.' Ophelia turned on her heel and raced back into her office, slamming the door so hard it felt like the entire building shook.

But Myrtle Parker wasn't the least bit convinced. She sat down and read the entire article from start to finish, wondering what on earth was going on.

Chapter 31

Maryam Moussa closed the lid of her suitcase and dropped Dr Hassam's secret phone into her handbag. Yesterday had been far more productive than she had expected, so this morning she would fly to Luxor – a day earlier than planned.

Nour had been curious about the change, but Maryam had searched Dr Hassam's calendar and found several people he was often in contact with in the other city. She was going to make their acquaintance – at least that's what she told

Nour, who offered to set up the appointments. But Maryam had done it already. All Nour was required to do was edit and print her itinerary and book another night's accommodation, then everything would be in place.

It seemed that Dr Hassam had been very enterprising during his time as Minister. Not only for Egypt, but for himself. He was clever too – a man who used all his charm and knowledge to get exactly what he wanted and, from what she had gleaned so far, it seemed his network for doing so was well established. All she'd had to do was say she was continuing Dr Hassam's work – exactly as he had done – and suddenly doors were opening.

Maryam never intended to stay in Cairo as long as she had. But life in Egypt had been far more comfortable than she had imagined. She hadn't loved her job, but it served a purpose and she was still young enough for life to throw some exciting new challenges her way – as she had been planning. She just hadn't expected this.

Lying unconscious in that hospital bed, Mustafa Hassam had no clue that his ill health had handed Maryam everything she needed to start over again on a platter.

Her own phone rang. Maryam pulled it out of her pocket and looked at the screen.

'Yes Nour, I'm on my way now,' the woman said. 'Is there a problem?' There was a long pause while Maryam listened.

'Wonderful,' she squeaked. 'That's very good news.' But it was hard to talk when it felt as if the breath had just been sucked from her lungs. Nour reported that Dr Hassam had briefly woken up before dawn. The doctors said that it was only a matter of time before he fully regained consciousness. Maryam was going to have to work fast or her plans would be completely derailed.

'Hurry up, children,' Barclay Ferguson called as the group grabbed their luggage from under the bus and raced toward the check-in area. 'Miss Cranna, please make sure that there is nothin' left behind and I'll forge ahead with Mr Salah and get the process started.'

The man's stylish linen suit was covered in wet patches and he mopped his brow with his handkerchief. Despite being picked up before dawn, a huge traffic jam in the city meant they were late to the airport. Akil Salah had been on the phone constantly and said that he was sure they would still make their flight, though Barclay had not shared his confidence.

Masud was helping the driver remove the suitcases from the bus, lining them up on the footpath. The boy's own large satchel was draped over his shoulders. He could not afford to let it out of his sight for a second – not considering what it contained.

Yesterday, he had made a promising contact. The man he'd spoken to had said that he might be able to help, but that he needed to see the wares first to assess their value. Last night, Masud had undertaken a dangerous trek back to the pyramids with one funerary figure in hand and photographs of the others on his phone. The man had seemed very pleased and said that he would make contact again in Luxor.

His parents had been at the hospital when he slipped out and his grandmother had been in her room watching soap operas. If they ever found out what he was doing he would be in terrible trouble, but this was for Jabari. All the trouble in the world would be worth it to see his little brother well again.

Masud passed Millie her suitcase as the children came forward to collect their bags. She gave him a smile and hoped that he was okay. That morning before they'd left the hotel she'd finally shown Alice-Miranda the photographs of the boy with the men at the Sphinx. They'd been too distracted last night by Miss Reedy's revelation to Alice-Miranda about what was happening at school. The girls agreed that it seemed more than a little strange for the boy to be with those fellows, especially after what Mr Salah had said. Today, Millie found herself watching Masud like a hawk. During the bus ride to the airport he'd sat in his usual spot behind the driver and kept to himself. Hopefully she'd get a moment to chat with him sometime. The last thing she wanted was for Masud to be in any trouble.

'Here, Alice-Miranda, I'll take that.' Sep grabbed the top of the girl's bag.

'No, let me.' Neville grabbed the handle on the side.

The pair wrestled over the case for several seconds.

'Boys! Please stop!' Alice-Miranda shouted, silencing everyone around her too. 'I am more than capable of taking my own bag and I'd much prefer if one of you helped Caprice. I can look after myself.'

Neville and Sep looked at each other, shame-faced, and scurried away. Neither of them had ever heard Alice-Miranda speak like that before and it was unsettling to say the least.

'I'm sorry! I didn't mean to sound cross,' the girl called after them, but they were gone.

'Oh, thank goodness you finally told them off,' Sloane said, shaking her head.

'Finally?' Alice-Miranda frowned.

'Honestly, the way Sep has been simpering all over you since we arrived is sickening – especially when it's clear that you prefer Neville. I mean, who wouldn't? Sep is . . .' She hesitated and wrinkled her nose. 'Well, Sep.'

'Don't be mean. Your brother's sweet,' Jacinta said with a smile.

Alice-Miranda's brown eyes widened and for a moment she looked completely shocked.

'Seriously? You hadn't worked that out?' Sloane said.

Alice-Miranda bit her lip and slowly shook her head.

'Well, now you know,' Sloane said. Jacinta nodded.

Alice-Miranda thought for a moment. She liked both boys very much, but she wasn't ready to be anyone's girlfriend. She'd have to chat with them later. Breaking someone's heart wasn't on her to do list – she wasn't even a teenager yet. All of a sudden her head was in a spin. Was she really so naïve that she hadn't noticed?

'Are you okay?' Millie asked when the girl reached the check-in queue.

'I'm not sure. But Sloane and Jacinta just pointed something out that's made me feel very silly – and a bit mean,' Alice-Miranda said.

'Are you going to share?' Millie asked.

Alice-Miranda told her what had happened. Millie grinned. 'I love you, Alice-Miranda Highton-Smith-Kennington-Jones, even if you have no idea when it comes to boys.' She hugged her friend tight.

Chapter 32

After the short flight to Luxor, the children were soon on a bus heading for the animal sanctuary, where they would work for the remainder of the day. It was quite literally nine minutes from the airport and, given their early departure, they would arrive just before ten.

Mr Salah explained to the children that the charity had been set up by a young woman named Barbara who had come to Egypt on a holiday and never left. Miss Cranna chipped in that she and

Barbara were actually distant cousins, though they didn't know each other very well.

'What sort of animals do they have?' Caprice asked. 'Are there . . .?'

'Camels? Yes, Miss Caprice, I am afraid that there will be camels. But there are also horses, mules, donkeys and dogs,' Mr Salah replied, to chortles of laughter.

'Well, I'm not looking after any of those rotten –' Caprice began, but the man cut her off.

'Camels,' he said into the microphone. 'I suspect that everyone on this bus is well aware of that fact already.'

The children roared with laughter. Even the teachers were doing their best to suppress giggles. The girl did make herself quite the target at times.

'Fine, laugh if you want to but at least I won't be the one with camel slobber all over me this time,' Caprice huffed.

The animal sanctuary was located in a green belt between the town of Minshat Al Ammari and the city of Luxor. The lush pastures formed part of the Nile Delta, which provided rich farming land along the riverbanks and for a few miles inland.

Sloane raised her hand. 'Does it flood here, Mr Salah? It's so green.'

'For thousands of years that was the case. Every summer there would be a great inundation – our people called it akhet – but then in the 1960s the Aswan Dam was constructed and now the flooding is controlled.'

'That's why they had to move Abu Simbel to a higher place, or the monuments would have been lost forever,' Alice-Miranda said. 'I wish we could see it but it's such a long way from here.'

'That is true,' Mr Salah said. 'You will just have to come again sometime.'

Alice-Miranda nodded. 'Yes, please.'

When the bus pulled up outside the animal shelter, the children were instructed to take only their small day packs and water bottles. Their luggage would be driven ahead to their accommodation, a guesthouse right on the edge of the Valley of the Queens. Mr Salah said that it was owned by an old friend of his and that he and Mr Ferguson had stayed there many times before.

The group exited the bus and milled about at the entrance to the facility.

'Masud, what are you doing with your bag?' Akil asked his son. 'You do not need to carry that with you.'

Millie and Alice-Miranda watched the boy.

'It is fine, Baba,' Masud said. 'I would prefer to keep it close.'

Akil Salah shook his head. 'Unless you have bars of gold in there, there is no reason to lug it about. Hurry – before the bus leaves – take it back. You have a smaller pack for your water and our lunch is being provided here. I do not understand this strange attachment.'

'But . . .' Masud began. His father cast a glare that Millie and Alice-Miranda had seen aimed at Nenet when she was biting one of the other camels yesterday.

The boy's shoulders slumped and he reluctantly went back to the vehicle to place his bag inside, then returned to the group.

His father nodded but it was clear that there was something amiss.

'We should try to talk to him,' Alice-Miranda said. 'He seems upset.'

Millie agreed as a wiry woman with stark white hair charged through the front gate and waved her arms about to get everyone's attention. She introduced herself as Barbara and told them all about the shelter and the charity associated with it. The Queen's Colours group would be attending to a long list of jobs that needed doing, from mucking out stalls to hand-feeding baby animals to washing and grooming and cleaning and sorting tack and other donations.

Madagascar made a face. 'That's the *young* woman who established this place?'

'She must have got old,' Caprice replied. 'People do that, you know.'

'Well, duh,' Madagascar glared at the girl. Their love affair seemed to be taking a wrong turn. 'There is no way I am going to be carting poop around all day – that's disgusting.'

Caprice wrinkled her nose but didn't say anything.

Philippe had been listening to the girls' exchange. 'I honestly don't know why you are part of this program. The Queen's Colours is for kids with grit and determination. The only thing you are determined to do is get out of everything and do as little as possible – it's a joke. You bring the rest of us down.'

'Excuse me!' Caprice exclaimed. 'You don't know anything about us. And just for the record, *I* wasn't complaining.'

'Except about the camels, for the thousandth time,' the boy replied. 'If *I* was your teacher I would have sent you home by now for all your whining. Do you know how lucky you are? How many children would give anything to have these opportunities? But all you do is gripe and moan.'

Caprice's and Madagascar's jaws almost hit the ground. The pair of them pushed through to the front of the group, their faces red – and not only from the heat.

'I think I'm in love,' Sloane said, looking at Philippe with new-found respect.

'The boy certainly knows how to read people,' Mr Plumpton said, fanning his face with a magazine he'd taken from the plane. Sloane blushed, not realising she'd been heard.

The children were quickly taken inside the walled premises of the sanctuary, where there were yards, stables and offices, as well as some accommodation for workers and volunteers. Barbara and her team had been given a list of names prior to the group's arrival and there was a roster written on a large white board with everyone's tasks outlined.

From the looks on Caprice's and Madagascar's faces, they were on mucking-out duty first up – which served them right after their earlier outbursts.

'Look – we're on bath time,' Alice-Miranda said to Millie with a smile.

Masud was standing off to the side of the group. 'Do you have a job?' Millie asked him.

He shrugged and didn't answer. Alice-Miranda scanned the board.

'Yes, you do. You're with us,' she said.

Masud gave a slight nod, but there was no sign of the enthusiasm he'd shown at the dig site or with the camel herd.

The children set to work. They had a couple of hours on their first task before lunch and then their second and third activities in the afternoon.

Alice-Miranda, Millie, Masud and Neville were given a quick demonstration of how to wash a large beast before they were paired up to start their work. It turned out there was an impressive queue of animals waiting for their baths.

'Do you want to go with Masud?' Alice-Miranda asked Millie, who nodded. 'See what you can find out.'

Millie didn't mind, although she wondered if Alice-Miranda was looking for a moment alone to break it to Neville that, while they were good friends, she wasn't interested in anything more at this stage. Millie hoped he'd take it well and that Sep wouldn't get the wrong idea and think he was in with a shot.

'Hello you,' Millie said to the mule that was tethered to the hitching rail. A name plate on the animal's halter said he was Ringo.

'Are you a star?' Millie asked, giggling at her own joke. Ringo snickered, then began to make a noise that sounded a bit like a violin in a scary movie. It was not quite the hee-hawing of a donkey but neither was it the whinny of a horse – which stood to reason given the beast was the offspring of a female horse and a male donkey.

'Oh, that's a horrible sound.' Millie wrinkled her nose as Masud took the hose and wet Ringo down.

'You know they whimper too – like a baby – when they are worried about something,' the boy said, while Millie got the sponge and bucket of soapy water and began washing the animal's brown coat.

'I did not know that,' she replied, glad that the boy had finally said something. 'I have a pony called Chops and he's lovely. He's quiet as a mouse, unlike Alice-Miranda's boy, Bonaparte. That one's a beast in every sense of the word. Actually, I think Bony and Nenet would be best friends.'

Masud grinned. 'Nenet is not friends with anyone – and some of those other camels are her sisters.'

'Do you have any sisters?' Millie asked. 'I don't. I'm an only child and so is Alice-Miranda – but we're best friends and she's the closest thing to a sister that I'll ever have.'

Masud walked around and washed some of the sudsy water off the mule, who was flicking his tail and seemed to be enjoying the experience.

'No,' he said.

'What about brothers?' she asked, then noticed the sad look on his face. 'Sorry, it's none of my business.'

But Masud nodded. 'I have a little brother. His name is Jabari and he is my sunshine.'

Millie felt her eyes suddenly fill with tears. 'That's a beautiful thing to say about him. Does he ever come out with you? To show the camels?'

'He used to,' Masud said.

Millie's stomach tightened. Clearly there was something in those words, but she didn't want to ask.

Masud changed the subject. 'There is a lot of mud caked under this flank,' he said. 'You will have to get up there closely.'

Millie hopped around and began washing the mule's underside.

'I need to find a hoof pick,' Masud said, and hurried away.

It seemed that their conversation was over for now.

Chapter 33

'I'm pooped,' Sloane said, stretching her aching arms above her head.

'Quite literally,' Chessie agreed. 'I don't think I've ever seen that much manure in my life.'

'True, but I feel like we really contributed there today,' Jacinta said. 'Barbara works so hard and she's saved thousands of animals. I think I'd like to spend some time working with her on my gap year.'

Millie grinned. 'That's a great idea! Count me in.'

'How did you find it, Caprice?' Alice-Miranda asked the girl, who had just exited the bathroom and was towel-drying her hair.

'I suppose it wasn't *that* bad,' Caprice replied.

'Oh, come on,' Alethea said. 'I saw you with that gorgeous donkey foal – he was following you around everywhere. You fed so many babies. Barbara said that you were a natural.'

Caprice shrugged. 'Some of the things Barbara showed us were so heartbreaking. It must be hard for her, not being able to save all the animals that come into her care.'

'Who knew? She has feelings?' Millie whispered to Chessie, who bit back a smile.

Alice-Miranda grinned at Caprice. 'Yes, I agree it was terribly confronting but overall I think it was a good day.'

The group had arrived at the guesthouse just before six and been directed to their rooms. Unlike the glamorous hotel in Cairo, their accommodation here consisted of two bunk rooms for the children – the girls together in one and the boys across the hall. The teachers, Mr Ferguson and Miss Cranna had their own rooms in the same wing. The place seemed to be set up to cater for schools and backpackers as well as individual trav-ellers. Mr Salah said that there were often groups of archaeologists staying too.

The girls' dorm consisted of six sets of bunk beds and a large bathroom with two showers, from which Britt and Madagascar had just emerged, wrapped in towels. The room was a hive of hair brushing and chatter.

Miss Cranna poked her head around the door, pleased to see that everyone appeared to be getting on well. She had been a little apprehensive about all of the girls bunking in together, knowing there were some strong personalities.

'Evenin', girls,' she said. 'Dinner is in ten minutes, so ye'll need to get a wriggle on. The dinin' room is through the reception area at the back of the buildin' and I have to say the view of the desert is quite somethin'. Oh, and have any of you seen a brown satchel-style bag in here? Masud Salah's has gone missin' and the poor boy is quite beside himself.'

Millie looked across at Alice-Miranda and raised her eyebrows.

The other girls shook their heads.

'We'll have a look,' Millie said.

Morag Cranna bid them farewell and headed across the hall to the boys' dorm where there was an amateur tag-team wrestling match underway – albeit a friendly one.

A few minutes later the girls spilled out of their room, heading for dinner. Alice-Miranda and Millie stayed behind, checking under the beds and in the corners to see if there was any sign of the lost bag.

'I don't blame Masud for being upset given he really didn't want to leave it on the bus in the first place,' Alice-Miranda said. 'There must be something in there that's important to him.'

Alice-Miranda searched behind the girls' suitcases and in the cupboard while Millie lay on the floor and checked under each of the bunks. She was about to give up when she spotted a brown strap. It looked as if the bag must have been put onto one of the bottom bunks but had fallen down the gap between the bed and the wall.

'Found it!' she exclaimed, then wriggled into the narrow space and grabbed the satchel. It was much heavier than she had anticipated. As Millie inched her way back out she saw that the flap had come undone. When she pulled on the strap there was a thud and the bag was suddenly much lighter. Something must have fallen out.

'Can you take this?' Millie asked Alice-Miranda, who was on her tummy now too. The other girl reached in and pulled the strap. Millie wormed her way back under the bed and felt around until her hand hit something hard. She grabbed it and backed out.

'What's that?' Alice-Miranda asked.

The object was wrapped in a cloth and was heavy for its size.

Millie laid it on the floor and removed the covering.

'Oh, that's lovely,' Alice-Miranda gasped as the girls stared at the golden figurine. 'It's a shabti, isn't it?'

Millie nodded. She picked it up and studied it more closely, quickly realising that she could read some of the inscriptions. Her stomach twisted. 'This is actually a funerary figure, and I have a feeling this one didn't come from the souk.'

'What? Why would you think that?' Alice-Miranda asked.

Millie pointed at the hieroglyphs and quickly told Alice-Miranda what Harry, the archaeologist leading her group at Saqqara, had told her about the meaning of some of the pictures relating to King Khufu. This figurine had those same markings. Masud had asked a lot of questions and they'd even had a discussion about what something from Khufu's tomb would be worth if anything ever turned up.

'You think this could be real?' Alice-Miranda said, frowning.

Millie nodded. 'It's so heavy, and that gold colouring is different to the shabti I bought in the market.' The girl quickly rummaged around in her bag and laid her statue next to Masud's on the bed.

'You're right,' Alice-Miranda said. 'Yours is brassy, but this one looks just like the gold statues and artefacts we saw in the museum.'

Alice-Miranda's eyebrows jumped up. 'But surely Masud would know the risks better than anyone, wouldn't he?' The girl thought for a moment and bit her lip. 'Do you think that's why he was talking to the man at the Sphinx? His father said that fellow wasn't to be trusted – that he had a bad reputation. Surely Masud is not planning to sell this on the black market?'

Millie shrugged. 'Who knows? But if he does he could be in terrible trouble.'

'We still need to give his bag back,' Alice-Miranda said. 'Maybe we're wrong. He seems such a lovely boy and I feel awful that we've been snooping.'

'We didn't,' Millie said. 'That statue fell out and if I hadn't realised, it could have been under there for days – maybe years going on the amount of fluff and dust on the floor. I don't think anyone's run a vacuum under there for a long time.' Millie rubbed her nose to try to stop a sneeze that was building.

She pulled out her camera and began to take photographs of the piece from all angles. She figured it was insurance – just in case something happened.

'That figurine isn't proof he's doing anything wrong. Maybe it's an excellent reproduction – or an heirloom that's been in Masud's family for a long time,' Alice-Miranda said.

'And maybe, for whatever reason, he's about to do a deal with some very bad people. I agree we'll give his bag back but we're going to have to keep a close eye on him,' Millie said. 'I think there's something going on with him.' She explained the conversation she'd had with Masud earlier in the day about his little brother.

'When we were at the Great Pyramid yesterday, Mr Salah got teary when I mentioned there's nothing worse than seeing animals and children in pain – he said it was because he was thinking about the horses and donkeys but I wondered if there was something more,' Alice-Miranda explained.

Millie wrapped the statue in the cloth and placed it inside the bag. She was tempted to see if there was anything else interesting inside, but she resisted the urge.

'Come on,' Alice-Miranda said. 'We have to go and find him – now.'

Chapter 34

Alice-Miranda and Millie hurried to the colour-ful dining room to find it alive with chatter. Mr Ferguson was busy making the acquaintance of a group of archaeologists the children were going to work with in the Valley of the Queens, while the rest of the group milled around the tables.

Millie had brought Masud's bag with her as the girls had no idea which room he was in. They hoped he was here, otherwise they would give it to his father.

Alice-Miranda glanced around and spotted the boy as he practically sprinted towards them.

He tore the satchel from Millie's shoulder. 'You found it!'

'Yes, we did,' Millie rebuked. She screwed up her nose and rubbed the top of her arm. 'You can thank us if you like – and get me an ice pack.'

The boy looked sheepish and cast his eyes to the floor. 'I am sorry. Thank you, Miss Millie.' He scurried away to a corner. The girls watched him open the flap and rummage around, a look of relief spreading across his face.

'That's not a kid who's just got a worthless souvenir back,' Millie said.

Alice-Miranda could only agree.

They watched as Masud approached his father. The boy showed him the now-closed bag and then he bolted, presumably to put it in his room.

'Alice-Miranda,' Sep called out. He'd saved her a seat.

'Really?' Millie whispered.

'It's okay,' Alice-Miranda replied. 'I'm going to tell him the same thing that I told Neville, and then perhaps the boys can be normal with each other again instead of fighting over me like I'm some sort of prize – which I'm not.'

Millie grinned. 'You can't help being adorable.'

Alice-Miranda gave the girl a nudge. 'Ha ha, you know that's not true. Anyway . . .' she started, then stopped, her eyes drawn to something – or someone.

'What?' Millie asked as she turned around. 'Oh. I didn't think *she'd* be staying here.'

Standing in the doorway, Maryam Moussa looked as if she'd just been bailed up by a bask of Nile crocodiles. The owner of the guesthouse, Mr Tadros, who had greeted the children effusively upon their arrival was beside her, pointing and chatting, but the expression on Maryam's face said that she would have preferred to be anywhere but here.

'Hello Miss Moussa,' Alice-Miranda called and gave a wave.

'I'm going to sit with the girls,' Millie said, leaving her friend to it. Alice-Miranda was far better at public relations and Maryam Moussa hadn't exactly endeared herself to the children so far.

The woman muttered something, then plastered a smile on her face. 'Oh, hello. You're here.'

'I don't think we've ever been properly introduced. I'm Alice-Miranda Highton-Smith-Kennington-Jones,' the girl said, extending her hand.

At the mention of the name, Maryam flinched. 'Kennington-Jones?' she said aloud.

'Yes, that's Daddy's surname. He's Hugh and Mummy is Cecelia Highton-Smith. They didn't really know what to call me so they gave me the lot – it's a bit much, isn't it?' The girl grinned. 'Are you staying here too? It's very cosy, though I don't imagine you're in a bunk room like us girls.'

Maryam looked at their host, her eyes widening in alarm.

'Oh no, Miss Moussa is in the Ministerial Suite. We keep it especially for Dr Hassam as he is here very often.'

Maryam blanched, wondering how the man would feel about his exclusive room being given to her, but it certainly sounded a lot better than bunk beds.

'We are honoured that the Minister has chosen our humble establishment as his place of residence in Luxor for nearly twenty years,' Mr Tadros said. 'He says that it is because of our most excellent food and comfortable beds – as well as the sweet-smelling complimentary personal products – however, I think our proximity to the Valleys of the Kings and Queens is more likely the real reason. That, and the fact that he has very good friends nearby.'

'What friends?' Maryam asked. To her great disappointment, today had been a spectacular waste of time. She hadn't been able to make contact with any of the people she'd been hoping to meet.

'Well, as you are the Acting Minister, Miss Moussa, I can tell you that one of them is an important businessman – Mr Farouk. He is very rich. There is a jet at the airport on standby for him at all times due to his frequent travels,' the man explained. 'He and Dr Hassam often dine together with another friend. In fact, Mr Farouk usually sends the jet to collect Dr Hassam from Cairo.'

Maryam wrinkled her nose. Nour hadn't mentioned that to her.

'What sort of business is Mr Farouk in?' Alice-Miranda asked, curious about what would take him travelling so often.

'Mattresses,' the man replied.

'Mattresses?' Alice-Miranda said, somewhat surprised.

Mr Tadros chuckled. 'Mr Farouk has the largest bedding manufacture company in Egypt, and he is also in Turkey, Africa and the Middle East. In fact, the mattress you will sleep on tonight comes from his Dozy Head brand. They are extremely comfortable, particularly as they are brand new. The man is very generous and replaces every bed in this establishment for me twice a year at no cost. The savings enable me to purchase the finest Egyptian cotton sheets. One thousand thread count.'

Alice-Miranda frowned. 'Why would he do that? It doesn't sound like good business practice.'

'Because he is a most kind and philanthropic man. You see, the mattresses are then shipped across the border into Sudan where he donates them to charities. And because they are second-hand there are no taxes to be paid or need for inspections. It is a win-win for everyone. Especially for my guests, who all tell me that they sleep like babies while they are here.'

Maryam Moussa frowned too, clearly deep in thought.

'Oh, that is kind,' Alice-Miranda said.

'I will organise your table, Miss Moussa – it is in a separate room. Dr Hassam prefers this to protect his privacy and give him some time away from the glare of his admirers. Is this to your liking?' Mr Tadros asked.

Maryam nodded. 'Yes, please – the sooner the better.' The man hurried away, leaving the woman standing with Alice-Miranda.

'We're looking forward to being on the dig with you tomorrow,' Alice-Miranda said. 'Mr Salah mentioned that one of your PhDs was all about Hatshepsut – what a woman. Who could have imagined she would crown herself Pharaoh? It must have been outrageous at the time, especially given the Egyptians really didn't have a word for Queen.' Alice-Miranda gave a beaming smile. 'And please don't be nervous. We're just kids and you're the expert.'

'Who said I was nervous?' Maryam asked.

'Well, it looked that way at the museum the other day. And I can't say I blame you. You've stepped into some very big shoes. Mr Salah said that there was a lovely double-page article in the newspaper about you yesterday. He was the one who told us you were an expert on Hatshepsut,' Alice-Miranda replied.

Maryam blinked. An article? She had told Nour that she had no desire for any media attention.

How dare the woman allow this to happen? The last thing she wanted was her face to be splashed all over the papers.

Alice-Miranda turned and saw a couple of waitresses delivering food to the tables. 'I'd better go – I think our dinner is arriving. See you in the morning.'

Maryam Moussa smiled tightly and gave a half wave as Alice-Miranda spun on her heel and hurried back to the table where Millie was sitting with the other girls. She was pleased to see Sep at another table next to Neville, and waved at him to sit down and stay there. She indicated she would sit with the girls tonight. Surely Neville and Sep could patch up their friendship without her coming between them.

'Was Miss Moussa any more enthusiastic than the last time we saw her?' Millie asked.

'Not especially,' Alice-Miranda said, 'but I think we should do what we can to make her feel more comfortable.'

'Why?' Sloane said. 'She's a total fake. Mr Salah knows way more about Egyptian history than she does.'

Britt frowned. 'Let's see how she is tomorrow. Perhaps Miss Moussa will dazzle us with her knowledge. Hopefully she will wear some more appropriate shoes.'

'We should give her a chance while she's finding her feet,' Chessie said.

'And meeting with dodgy crooks.' Millie motioned towards two men who had just arrived and were standing in the doorway.

'Oh my goodness, isn't that the fellow we saw her with at the Sphinx?' Alice-Miranda said.

Millie nodded. 'The one that Masud was talking to as well when we were leaving.'

'What do you mean?' Britt asked. Millie shook her head. She'd tell the others later, when there was less chance of being overheard.

'I wonder who that other guy is,' Sloane said. He was dressed in a finely tailored charcoal-coloured suit, and had a long grey beard and hair to match.

They didn't have to wait long to find out. Mr Tadros greeted the fellow with open arms. 'Good evening, Mr Farouk, how wonderful to see you again. And Mr Zoheir – it has been a while.'

Alice-Miranda knew immediately who Mr Farouk was, having just been told all about him. And now they had a name for the man from Cairo as well.

'Good evening, Mr Tadros,' Mr Farouk replied. 'We understand that Miss Moussa is in residence this evening.'

The man nodded.

'Ah, I was just telling her about you and your friendship with Dr Hassam,' the man replied.

Masud Salah had returned to the room a few minutes earlier and was sitting on a table with his father. Millie watched as Mr Salah stood up and walked over to speak to Mr Ferguson and Miss Cranna, leaving Masud alone.

'This way, gentlemen,' Mr Tadros said with a broad smile. 'Miss Moussa will be delighted to meet you.'

Mr Farouk followed him, Mr Zoheir close behind.

Millie nudged Alice-Miranda, who was already trailing the men with her gaze. As Mr Zoheir passed by Masud's table, he whispered something to the boy. Millie and Alice-Miranda both saw Masud swallow hard and mumble something in reply.

He looked terrified.

'There's something going on,' Millie said.

Alice-Miranda nodded as the three men disappeared behind a screen.

★

After dinner, the children moved to the lounge area. There they were treated to an enthusiastic lecture from Mr Salah about Luxor, which had been known as Thebes in ancient Egypt and was the capital during the period known as the Middle Kingdom. He also gave them a fantastic overview of the history of the Valley of the Kings and Valley of the Queens, with an audio-visual presentation too. The man's knowledge was extensive and he peppered his words with humorous anecdotes to keep the children entertained.

'That man is a walking history book,' Sloane said. 'I don't think there is anything he couldn't tell us about this country. He should be the Acting Minister for Antiquities, not Miss Moussa.'

'I tend to agree,' Lucas said.

Alice-Miranda had tried to sit near Masud, but Sep had saved her a seat again and she didn't feel like she could brush him off for the second time that night. She noticed that he'd smirked at Neville, which really wasn't fair.

Mr Salah finished his talk and the children were given time to get some drinks and go to the loo before their next round of activities, which Miss Cranna promised would be lots of fun, as well as a test of their knowledge and skills.

'Sep, can I talk to you for a minute?' Alice-Miranda asked.

The boy grinned. 'Of course. What's up?'

'Do you mind if we step out onto the terrace?' the girl said. She turned and frowned at Millie and Chessie, who were waving their hands, telling her to hurry up. Neville was chatting with Sloane and watching anxiously.

'You know she doesn't want him to be her boyfriend *either*,' Sloane said to Neville. 'I mean seriously, who *would* want that? It's Sep.'

Neville grinned. 'She told me. And I understand, I really do. It's just that I adore her.'

Sloane giggled. 'We all do, but she's not ready for romantic entanglements – yet. I always forget that she's younger than the rest of us.'

'Me too,' Neville said. 'What about you? Is there someone special in your life, Sloane?'

'Why – are you keen? You know you're on the rebound, Nev, so I'd have to turn you down,' the girl said with a huge smile.

'Haha, very funny. But hey, you're not that bad, not really,' Neville replied.

Sloane punched his shoulder.

'Ow. You do know that I was in the middle of an epic wrestling tournament before dinner and

324

I am planning to finish Hunter off before bedtime?' Neville said, rubbing his triceps.

Alice-Miranda and Sep reappeared and while the boy looked sheepish at least he didn't seem too upset.

'I'll get us some drinks,' he said, and hurried away.

Millie raised her eyebrows.

'We're fine,' Alice-Miranda replied. 'I'm going to the bathroom.'

The toilets were down the hallway past the reception area. Alice-Miranda charged inside to find both cubicles empty. A few minutes later she was about to flush when she heard a man's voice. It sounded like it was coming from outside the open window that sat high up on the wall.

'You said that one of them was made of solid gold? Where is it?' the man hissed.

'I will bring it as soon as I have the money for these,' a boy replied.

Alice-Miranda knew at once that the boy was Masud Salah. And she had a fair idea who he was talking to.

'We had an agreement. You lied to me,' the man said. His tone was menacing.

'No. I promise,' the boy replied. 'I have it.'

Alice-Miranda climbed up on the toilet seat and tried to pull herself up to see outside, but the window was too high. At least she could hear more clearly.

'We do not take kindly to double dealers, Masud. I want the gold figurine by tomorrow and then you will have your money. Remind me of how much that was?'

'One million American dollars,' the boy said.

Alice-Miranda's hand flew to her mouth to stop herself from gasping.

The man chuckled. 'I do not recall that amount.'

'You agreed. The gold funerary figure alone is worth ten times that amount – probably more,' Masud said, his voice wavering. 'You told me you would pay that.'

'I will give you half,' the man replied.

Alice-Miranda's heart was pounding.

'Half?' Masud said. 'But that's not enough.'

She could hear the desperation in the boy's voice. What on earth could he possibly need a million dollars for? He was just a kid. Perhaps his family was in some sort of trouble? She wouldn't have thought that, looking at his father, but Akil *had* had that moment after she'd mentioned children in pain . . .

'I tell you what, Masud. You bring the gold figurine and anything more that you have – and I know that you have more – and I will give you seven hundred and fifty thousand US dollars. That is a fortune in anyone's language,' the man said.

'Where?' Masud asked.

'You are visiting Deir el-Bahri tomorrow?' the man said.

'Yes,' Masud replied.

'I will be in the shrine of Hathor at two o'clock,' the man said.

'But I will be helping my father with the group,' Masud replied.

'Surely you can make an excuse to go to the bathroom,' the man scoffed. 'Unless you do not wish to make the sale?'

'I will be there,' Masud spat.

'Do not be late, and come alone or the deal is off. Now get out of here.'

Alice-Miranda heard footsteps running on the gravel. She was about to leave too when the man spoke again.

'He's just a stupid kid, but I do believe that he is about to make our fortunes,' the man said.

There was a pause. He was on the phone.

'Do not worry – I am not planning to pay him a cent. But after this, my friend, we will be richer than the Pharaohs.'

The situation was worse than Alice-Miranda first feared.

The door to the hallway swung open and a loud voice echoed through the bathroom. 'Alice-Miranda, are you here?' Millie called.

The girl practically fell off the toilet, pressing the button to flush on her way down and landing with a thud.

'Miss Cranna wants to start the game and we're all waiting for you – and Masud. You didn't see him on your way in here, did you?' Millie asked.

'I'm coming,' Alice-Miranda said as she walked out and washed her hands.

'Are you okay? You look as if you've seen a ghost,' Millie said.

'Masud's in big trouble,' the girl replied. She explained what she'd just heard.

'Wow. Who knew that going to the toilet could be the bringer of such bad news – first Jacinta and school, and now this,' Millie said.

'We have to stop him. He could end up in prison at worst and penniless at best,' Alice-Miranda said.

'Should we go and talk to him – or to his father?' Millie said.

'I don't know. He must have a reason for what he's doing and I don't want him to get into any trouble,' Alice-Miranda said. 'Let's think about it.'

Millie chewed her lip in worry, then nodded and grabbed her friend's hand as the pair scampered out the door.

Chapter 35

Alice-Miranda and Millie rejoined the group, who had just started an energetic game of Egyptian-themed charades. Britt and Henry had everyone in stitches as they tag-teamed one another to act out an interpretation of a famous hieroglyphic relief depicting family scenes – including milking cows, riding camels, baking bread and playing musical instruments. It was their double act on mummification, though, that brought the house down. Henry lay prostrate on the floor while Britt pretended to remove his brain with an imaginary hook and place it into an imaginary jar. It didn't take long for the others to shout out exactly what she was doing.

'That was brilliant, kids!' Mr Ferguson clapped loudly. 'But I'm afraid it's time for bed.'

His words were met with groans of disappointment from the children.

'Ye'll need to be at breakfast by half past seven to be on time for a very exciting day at Deir el-Bahri. The team of Polish and Egyptian archaeologists workin' there have found some particularly interestin' new prospects. I was chattin' to a couple of the leaders here earlier and they believe they are on the cusp of somethin' marvellous.' The man rubbed his hands together. 'I canna wait. It's goin' to be grand.'

'Imagine if we helped crack open a new tomb? That would be incredible,' Neville said.

'And highly unlikely,' Sep replied.

'Yeah, but just *imagine* it,' Neville said. 'We'd be famous, like Howard Carter and Lord Carnarvon.'

'Or Dr Hassam,' Alice-Miranda added. 'He's found loads of artefacts and new tombs over the years. I do hope his health is improving. It would have been so lovely to meet him.'

The children headed off, with firm instructions that Miss Reedy and Mr Plumpton would be checking for lights out in thirty minutes.

'What were you going to tell us about those men at dinner?' Britt asked Millie and Alice-Miranda as they walked to their room. The boys had all charged off, eager to restart their wrestling tournament. Madagascar, Caprice, Alethea and Gretchen had also gone ahead so they could play a quick game of cards.

Alice-Miranda explained what Mr Tadros had said, and Millie told the girls what they'd seen at the Sphinx. She left out the part about Masud meeting with Mr Zoheir, after what Alice-Miranda had told her following her trip to the toilet and knowing what the boy had in his bag.

'Do you think Miss Moussa is up to something?' Britt asked. 'She won't last long as the Acting Minister if she's found to be cavorting with criminals.'

'We don't know what to think,' Millie said.

Alice-Miranda motioned towards the end of the hallway, where Maryam Moussa was disappearing up the stairs. 'But we could ask her,' she said.

'What? No way. She's not going to tell us anything,' Millie said.

'There's only one way to find out,' Alice-Miranda said. 'Are you coming?'

Millie looked at the other girls.

Britt, Sloane, Chessie and Jacinta shook their heads.

'We'll leave the interrogation to you,' Sloane said. 'But you can tell us about it later.'

'Come on,' Alice-Miranda said to Millie. The red-haired girl rolled her eyes.

'Do you think there might be a time – just once – that we go away on a trip and there's no mystery, no drama and no funny business going on?' Millie said.

'I hope not,' Alice-Miranda replied. 'That would be a bit boring.'

'I think I'd like to try it,' Millie said. The other girls grinned.

'We'd better hurry or we won't know which room she's in,' Alice-Miranda said.

'If we're not back before Miss Reedy does her rounds just put some pillows in the bunks and make it look like we're asleep,' Millie said. 'I don't want to miss out on my Diamond Queen's Colours because of little Miss Marple here.'

★

Maryam Moussa had just kicked off her shoes and was about to run a bubble bath when there was a loud knock on the door.

'I don't need anything – thank you,' she called.

She'd ducked down to reception to get a map; it had been a pain, trying to see the scope of the valleys on her laptop. The device was still sitting open on the desk, with an overview of Hatshepsut and her mortuary temple on the screen. Hopefully the last-minute study would be enough.

Maryam had to admit the room was a lovely surprise. It was a proper suite with a lounge area, a king sized bedroom and a bathroom fit for a Pharaoh. No wonder Dr Hassam enjoyed spending time out here. The food at dinner had been excellent too – and the company *very* interesting.

She walked into the bathroom and turned on the taps. She had just begun to unbutton her blouse when there was another, more insistent, knock.

'Look, I told you already . . .' She hurried across the room and opened the door, stunned to see the child called Alice-Miranda and her friend standing there. 'What do you two want?'

'Hello Miss Moussa,' Alice-Miranda said. 'We were just worried about you and came to see that you were all right.'

'Why wouldn't I be?' Maryam demanded.

'Well, yesterday we saw you at the Sphinx with a man that Mr Salah said has a very bad reputation. And then he was here tonight,' the brunette explained.

Maryam could feel her temperature rising. 'I don't know why you think the company I keep is any of your business,' she said.

But the child was undeterred. 'Mr Salah said the man Mr Tadros called Mr Zoheir has links to the criminal underworld and is involved in antiquity trading on the black market.'

Maryam's jaw dropped. 'What are you talking about?'

'And as you were having dinner with him and his associate, Mr Farouk, we were just concerned, that's all,' Alice-Miranda explained.

'Come inside, now!' Maryam demanded, her mind racing. She motioned for the girls to sit on the couch. She couldn't let these children bring everything unstuck – not now. She was too close to getting what she wanted, there was no plan B this time.

'We didn't mean to upset you, Miss Moussa,' Alice-Miranda said. 'It's just that you've only been in your job for such a short time and perhaps you didn't know about the rumours.'

Maryam was thinking through a hundred different scenarios, but it was the obvious one that jumped out at her. Tell them the truth – or part of it, anyway.

'You seem like lovely girls who obviously care very much about doing the right thing, but you must swear that what I am about to say goes no further than this room,' Maryam said. She looked at the pair sternly.

Alice-Miranda and Millie nodded.

'Since coming into this position as Acting Minister I've learned that all is not what it seems, and now I have a small window of time to gather evidence to put an end to this corruption. I have become aware that Dr Hassam has been at the heart of a large-scale fraud, robbing the Egyptian people of their heritage while making millions of dollars for himself and his partners,' Maryam said.

'No!' The two girls gasped in unison.

'That's terrible,' Alice-Miranda said. 'The man is loved like a god here in Egypt.'

'Yes, except that he has the heart of a devil,' the woman replied.

Millie and Alice-Miranda glanced at each other, stunned by Miss Moussa's revelation. As they turned back to face the woman, they spotted the open laptop and the website on the screen. Millie nudged her friend.

'What are you looking at?' Maryam asked as she turned around. 'Oh – you must think I'm stupid or something. I was just working out how to couch my language in layman's terms tomorrow to make it easier for you all. I tend to speak at a university level if I don't remind myself not to.' She jumped up to close the lid before sitting back down.

'Where was I?' She paused to gather her thoughts. 'Yes, in order to bring an end to this evil ring of thieves, I must gain their trust and make them believe that I too will continue Dr Hassam's work, exactly as he has done for many years.'

'So you're pretending to be friends with them?' Millie said.

Maryam nodded. 'Not friends, exactly, but business associates. I have made them believe Dr Hassam had already brought me into the fold.

In my previous role, I was in charge of cataloguing and had access to sensitive information about where artefacts were stored and how they were moved between museums. Having Dr Hassam's secret telephone in my possession – which he uses to communicate with the men – has given them faith that I am indeed part of this and will do nothing to compromise their activities.'

'But that's not true?' Millie asked.

'No.' Maryam shook her head. 'I found the phone by accident, but I have long had my suspicions about Dr Hassam. They have just been confirmed.'

'Do you know who they sell to and how they move the goods out of the country?' Alice-Miranda asked.

'I have some idea of their buyers, but how they move the goods remains a mystery – although Mr Farouk's private plane probably helps. Mr Salah is right in saying that there have been whispers for years about this sort of trade. It has been impossible to prove it until now,' Maryam said.

Millie raised her eyebrows. 'Have you got a plan?'

'Not exactly,' Maryam said, which wasn't technically true. She had a very good idea of what she was going to do, but didn't feel the need to share that much information with these two.

Millie looked at Alice-Miranda and widened her eyes.

'I think we could help you, and in doing so save a friend from a terrible fate,' Alice-Miranda said.

Maryam looked at the girl. 'What are you talking about?'

'Masud Salah is planning to sell what we think are very important antiquities from the tomb of Khufu,' Alice-Miranda began.

Maryam frowned. 'I don't believe it. Khufu's tomb was emptied of its treasures thousands of years ago. If anything was found it would be price-less.' That was one fact she knew for sure.

Millie still had her camera slung around her neck. She'd fetched it after dinner to take some group shots and record videos of their charades.

She scrolled through the frames, then held the camera out for Miss Moussa to see one of the pictures she'd taken of the gold figurine.

'Oh!' Maryam recoiled. While she was no expert, she knew that what she was looking at was something special. 'Do you know where he got this?'

The girls shook their heads. 'We don't know anything. We were going to speak to him and his father.'

'No! You mustn't,' Maryam ordered. 'But I need to hear exactly what he was planning and how this information has come to you.'

Alice-Miranda explained everything and Maryam nodded. This couldn't have been more perfect if she'd devised it herself and it was much simpler and swifter than her original plan. Finally Dr Hassam and his cronies would get what was coming to them – and Maryam would have her ticket to freedom.

Chapter 36

Alice-Miranda and Millie had both left Maryam Moussa's room last night feeling quite overwhelmed. Miss Moussa promised that there wouldn't be any repercussions for Masud, but they'd still been worried about the boy. Back in their room, they'd told their friends only that the woman had invited them in for a chat and had been much friendlier than the other times they'd met her. She'd thanked them for letting them know about Mr Zoheir's reputation and said she'd had no idea.

This morning, the dining room was abuzz with chatter. They were partway through breakfast when their host, Mr Tadros, hurried in with a large envelope. He scanned the crowd before heading straight for Alice-Miranda.

'Ah, good morning, Miss Alice-Miranda. A lady called Mrs Parker sent you some documents via fax machine overnight. Fortunately we still have one of those dinosaur devices. The pages are enclosed. Enjoy your breakfast,' the man said, handing her the envelope.

'Thank you, Mr Tadros,' the child replied.

Millie looked at her expectantly. 'Well, come on.'

'I can't open it here,' she said.

'Yes you can – we all know,' Sloane said. Millie, Alice-Miranda, Chessie, Sloane, Jacinta and Britt had managed to get a table together this morning.

Alice-Miranda pulled out the wad of papers and scanned the first one: a map of the school grounds. What followed were plans of buildings and construction projects that had happened over the years, fundraising documents pertaining to capital works and inventories for furniture. When it came to anything with Miss Reedy's signature, though, it was all just daily business – there were no bank documents or legal papers. The only thing out of the ordinary was what was apparently a copy of the deed to the school, given that, according to what Miss Grimm had said to Miss Reedy, the teacher had signed over the original to Mr Badger and he'd personally collected it. This was obviously a very old document, with flowery handwriting and a title that said, 'This Conveyance' in old English lettering. There were stamps and seals and signatures – though none of them belonged to anyone Alice-Miranda recognised.

'Anything?' Sloane said, sipping her tamarind juice.

Alice-Miranda shook her head. 'I don't think so. I suppose it's helpful for Uncle Lawrence if he shoots the movie at school – at least he'll have all the plans and know where everything is – but as far as shedding any light on Mr Badger, there's nothing.' She put the papers back into the envelope.

Shoulders slumped around the table and several of the girls rested on their elbows.

'This can't be the end,' Millie said.

'No,' Alice-Miranda agreed. 'Something will turn up. We have to keep faith. In the meantime,

I'm going to give Mrs Parker a quick call and thank her. I'm sure it would have taken ages to find all this.' She hopped down and left the room.

Madagascar and Caprice were watching the girls from the next table, wondering what they were up to.

'What was that all about?' Madagascar asked.

Caprice shrugged. None of the others on their table had been looking. They were too engrossed in a discussion about what they were going to see today.

Madagascar slid out of her seat and walked over to Millie.

'I hate Mr Badger for stealing all the money,' Jacinta blurted.

'Are you talking about Mr Badger from Badger and Woodcock?' Madagascar interrupted them, startling Millie, who almost fell off her chair. 'Mummy told me last night that he's a thief and a scoundrel. It's lucky *they* never invested anything with him. Why do you hate him, Jacinta? Are your parents broke or something?'

'No, it's the school!' she retorted, then clamped her hand over her mouth. The last person in the world she wanted to know about this was Madagascar Slewt.

Caprice had walked up beside Maddie in time to hear Jacinta. 'What?' she demanded. 'Has the school lost all its money?'

'Forget it. It's nothing for you to worry about,' Sloane said.

'Just think, Caprice – if that rubbish little school of yours closes down you'll be able to come to Bodlington with me,' Madagascar said, with a smirk. 'It's so much better – the work is easy and the teachers are stupid.'

Caprice turned to the girl. 'But I don't want to go to Bodlington. I want to stay at Winchesterfield-Downsfordvale with my friends.'

'You don't have any friends – they all hate you,' Madagascar said with a glare.

'Maddie!' Millie hopped out of her seat and stood up. 'That's a horrible thing to say. Of course Caprice has friends, though I doubt she'd have any if she teamed up with the likes of you.'

Madagascar's face was turning red. 'How dare you speak to me like that? You're my cousin – seven hundred times removed or something and thank goodness for that, because who would want to be closely related to you. And you're on a scholarship. Your parents are too poor to be able to pay for a good education.'

By now the entire dining room was looking their way. Miss Reedy and Mr Plumpton had stood up and were ready to pounce, while Miss Cranna and Mr Ferguson were both sporting looks of horror.

Millie was about to retort, but Caprice got in first.

'Take that back, Maddie,' she demanded, eyeballing the girl.

'What? You hate her. You told me she's always mean to you,' Madagascar scoffed. 'She was horrible to me when we were little too – always stealing my toys.'

'That's not true!' Millie said. 'More like the other way around.'

'Millie is a bright girl with a kind heart, and even though she and I tease each other mercilessly I know that if push came to shove she would have my back,' Caprice yelled. 'Unlike you!'

Millie swallowed hard.

'And for your information, you horrible little snob, I'm on a scholarship too, because although my mother is Venetia Baldini – the famous celebrity chef – hospitality is hard and she's had more than her fair share of ups and downs, so in order to help her and Daddy I applied for one myself. And there is nothing wrong with that!'

Madagascar Slewt stamped her foot. 'I hate you, Caprice Radford. I hate all of you and this stupid program – which, for your information, I paid girls at my school to do for me. What a joke!'

Madagascar fled from the room, Miss Cranna taking off after her.

The other children were so stunned they didn't say a word.

Millie looked at Caprice. 'Wow. Thank you.'

Caprice nodded. 'It's okay. And for the record, I suppose we've fallen into a bad pattern but I meant what I just said – that I know you'd have my back in a crisis.'

'I would,' Millie said, and brushed a tear from her eye. The other girls did as well.

'Could I sit with you? And maybe you could tell me what's going on? It sounds like my life might be affected too,' Caprice said.

'Sure,' Sloane agreed.

Caprice hopped up onto the seat Alice-Miranda had vacated only minutes before. And while all of the girls were still holding out hope that the school could be saved, they quickly told Caprice everything they knew.

★

347

Alice-Miranda was standing by the reception desk when Madagascar Slewt ran past her, Miss Cranna hot on her heels.

'Is everything all right?' she called, but neither of them stopped. She was waiting to ask Mr Tadros if he could help her use the payphone around the corner, but he'd just picked up the phone on the counter when she arrived. He nodded and put his hand over the mouthpiece.

'It is a call for you from Russia,' the man said. 'This fellow says his name is Lawrence Ridley. Is it possible he is the movie star by that same name?'

Alice-Miranda's eyes lit up. 'Yes! He's my uncle,' she said as she took the handset.

'Oh my!' Mr Tadros said with a grin. 'The famous Lawrence Ridley called my guesthouse. Please tell him that if he would ever like to stay I can do an exceptionally good deal – at least fifty per cent off. Actually, he can come for free if he would like. I will put him in the Ministerial Suite.'

Alice-Miranda nodded. She didn't want to be rude but she was bursting to talk to her uncle. She took the phone and scurried away to the funny little pay-telephone box around the corner so she could have some privacy.

'Uncle Lawrence! Finally!' Alice-Miranda exclaimed.

But the news was not what she hoped. Her brilliant plan to have her uncle set his directorial debut at Winchesterfield-Downsfordvale was not to be. Lawrence had just signed a deal to become the next Drew Tate, a superspy hero beloved by generations, and the contract strictly forbade him from filming other projects until he'd finished all obligations associated with that character. By the time he could make his own movie, it would be far too late.

'Thank you anyway, Uncle Lawrence – I know you'd help if you could. Give the twins and Aunt Charlotte hugs from me. See you soon,' the child said, and hung up. She walked back to the reception desk.

'You look very sad, Miss Alice-Miranda,' Mr Tadros said as she returned the phone to him. 'Not like a girl who is lucky enough to have Lawrence Ridley for an uncle.'

'Indeed,' she said, then paused before repeating slowly, 'indeed . . . Deed – Mr Tadros, that's it! May I use your phone again?'

He nodded. 'Yes, of course.'

Alice-Miranda ran back around to the little booth and called Mrs Parker, hoping upon hope that her hunch was right.

Chapter 37

It was fortunate they hadn't been due at Deir el-Bahri until nine o'clock, because Alice-Miranda's realisation had led to a flurry of phone calls and activity.

First, the girl had broken the news to Miss Reedy and Mr Plumpton. The copy of the deed Mrs Parker had faxed hadn't been a copy at all. And there was certainly no signature from Miss Reedy signing it over to Mr Badger – which had been the thing that tipped Alice-Miranda off.

She knew all about the importance of signatures after Queen Georgiana's cousin, Lloyd Lancaster Brown, had attempted to overthrow the woman a couple of years back, alleging that his father had never signed his abdication document. Had the original not been found, this 'evidence' would have handed Lloyd the throne.

In this case, it seemed Mr Badger had somehow convinced the bank of his ownership of the property – probably forging Miss Reedy's signature on a copy of the deeds that he had somehow got his hands on.

Once Mrs Parker had in turn spoken to Miss Grimm, the good news had come thick and fast. The headmistress had contacted the police, who had then arrived with the documents Mr Badger had used to take out loans with the bank – which Mrs Parker promptly pointed out *all* contained forged signatures. She had copies of other papers Livinia had actually signed and could spot the difference a mile off. The only thing Miss Reedy had ever consented to was the rollover of their term deposits. Mr Badger had conned the bank completely, falsifying all of the loan documents. The bank had no recourse over the school and

would have to continue their pursuit of the duplic-
itous Mr Badger for their money. Miss Grimm had
been due to sign the sale papers that very morning,
so the timing couldn't have been better. As for the
school's savings, the bank would have to wear their
reimbursement too.

There were celebrations all round, though
Mrs Parker couldn't understand for a second why
Miss Grimm hadn't confided in her – she could
have easily solved the problem.

'Myrtle will be insufferable after this,' Millie
said later. The children were looking out across
the Valley of the Queens from the top terrace
of the mortuary temple of Hatshepsut, where they
were finishing up their tour of the edifice.

'I don't mind. Who knows what would have
happened if it wasn't for her,' Alice-Miranda said.

Chessie shook her head. 'No. If it wasn't for you
and your plan with Lawrence, Mrs Parker would
never have found that deed, so it was a chain of
events, you might say – one good thing leading
to another. Well, except that he's not making the
movie at school.'

'Yes,' Miss Reedy looked at Alice-Miranda, a
beaming smile on her face. 'You saved the day,

my dear. Now, finally, we can all enjoy this trip and stop worrying.'

Josiah Plumpton raised his wife's hand to his lips and kissed it.

'And my darling wife has been completely exonerated,' the man said.

Alice-Miranda nodded, though she didn't quite feel the same. It was wonderful that things at school had taken a turn for the better, but she was still worried about Masud.

The boy had been trailing around after his father all day and, although he had left his large satchel back at the guesthouse, he hadn't once removed a smaller bag that was slung across his body from shoulder to hip. She had a very good idea of what that contained and could only imagine how nervous the boy was, knowing that he had a rendezvous booked for two o'clock.

Miss Moussa had assured Alice-Miranda and Millie that she would have the authorities there to intercept the exchange. It would then be a matter of unravelling the links from Mr Zoheir to everyone else – though the woman said she had a clear line to Dr Hassam.

Part of Alice-Miranda wanted to warn Masud – and then he could abandon his plan altogether – but

Miss Moussa said that the sting was a matter of national importance and they couldn't tell a soul what was going on. Jeopardising the whole operation would be a huge mistake.

'Are you all right?' Britt asked Alice-Miranda as they walked towards the dig site where they would be spending the rest of the afternoon.

'Yes, of course.' Alice-Miranda squeezed her friend's arm.

'You still look as if your school is about to close down,' Britt said. 'Not like the girl who saved it.'

'I was just thinking about this place,' Alice-Miranda said, which wasn't entirely a lie. 'It's incredible to imagine life here thousands of years ago. You know me – I like to ponder.'

'Okay. But if something else was the matter, you'd tell me, wouldn't you?' Britt said.

Alice-Miranda smiled at her friend but was saved from answering by Mr Salah, who called their attention.

'Children, we are now entering Hathor's shrine,' the man said. He was due to hand over to Miss Moussa at the dig site soon, though there had been no word yet of her arrival.

'I would like you to consider the differences in the depictions of Hatshepsut here to the very

355

masculine statues and reliefs we have already seen. Out there, she wears the false beard of the Pharaohs and if we did not know better we would say that she was a man. In this temple, the portrayals are softer and more feminine. This was a private place for her to be her real self,' Mr Salah explained.

'I love this stuff,' Neville said. 'Seriously, I think this trip has sealed my fate for university.'

Once they had finished their tour, Mr Salah led them to the side of the funerary complex where the archaeologists were working. It was a large area, sectioned off with string lines and crawling with human excavators. Apparently they were hopeful that there were some additional tombs here.

'Ah, there you are, Miss Moussa,' Mr Ferguson called out as the woman walked towards them. 'We wondered if you'd arrived.'

'At least she's wearing more sensible clothes,' Britt commented. Today Maryam Moussa looked every inch the archaeologist in her beige trousers and a mid-sleeved shirt, with sandshoes on her feet and a scarf covering her fedora-style hat.

'Hello Mr Ferguson, I've just been catching up with the team about what they've found,' Maryam replied with a smile. She waved at the children.

'Is that the same person we met a couple of days ago?' Sloane asked.

'It's almost as if she's given herself permission to enjoy what she's doing,' Millie said. She wondered if the spring in the woman's step had more to do with the fact that she was soon to be headline news for smashing apart a black-market trading ring that had been robbing the country for years.

There was something about her plan, though, that had Millie perplexed. Unless Miss Moussa knew a lot more about Mr Farouk and Mr Zoheir's misdeeds than she'd told the girls, her only evidence was completely reliant on one deal that was to be brokered this afternoon. And Alice-Miranda had overheard that Mr Zoheir was intending more of a robbery than a transaction. Until the goods were on-sold, he could probably just make up some nonsense about finding them himself and get off scot free. Something wasn't adding up. Millie resolved to keep a close eye on Miss Moussa until she figured out exactly what was going on.

While Millie had been musing, Maryam had invited the children to gather around and had begun to tell them what the excavation had revealed so far. There had been quite a lot of jewellery and cartouches uncovered, but the most exciting find was a seemingly cavernous space that the team had identified with their ground-penetrating radar. They were still looking for the entrance, which was where the children were going to help today. Anything else they came across would be a bonus.

The students were once again split into teams – this time of five – and allocated a work area with an archaeologist in charge.

Alice-Miranda was with Britt, Lucas, Aidan and Junior.

'Miss Moussa seems to have found her feet today,' Mr Ferguson noted to Mr Salah, who nodded.

'Yes, it is good to see. I was concerned that she was ill-suited to the position, but perhaps it has just taken her a few days to get the hang of things,' Akil replied. 'Dr Hassam would be pleased – though we are all hoping that he is well again soon.'

'Masud,' Maryam called. 'Would you like to come and join us?'

The boy flinched, wondering how she knew his name. Millie flinched too – wasn't the woman making things a bit obvious?

Maryam was working with Chessie, Gretchen, Hunter, Henry and Sloane, and immediately whisked them away to the far corner.

It was amazing how fast the time flew by as the children dug and sifted and brushed the sand from anything they found. It seemed they had arrived on a particularly fruitful day, with many shouts of excitement from the teams or the other adults working on various parts of the site as ancient pieces were unearthed – mostly pottery and a few pieces of metal so far, but thrilling nonetheless.

Lunch provided a welcome break from the heat of the desert sun. Miss Cranna had organised food to be brought out from the guesthouse – delicious pita bread and barbecued lamb skewers, hummus and other dips and savouries like pickles.

While they ate, the children busily compared notes about things they had found. There had been great excitement in particular when Caprice had unearthed a gorgeous jewel representing Horus the falcon. Mr Salah said that it had most likely been worn as a brooch.

The girl had not been best pleased when the piece was taken away by one of the archaeologists to be tagged and documented, knowing she would never see it again, except perhaps in a museum. She did ask if there would be some sort of acknowledgement that she found it.

Alice-Miranda was only half-listening to her friends talk. She had noticed a man working a couple of sections across from her, watching everyone else and doing very little digging. He was clean-shaven with short dark hair and there was something familiar about him.

'I'm going to take some pictures,' Millie said.

'I'll come with you,' Alice-Miranda replied. 'There's someone I want to say hello to.'

Millie frowned and Alice-Miranda whispered something that caused the girl to recoil.

The friends walked across the sand. Alice-Miranda tapped the fellow on the shoulder. He leapt into the air like a rocket, then took stock of who was standing in front of him.

'You scared the life out of me, miss,' he said.

'And now you're scaring the life out of us, *Ahmed*,' Alice-Miranda said. Millie glared at him.

'No, that is not my name,' the man said, shaking his head.

Millie held her camera up.

'Say cheese!' she said, and pressed the shutter.

'Cheese.' He grinned broadly and there it was: that gold tooth yet again.

'Seriously – who are you and why do you keep turning up everywhere?' Millie demanded.

'I do not know what you are talking about.' The man shook his head.

'Yes, you do. Why did you ask if our teachers were treating us well? Are you some sort of child-protection agent or something?' Alice-Miranda asked.

The man shook his head again.

'We're not letting you leave until you tell us who you are. If you don't, I'll take this picture to the police and tell them that you've been following us all over Cairo, and now to Luxor. We're just kids. I don't think that sort of thing would go over very well with the authorities,' Millie threatened.

'No. No, no, no, please do not do that,' the man said, waving his hands like windscreen wipers. 'It is true my name is Ahmed, but I am not a taxi driver, nor a souvenir salesman, nor a dancer.'

'No surprises there,' Millie said.

The man looked mysteriously to his left and right. 'I am a private detective,' he replied, pressing his finger to his lips.

Alice-Miranda frowned. 'Okay, but what do you want with us?'

'I was hired by Mr Woodcock of Badger and Woodcock Accountants to follow your teacher – the very tall and slim one known as Miss Reedy – to see if she and Mr Badger were working together.'

'What? You've got that all wrong,' Millie said. 'Miss Reedy is totally innocent. We found out this morning that she never even signed those papers. Mr Badger forged the documents. Hasn't Mr Woodcock called you?'

'Yes. He released me from his services first thing this morning, but I was already here and my place had been arranged on the dig. I have never had such an opportunity before. Perhaps I will find some treasure,' the man said.

'I can't believe Mr Woodcock thought Miss Reedy would have been involved in Mr Badger's Ponzi scheme. She's the most honest person you'd ever meet,' Alice-Miranda said.

'Yes, I must admit that I have felt bad for following you, but Mr Woodcock was suspicious given that she left the country and Mr Badger has gone missing too. That's why he hired the best private detective in Cairo, perhaps in all of Egypt,' Ahmed said. He pulled a card from his trouser pocket.

'This says you're the best taxi driver in Cairo,' Millie said, passing it back to him.

'Sorry, wrong card – here it is,' he said, then looked and put it back. 'No, that was for Tanoura dancing.'

The man pulled out a third card. He passed it to the girls.

'Ahmed Ally. Private Investigator,' Alice-Miranda said. 'Well, it's lovely to finally make your acquaintance properly, Mr Ally.'

'Yes, miss. Might I say that if ever you two would like jobs in the private-investigation industry when you are older, I would be happy to recruit you to my team,' the man said.

'How big is it?' Millie asked. 'Your team?'

'At the moment it is just myself and my assistant, who is also my wife, but she is an excellent researcher and has infinitely better computer skills than I do,' Ahmed said with a smile. 'She is also very beautiful and an outstanding cook.'

The girls giggled. 'You're a funny man, Mr Ally.'

'And you are very perceptive for children – my disguises are among the best and yet you could still tell that it was me.'

'Perhaps I could make one small suggestion – you probably should get rid of your gold tooth. It's a bit of a giveaway,' Alice-Miranda said.

'I am afraid I cannot do that. I was given this tooth from my grandmother. It is a family heirloom.' The man grinned again.

Alice-Miranda and Millie looked at each other, wondering exactly what that meant. But it was probably best not to ask.

'Anyway, I have been given a new assignment in the past hour,' the man said.

'Then why are you still here?' Millie asked.

'Because as fate would have it, I have been tasked with investigating our new Minister, Miss Moussa,' he said. 'Dr Hassam's personal assistant has asked me to look into some concerns. It is such good luck that she is here with your group.'

'You do realise you probably shouldn't have told us that,' Millie said.

'Yes, that is true,' he said, grimacing.

'Why does Dr Hassam's assistant have concerns?' Alice-Miranda asked.

'I cannot tell you. I am a professional,' the man said, apparently just remembering that fact. 'But if you see anything that is unusual or troubling, please – you have my card.'

The girls nodded and walked away.

'I've got a bad feeling about Miss Moussa's plan,' Millie said, glancing across at the woman, who was smiling and chatting and seemed like a completely different person to the one they'd met on the previous days. She explained her misgivings to Alice-Miranda, who nodded.

'I hate to think we've done the wrong thing telling her about Masud,' Alice-Miranda said.

Millie shrugged. 'I know. I feel bad for him. He's a nice kid and his father is fantastic. I just don't understand why he's doing it.'

Alice-Miranda looked at her watch. It was almost half past one and Masud was due to meet Mr Zoheir at two.

'Let's go and find him – make sure he's okay,' Alice-Miranda said. The girls walked back towards the tent that had been set up to cover the catering and give shade to the workers.

'There he is!' Millie spotted Masud sitting on his own near the base of the cliffs. A scrawny younger boy ran towards him. The lad handed over what looked like a note, then scampered away again.

'I wonder who that is,' she said.

Masud unfurled the paper and quickly stood up. Something had rattled him.

'He's going somewhere,' Alice-Miranda said. 'Come on – we should follow him.'

Miss Cranna had just begun passing out sweet feteer – a flaky, layered pastry with a variety of stuffings – caster cream, banana, chocolate and nuts. Everyone had stopped work to join the dessert line.

'Britt,' Millie called out. 'We're just going to get some pictures from the top terrace. We'll be back soon.'

The girl nodded.

Ahmed Ally was looking at Miss Moussa. As he watched her stalk off towards the temple, his phone buzzed in his pocket. He pulled it out to read the message. 'Oh, Miss Moussa, that is a big concern,' he said to himself, then hurried after her.

Chapter 38

'He's heading towards the temple,' Millie said as the girls followed Masud at a safe distance, ducking in and out of the columns and around the colossal statues that adorned the outside of the building. The complex was a labyrinth of rooms, tombs, grand courtyards and alcoves.

Most of the tour buses had gone. It was lunchtime, and too hot to be out in the middle of the day. Apart from their group, it seemed as if the place had been abandoned.

'Perhaps Mr Zoheir decided to bring their meeting forward. If that's the case, then Miss Moussa's plan will be thwarted. Her people won't be here yet,' Alice-Miranda said. Apart from an older couple who were leaving, there was no one around.

'Then we should stop Masud,' Millie urged. 'If he gives away the evidence we'll have no way of proving what Zoheir and Farouk are really up to – and Dr Hassam.'

The girls still hadn't caught up to the boy when Masud headed inside Hathor's shrine.

Millie was about to call out to him when Alice-Miranda grabbed her arm.

'Millie – look – it's Miss Moussa!' she whispered. 'What's she doing here? Come on.'

The girls crept inside, darting among the sacred statues and reliefs. They hid behind a pillar just in time to see Maryam Moussa approach the boy.

'Hello, Masud, thank you for your work out there today, but now . . . I believe you have something I want,' Maryam said. There was a menace in her voice that the girls hadn't heard before.

Millie gasped and tugged on Alice-Miranda's shirt. 'What's she doing? This wasn't the plan.'

She grabbed the camera around her neck and began to record a video.

The boy shook his head.

'I know what you have inside that bag, and as Acting Minister of Antiquities I order that you pass it over to me – or I will have you charged with theft and take away your father's licence to operate as a guide,' the woman threatened.

Masud flinched. 'No. You cannot do that. Where is Mr Zoheir?'

'I believe he is due at two. What a shame you will have nothing for him,' she growled. 'Now hand over the artefacts.'

'Not until you give me the money,' Masud demanded.

'I am not paying you to take back the treasures of Egypt. I am giving you an opportunity to keep your family together and your father in work,' the woman scoffed.

Millie looked at Alice-Miranda. 'I can't believe this!' she whispered.

Masud was trembling. 'That is exactly why I am making a deal – for my family, to save my little brother's life!' the boy spat.

Millie's hands shot to her mouth. That's what Masud had meant when he said that his little brother didn't come out with him anymore. The boy was sick.

'What are you talking about?' Maryam asked.

'Jabari has leukaemia and we must take him to America to have a bone-marrow transplant. I need the money to pay for his treatment,' the boy said, his voice cracking.

'Oh my goodness,' Alice-Miranda whispered to Millie.

'Well, *I* need the statues too,' Maryam said. 'I refuse to spend another moment living this life.'

'But you are the Minister,' Masud said.

'Dr Hassam is the Minister and he has awoken from his slumber, so I will be leaving the post,' the woman said. 'Of course, he will be leaving it too after the message I sent to the Chief of Police this morning.'

Alice-Miranda wondered why she would need to leave her job if she had already told the police what Dr Hassam was up to, and – if she was taking the figurine now – how would she ever prove the other men's involvement in the smuggling ring's guilt.

'There will be no escape for him, but the money will allow me to disappear – again,' Maryam said.

Millie and Alice-Miranda looked at each other, wide-eyed at this revelation.

There was a shuffling sound behind the girls. Alice-Miranda turned to see Ahmed Ally tiptoeing towards them.

'What are you doing here?' Millie whispered fiercely.

'I followed Miss Moussa. She is a very bad woman,' he said.

'We know,' Alice-Miranda agreed. Millie nodded.

'She is also a total fraud!' He dug his phone out of his pocket and held it up for the girls to read the screen.

'Well, that makes sense,' Millie whispered.

'The woman is as much an Egyptologist and archaeologist as I am a licenced taxi driver and Tanoura dancer – which is to say that she is neither of those things,' Ahmed said. 'Maryam Moussa is not even her real name. This woman did not exist until twelve years ago.'

'Who is she then?' Millie asked.

'My wife is still trying to find that out,' the man replied.

It was just as well that the girls and Ahmed were hidden from view of the entrance as well as

371

from Masud and Maryam, because a man had walked inside while they were distracted. It was ten minutes to two.

Alice-Miranda spotted him first. 'Uh oh, this is about to get interesting.'

Maryam had ducked out of sight as footsteps fell on the stone floor.

'Hello Masud,' Mr Zoheir said. 'You are early.'

Masud spun around, startling briefly as his gaze swept across the columns and he spied the others too. Alice-Miranda raised her finger to her lips.

'Do you have what I need?' Mr Zoheir asked.

Masud nodded. 'I want the money first.'

'Of course, Masud,' the man said. 'I have it here.' He set a duffel bag down on the floor.

'Show me,' the boy said, taking his own bag from his body.

'We have to do something,' Millie whispered as the man reached for the boy's bag. Her heart was racing.

'Masud, no! It's a trap!' Alice-Miranda cried out.

The boy spun around. Maryam Moussa rushed from her hiding place, reaching for the bag.

'What are you doing, you stupid woman?' Mr Zoheir yelled, lunging for Masud.

But they were both too slow.

Masud flicked the bag's strap over his foot and kicked it into the air. It seemed all of that football practice wasn't in vain after all.

'Millie!' the boy shouted. She raced from her hiding spot and caught the bag then passed it to Alice-Miranda, who sprinted onto the terrace. Meanwhile the duffel bag fell from Mr Zoheir's shoulder, spilling open its contents.

'What's this?' Masud looked at the worthless pieces of paper lying on the ground.

'Come back here!' Mr Zoheir took off after Alice-Miranda, who was already being pursued by Maryam. The girl charged along the terrace, desperately searching for a fast way back to the dig site, where surely there was safety in numbers. Millie, Masud and Mr Ally were in pursuit.

'How did you know I was here?' the boy asked, panting.

'Alice-Miranda heard you with Mr Zoheir last night in the garden,' Millie said.

'Why didn't you warn me what he was planning?' the boy demanded.

'I'll explain later! We've got to get to her before they do,' the girl puffed.

Mr Ally was yelling into his phone. 'Yes, brother, you need to come right away!'

At the front of the pack, Alice-Miranda dodged in and out of the columns, trying to shake the nefarious adults, to no avail. 'Help!' she shouted, hoping to get the attention of those at the dig site below. 'Help me!'

The bag was starting to weigh her down, but there was no way she was going to leave it behind for either of those two crooks.

Down at the refreshment tent, Sep frowned and looked up. 'Did anyone else hear that?'

'There! It's Alice-Miranda!' Neville yelled.

'Good heavens, what's going on?' Mr Ferguson said as he caught sight of the girl, who was now charging along the edge of the temple – precariously close to the twenty-foot drop to the ground below.

'Alice-Miranda!' the man called. 'What's the matter?'

But the girl was too out of breath to answer.

Maryam Moussa and Mr Zoheir sprinted into view. 'That man! What is he doing up there?' Mr Salah shouted.

The group on the ground watched in horror as Mr Zoheir ran at the girl and grabbed her around

374

the middle. Alice-Miranda kicked him hard in just the right spot and he let go, doubled over in pain, but Miss Moussa was still hot on her heels.

'Here!' Alice-Miranda shouted down to her friends. 'Catch!'

She hurled the bag over the side of the temple.

'Noooooo! You stupid child!' The woman ran to the edge and watched it fall, Mr Zoheir staggering up behind her.

Caprice looked up with her hands out-stretched. She lunged for the bag but it was too heavy. Although she managed to cushion its fall a little, the bag slipped between her fingers and crashed into the patch of ground where she had been digging – with such force it smashed right through the surface, not stopping until it reached the bottom of the gaping void Caprice was stunned to see appear beneath it.

The archaeologist in charge of the site ran to see what had happened. He fell onto his knees and grabbed the torch from his belt, shining it into the hole.

'We've found it!' he screamed. 'It's the entrance! The entrance to the tomb!'

'Really?' Caprice's eyes were huge.

On the terrace above, Mr Zoheir and Miss Moussa were wringing their hands and screaming at the children and one another. Masud, Millie and Mr Ally had arrived close behind.

'What were you doing, you stupid woman?' Mr Zoheir shouted at Miss Moussa.

'You're going to prison! You and Mr Farouk and Dr Hassam,' the woman spat. 'I have witnesses who will attest to your intention to purchase antiquities and sell them on the black market.'

She looked at Millie and Alice-Miranda and Masud.

'Why would we testify for you?' Alice-Miranda said. 'You were planning to steal the funerary figures first.'

'What? No, I wasn't. I was helping your friend avoid getting himself into terrible trouble,' the woman said with a sneer. 'It's your word against mine.'

'You lied about everything. You were going to double cross Masud just as Mr Zoheir intended as well.' Millie pointed at her camera. 'I think you'll find that we have all the evidence the authorities need right here.'

By now Mr Salah, Mr Plumpton, Miss Reedy

and most of the children had raced up to the terrace.

'What trouble, Masud?' Akil Salah looked at his son.

The boy swallowed hard.

'It was for Jabari, Baba. I only did it for him,' the boy said, tears in his eyes.

'Mr Salah,' Alice-Miranda ran towards the man. 'I should have come to you but Miss Moussa said she would make sure that Masud didn't get into any trouble – that she needed him to break open the ring of thieves and help the country. I had no idea that your son was so ill. Masud only wanted to help get him treatment. He has found some very important artefacts – quite possibly the most important discovery of modern times.'

Akil Salah's eyes welled with tears too and he charged at the boy, hugging him tight.

'Oh, Masud, my son,' the man began to sob.

Alice-Miranda was distracted from their emotional moment by the sudden arrival of police everywhere on the dig site.

'Arrest that man,' Maryam Moussa ordered, pointing at Mr Zoheir.

'Arrest that woman!' Ahmed Ally said.

Miss Reedy looked at the man, who grinned at her. 'You! What are you doing here?' she blanched.

'It is all right, Miss Reedy. My name is Ahmed Ally and I am a private detective. My brother Mohammed is that police officer there. The whole family is very proud of him. I am merely Cairo's best private detective.'

Maryam fought as she was seized by a policeman. 'Take your hands off me!' she demanded.

The officer cuffing her baulked.

'No, no, no, no – put your hands back on her,' Ahmed ordered. 'She is not who she says she is. My wife is still looking for evidence of her real identity, but we do know that there is no trace of anyone called Maryam Moussa before she came to work at the Ministry.'

Alice-Miranda stared at the woman. The scar above Maryam's lip was clearly visible, and there was something else ticking away in her mind.

'Miss Moussa, may I ask how you got that scar?' Alice-Miranda asked, pointing to the same place on her own face.

'What? I had a mole removed,' the woman said, clearly taken aback by the question given her current situation.

Alice-Miranda looked at Britt, who nodded.

'Have you had a nose job, Miss Morsey?' Alice-Miranda asked. 'And do you wear coloured contact lenses?'

'What? No, of course not,' the woman replied, indignant at the questions. But she didn't even flinch at the change of name.

'But you are Gianna Morsey, aren't you? Or at least you were before you became Maryam Moussa,' the child said.

The woman looked as if she'd just swallowed a hippo. 'That's not my name. I'm not her. She died – a long time ago.' Maryam was speaking at a rate of knots.

'Who is Gianna Morsey?' Ahmed asked.

Livinia Reedy stepped forward. 'She's wanted back at home for running a Ponzi scheme, just like that scoundrel Elias Badger. You don't know him, do you?' The teacher stared at Gianna, who shook her head.

Alice-Miranda stepped forward. 'You stole money from my father and many of his friends and associates. You've been hiding here for years by the sound of it – using a fake name and false qualifications. When I told you my father's name last night, you reacted as if you had heard it before.'

'It's no wonder you hate having your picture taken,' Millie said. 'But kudos to your plastic surgeon – it's a good nose job.'

'Though that scar above your lip was a giveaway,' Britt said. 'And your eyes are so lovely and distinctive – with contact lenses.'

'I read in the newspaper that Gianna Morsey had brown eyes. When we were at Saqqara one of your lenses came out – we saw you had one brown eye and the other was green,' Alice-Miranda added.

Gianna's shoulders slumped in defeat while Mr Zoheir shook his head.

'Get them out of here,' Mr Ferguson said. The police grabbed the pair and shuffled them away.

Millie turned and hugged Alice-Miranda tight, Britt encircling them both before Millie broke away and hugged Masud too. While the boy didn't really know what to do in that moment, he leaned in and embraced the girl.

'Well, that was unexpected,' Alice-Miranda said.

'It certainly was,' Millie could only agree.

'Amazing,' Britt said.

'Hey!' Caprice shouted from the dig site below. 'What about this? It's pretty amazing too. If it hadn't been for my slippery fingers we never would have found it.'

'Whatever.' Madagascar rolled her eyes. She'd spent the entire morning sulking and hadn't spoken to anyone.

'No, Maddie – Caprice is right. Who knows what treasures lay beneath the surface, and to think we've been part of it – now that's something special,' Millie said, giving Caprice a huge grin. 'And it's all thanks to Masud's failed black-market antiquities career,' she added, smiling at the boy to show there were no hard feelings.

Despite losing the chance to raise the money for his brother's treatment, Masud felt curiously optimistic. He smiled right back at her.

Chapter 39

'Goodness me, what a day you have had, children,' Mr Tadros said as he greeted the group at the entrance to the guesthouse. 'For me too – I got to speak to a movie star.'

'It was certainly more excitin' than we had expected,' Mr Ferguson agreed. 'I think we should all get cleaned up for dinner and take a deep breath.'

Mr Tadros nodded. 'Yes, please hurry. We have a very important visitor waiting to speak to the children.'

Mr Ferguson frowned, but the other man didn't elaborate.

There was a buzz in the air as the students hurried to their rooms and rushed through the showers.

'I still can't believe that Miss Moussa was the lady who ripped off all those people years ago – just like Mr Badger has done now,' Chessie said.

'And that funny fellow, Mr Ahmed – what about him turning out to be a private detective?' Sloane said.

'Did you see the look on Miss Moussa-Morsey's face when she realised Alice-Miranda had said her real name?' Millie chuckled. 'She was never going to be able to deny it after that reaction.'

The girls were racing around the room finding clean clothes and brushing their hair.

'Do you think they'll send a news crew tomorrow when they open the tomb?' Caprice said. She was folding her dirty washing and frowning at the mess Madagascar had made all over the floor beside her.

'What? So you can be famous?' Madagascar scoffed. 'I'm glad I won't be here.'

Millie shook her head. 'You know, Maddie, it's not too late to apologise for what you said this morning. I can guarantee there is no girl here who wouldn't give you another chance – even though I doubt you deserve it.'

Caprice frowned, but when Millie raised her eyebrows the copper-haired girl nodded.

'She's right, you know. We all make mistakes – it's just that some of us have taken a lot longer to realise that they don't have to define us,' Caprice said.

'We have Alice-Miranda to thank for that you know,' Jacinta said. 'She's never given up on any of us, though I wouldn't have blamed her if she had.'

'Fine – I'm sorry,' Maddie whispered, her eyes welling with tears.

'Do you want me to come with you and you can apologise to Miss Cranna and Mr Ferguson too?' Millie asked. 'You might get bumped from the Queen's Colours program, but they'll probably let you stay for the rest of the trip. Otherwise it's going to be lonely flying home on your own tonight.'

'Okay. Just let me get dressed first,' the girl said sheepishly.

'We still don't know how Mr Farouk and Mr Zoheir have been moving the goods out of the country for all those years,' Sloane said, jumping down from her top bunk.

'What was that noise?' Alice-Miranda asked. 'It sounded like something clinking.'

'Do that again, Sloane,' Millie said.

The girl climbed back up top and bounced as she sat down.

'There – that!' Alice-Miranda said.

She sat on the bunk beneath Sloane's and felt the base of the mattress above.

She was about to ask the girl to repeat the action when there was a sharp knock on the door. 'It's me. Neville,' the boy shouted.

'Don't come in – Maddie's in her underwear,' Chessie yelled.

Madagascar smiled at the girl. 'Thanks.'

'What's the matter?' Millie yelled.

'You have to see this,' the boy said. The girls quickly finished getting dressed and charged out into the hallway, where Neville was standing in front of the wide-open door of the boys' room.

'What is it?' Alice-Miranda asked.

'Well, it's sort of bad but maybe good. We were having another wrestling match and this time Philippe said that we should pull the spare mattresses off the beds, so we did, and then Sep went down like a tonne of bricks and there was this thing poking out. It cut right through the fabric.'

'Oh my goodness, that's how they do it!' Alice-Miranda beamed. 'Did you pull whatever it was out?'

Sep, who was just inside the doorway, nodded. He held up the most beautiful necklace on a long gold chain. It was an ancient Egyptian scene set with blue lapis lazuli and other gemstones in a gold casing.

'They move the stolen goods out of the country inside the mattresses,' Alice-Miranda declared, grinning. 'It's genius.'

'There's something inside yours too, Sloane,' Millie said.

'Come on. We've got to tell Mr Ferguson.' Alice-Miranda took the necklace and raced away.

✳

'Good evening, children,' Mr Tadros said. The group was seated in the dining room together at two long tables, waiting for dinner to be served. Mr Ally had joined them at the behest of Mr Ferguson. 'Before you eat your meal tonight, I would like to introduce someone who has come especially to speak to you all. We are honoured to have him with us.' As the man stepped from around the curtain, Akil and Masud Salah's jaws dropped. Ahmed Ally's reaction was far more spectacular. He immediately flew out of his seat and ran toward the man with his hand outstretched.

'Who is that?' Lucas asked loudly.

Alice-Miranda frowned. After everything that had transpired, this was the last person she expected to see tonight.

'Dr Hassam, it is the greatest of honours to meet you.' Ahmed Ally shook the man's hand, then looked at his own as if he might faint. 'But forgive me, sir, aren't you a criminal in a coma?'

Mustafa Hassam gave the man a scornful glare. 'I woke up – and you should probably sit down.'

Ahmed nodded then spun around and raced back to his chair.

'Good evening, ladies and gentleman, boys and girls,' the man said. 'My name is Mustafa Hassam and I am the Minister for Antiquities.'

You could have heard a pin drop.

'I know that Miss Moussa has levelled some very serious accusations at me – at least to some of you – but I can assure you that I have in fact been working undercover with the police for a number of years now. Befriending the kingpins was a part of this operation, to unpick the one piece of the puzzle that has eluded me for all this time – how they were moving the antiquities out of the country. Now, thanks to you children, we know. Mr Tadros has explained what you found in the mattresses. An ingenious plan on their part – although unfortunately it means they will no longer be supplying new beds every six months now.'

The man continued to congratulate the children on their exploits. In one fell swoop, they had helped bring down a longstanding ring of thieves who had stolen tens of millions of dollars' worth of Egyptian history to be sold around the world and also uncovered Miss Moussa's fraudulent scam. He assured them that she would be extradited to face charges over the Ponzi scheme she had set up years before.

'Not only that, but today you have cracked open a tomb that appears to contain treasures to compare with that of the boy king, Tutankhamun. While we do not yet know the owner of the grave, it is one of the most exciting discoveries of modern times. Perhaps the most exciting of all, however, are the funerary figures that Masud found buried under his father's barn.'

Before the group had left the site, the archaeologists working there had retrieved the boy's bag from the cavern with a long hook. They'd realised at once the incredible significance of the find.

'And while I do not condone what you had planned to do with the collection, Masud, your intentions came only from a place of love and goodness, which is why I have decided that – no matter the cost – your brother will go to America and have his treatment, and I will personally pay for it. When the figures go on display in the new museum, there will be a plaque telling everyone about the boy whose camel kicked a stone and allowed him to discover one of the most important treasures of ancient Egypt.'

The room erupted with cheering and clapping and floods of tears. Alice-Miranda looked over at Masud as Akil Salah leaned across and wrapped his arms around his son. Sitting beside her, Millie squeezed her friend's hand and reached for a tissue in her pocket.

Dr Hassam raised his hands to silence them.

'And to thank you all for your part in this historic day, I would like to invite you to personally tour Abu Simbel with me before you depart for home. I am sorry, Mr Ferguson and Mr Salah, if this throws your itinerary into chaos but it is the least I can do.'

He looked at Alice-Miranda and Millie. 'And you, young ladies,' he said. 'Please come.' He motioned for the pair to step forward.

The girls stood up, wondering what they'd done to deserve this special attention.

Dr Hassam pulled two small boxes from his pocket and opened them, showing the contents. Inside each was a beautiful gold ankh covered in hieroglyphs.

'I hear you are both very brave girls. These are amulets to protect you now and always,' he said. 'A gift from my country, for your courageous actions.'

'Thank you, Dr Hassam,' Alice-Miranda said.

'It's so beautiful,' Millie said, blushing. 'But I don't think we really deserve them.'

The girls took a box each and returned to their seats, the other students eager to see the gifts up close.

Mr Ferguson stood and shook the man's hand. 'Thank you, Dr Hassam. Is there any chance I can persuade you to join us for dinner?'

'I was counting on it,' the man said. He walked to the spare seat beside Ahmed Ally, who almost fainted on the spot.

'What a trip,' Millie said, looking at Alice-Miranda, who had just put her necklace on. She helped Millie with hers.

'It has turned out to be quite the adventure, hasn't it?' Alice-Miranda said. 'And I wouldn't want it any other way, would you?'

Millie smiled at her friend and shook her head. 'Never.'

Just in case you're wondering . . .

The children spent a second day on the dig site. To everyone's great delight and astonishment, first indications were that the uncovered tomb belonged to the elusive and very beautiful Nefertiti, who until now was believed to have rested across the mountain in the Valley of the Kings. It was said to be the most exciting find since Lord Carnarvon and Howard Carter had cracked open Tutankhamun's resting place in 1922.

The children then spent a day touring the extraordinary sites of Luxor, Thebes and Karnak, and taking in the best of what Egypt had to offer, including their expedition south to Abu Simbel, where Dr Hassam dazzled them all with his knowledge.

Gianna Morsey, also known as Maryam Moussa, had fled to Egypt after ripping off hundreds of friends, family and business associates in a Ponzi scheme. She changed her name and appearance and lived the high life until a string of bad investments and a penchant for luxury shopping saw her burn through her funds and she had to get a real job. Her role in the Ministry was a means to an end, and when she was promoted to Director of Archives she had planned her own black-market sales ring. Dr Hassam had noticed the discrepancies in the storage lists right before his stroke. The Minister's illness had allowed Gianna to make the contacts she needed to try to expand her business. She had hoped to make enough money to disappear and start a new life – again – before he woke up. Selling Masud's find would have made her enough money to never work again in her life. She is now in custody awaiting trial. The Minister did acknowledge that she had saved his life, but he had to wonder whether – if her instincts hadn't kicked in and she realised the opportunity the situation presented – the outcome could have been very different. Thankfully Gianna must have had some shreds of decency left, despite her life of crime.

Dr Hassam is fully recovered from his stroke. As he told the children, he had been undercover for a number of years, trying to gather enough evidence to put an end to the black-market antiquities trading that plagued Egypt. He had been on the verge of a breakthrough right before he fell ill, though had the children not discovered that the artefacts had been smuggled inside the mattresses, he might still not have figured that part out. Interpol is in the process of retrieving a significant number of stolen items using the list of names he'd provided them. While Mr Zoheir had been caught, Mr Farouk had left the country in his private jet. The government has now frozen all of his assets and seized the bedding company. The authorities are confident that he will turn up somewhere soon.

Mr Badger has also disappeared into the ether. Whether he will be found remains to be seen, but at least Winchesterfield-Downsfordvale is safe from his grimy mitts.

Myrtle Parker has taken to her role like a duck to water and it seems that she will be in situ for some time yet. Her husband Reginald is quite enjoying his peaceful days at home and uninterrupted time to rehearse with his brother-in-law and bandmate, Stan.

Barclay Ferguson and Morag Cranna have recommended all of the students continue working towards their Diamond Queen's Colours Award except Madagascar, who will not be welcome to participate in any further activities. The girl accepted her fate with far more grace than anyone had expected. Morag and Barclay were surprised and pleased that the other students were prepared to give her another chance as a friend. Caprice and Millie are making progress and, while they might never be besties, they're getting on better than ever. The children can't wait to see each other again at the next group activity.

As soon as the children returned home they all undertook blood tests in case anyone was a match for Jabari's treatment. A few weeks later, Millie spent a night away from school. The only person who knew where she had gone was Alice-Miranda, who sent flowers to the hospital.

Jabari Salah has undergone a bone-marrow transplant, without even leaving Cairo, after an anonymous donor was found to be a match and the bone marrow was flown in by jet. All indications are that he is doing well. He is now recovering at home with Masud, his grandmother, Mama and Baba – and of course that cranky Nenet and her sisters.

Neville and Alice-Miranda still write to each other every week, and while the boy very clearly understands that she's not his girlfriend, he holds out hope that one day, when they're all grown up, that situation might change.

Alice-Miranda can't wait for that gap year, when she and her friends will travel the world. There's so much to look forward to and she's definitely expecting an adventure or two.

Cast of characters

Queen's Colours Egypt tour students

Alice-Miranda Highton-Smith-Kennington-Jones	Winchesterfield-Downsfordvale student
Millicent Jane McLaughlin-McTavish-McNaughton-McGill	Winchesterfield-Downsfordvale student
Jacinta Headlington-Bear	Winchesterfield-Downsfordvale student
Sloane Sykes	Winchesterfield-Downsfordvale student
Francesca Compton-Halls	Winchesterfield-Downsfordvale student
Caprice Radford	Winchesterfield-Downsfordvale student
Lucas Nixon	Fayle School for Boys student
Septimus Sykes	Fayle School for Boys student
Neville Nordstrom	Barcelona International College student
Britt Fox	Hartvig Skole student

Madagascar Slewt	Bodlington School for Girls student
Alethea Mackenzie	Mrs Kimmel's School for Girls student
Gretchen Bell	Mrs Kimmel's School for Girls student
Vincent Roche	Lycée International student
Philippe Le Gall	Lycée International student
Brendan Fourie	Todder House student
Junior Brown	Todder House student
Henry Yan	Mandeville College student
Hunter Martin	St Odo's student
Aidan Blair	Burns School student

Queen's Colours Egypt tour staff and teachers

Barclay Ferguson	CEO and tour leader
Morag Cranna	Assistant to Barclay Ferguson
Miss Livinia Reedy	Deputy Headmistress and English teacher at Winchesterfield-Downsfordvale
Mr Josiah Plumpton	Science teacher at Winchesterfield-Downsfordvale
Mr Hansie Pienaar	Todder House teacher

Winchesterfield-Downsfordvale staff

Miss Ophelia Grimm	Headmistress
Mrs Louella Derby	Personal secretary to the headmistress (currently on maternity leave)
Myrtle Parker	Village busybody and Mrs Louella Derby's maternity cover
Howie (Mrs Howard)	Housemistress

Others

Akil Salah	Tour operator
Esha Salah	Akil's wife
Masud Salah	Akil and Esha's son and assistant to Akil
Jabari Salah	Akil and Esha's son
Maryam Moussa	Director of Archives and Acting Minister for Antiquities
Dr Mustafa Hassam	Minister for Antiquities
Nour Badawy	Personal assistant to the Minister for Antiquities
Simeon Woodcock	Accountant
Elias Badger	Accountant and Ponzi scheme scam artist
Gianna Morsey	Ponzi scheme scam artist
Ahmed Ally	Cairo local
Mr Tadros	Guesthouse owner in Luxor
Mr Zoheir	Antiquities smuggler
Mr Farouk	Millionaire bedding manufacturer

About the author

Jacqueline Harvey taught for many years in girls' boarding schools. She is the author of the bestselling Alice-Miranda, Clementine Rose and Kensy and Max series, and was awarded Honour Book in the 2006 Australian CBC Awards for her picture book *The Sound of the Sea*. She now writes full-time and is working on more Kensy and Max adventures, and some exciting new projects too.

jacquelineharvey.com.au

Jacqueline Supports

Jacqueline Harvey is a passionate educator who enjoys sharing her love of reading and writing with children and adults alike. She is an ambassador for Dymocks Children's Charities and Room to Read. Find out more at dcc.gofundraise.com.au and roomtoread.org.

Enter a world of
mystery and adventure in

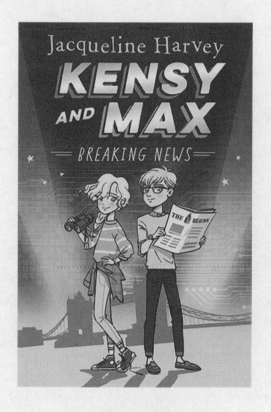

OUT NOW

CHAPTER 1

BKDIXKA

Max woke with a start as the car crunched to a halt. He yawned and looked around at his sister, who was still asleep in the back seat. Her blanket had slipped down and she was drooling on the pillow that was wedged in the corner. She wouldn't thank him for noticing.

The boy peered out at the jewel box of stars in the clearing night sky. It had only stopped raining a little while ago. On the other side of the car, Max could see what looked to be a hotel. A dull glow shone from one of the windows high in the roofline. For a second, he glimpsed a face, but it was gone as soon as it had appeared. 'Where are we, Fitz?' Max asked.

Fitz turned and gave him a weary smile. 'This is Alexandria,' he replied, as if that was supposed to mean something. 'Be a good lad and take the daypacks with you, and mind the puddles. No one will thank you for tramping mud inside.'

Fitz opened the driver's door and hopped out of the Range Rover.

Max stretched, yawning again, then reached over and gently shook his sister's leg. 'Kensy,' he whispered, 'we're here.'

The girl groaned and flopped her head against the pillow but didn't wake up. It was to be expected given they'd just spent the past sixteen hours driving from Zermatt, near the Swiss–Italian border, across France and then to England.

Fitz reappeared at the open driver's window. 'Don't wake your sister unless you want your head bitten off,' he warned with a wink.

Kensy let out a grunty snore, as if to agree.

Max heard footsteps on the gravel and looked up to see a tall man approaching. The fellow was wearing a red dressing-gown and matching slippers. His dark hair had retreated to the middle of his head and he sported large rimless glasses. Fitz walked towards him and the two shook hands.

As the men spoke in hushed tones, the boy slipped out of the car. The stars had disappeared again and fat drops of rain began splattering the driveway. Max quickly collected the packs from the back seat while the man in the dressing-gown retrieved their suitcases from the boot. Fitz swept Kensy into his arms and carried her through a stone portico to an open doorway.

'Are we home?' she murmured, burrowing into the man's broad chest.

'Yes, sweetheart,' he replied. 'We're home.'

Max felt a shiver run down his spine. He wondered why Fitz would lie. This wasn't their home at all.

The four of them entered the building into a dimly lit hallway. Without hesitation or instruction, Fitz turned and continued up a staircase to the right.

That's strange, Max thought. Fitz must have been here before.

'Please go ahead, Master Maxim,' the tall man said.

Too tired to ask how the fellow knew his name, Max did as he was bid. The hypnotic thudding of their luggage being carried up the stairs made the boy feel as if he was almost sleepwalking. They followed Fitz down a long corridor and eventually came to a bedroom furnished with two queen-sized beds and a fireplace. Max's skin tingled from the warmth of the crackling fire. He deposited the daypacks neatly by the door and shrugged off his jacket as the tall man set down their bags and drew the curtains.

'Sweet dreams, Kens,' Fitz whispered, tucking the girl under the covers.

Without any urging at all, Max climbed into the other bed. He had so many questions, but right now he couldn't muster a single word. The soft sheets and the thrum of driving rain against the window panes made it hard to resist the pull of sleep. He closed his eyes as Fitz and the tall man began talking. Max roused at the mention of his parents' names followed by something rather alarming – something that couldn't possibly be true. He tried hard to fight off the sandman to hear more, but seconds later Max too was fast asleep.